Sarah had a clear view of the stranger.

He sat facing the front entrance of the café, his eyes intent on the empty doorway. His light brown hair fell forward in a boyish wave over one side of his forehead. His features were strong, unyielding—despite his casual air, she sensed the self-assurance in him. A determined man with the persistence not to give up a search easily.

She drew a deep breath and crossed the space between the counter and the booth, her sandals making no noise on the worn wooden floor. She stood silently at the side of the booth, her body tense, her hands clenched at her sides.

Even if his reasons in looking for her were innocent, Sarah knew she was risking more than exposure, that she was in danger.

The very sight of Jordan Matthias disturbed her in a way no other man had ever done.

Dear Reader,

When two people fall in love, the world is suddenly new and exciting, and it's that same excitement we bring to you in Silhouette Intimate Moments. These are stories with scope and grandeur. The characters lead lives we all dream of, and everything they do reflects the wonder of being in love.

Longer and more sensuous than most romances, Silhouette Intimate Moments novels take you away from everyday life and let you share the magic of love. Adventure, glamour, drama, even suspense— these are the passwords that let you into a world where love has a power beyond the ordinary, where the best authors in the field today create stories of love and commitment that will stay with you always.

In coming months look for novels by your favorite authors: Kathleen Eagle, Heather Graham Pozzessere, Nora Roberts and Marilyn Pappano, to name just a few. And whenever you buy books, look for all the Silhouette Intimate Moments, love stories *for* today's woman *by* today's woman.

Leslie J. Wainger
Senior Editor
Silhouette Books

Carol Duncan

Stranger on the Shore

Silhouette Intimate Moments

Published by Silhouette Books New York

America's Publisher of Contemporary Romance

SILHOUETTE BOOKS
300 East 42nd St., New York, N.Y. 10017

ISBN: 0-373-07270-8

First Silhouette Books printing January 1989

Printed in the U.S.A.

CAROL DUNCAN

is a former newspaper journalist who turned in her press card, joined the diaper brigade and became a free-lance writer when her children were born. She claims to be a veteran of car pools, Cub Scouts and avoiding housework.

In addition to reading and writing, Carol enjoys family, friends, restoring antique furniture, poking around in secondhand stores and attending country auctions. She can also occasionally be induced to join her outdoors-loving family on camping and gold-prospecting trips—provided they assign someone else KP duty and allow her to take along a good book.

Carol was born in Knoxville, Tennessee, home to her family since the 1780s. She attended high school and college in California, married, then resettled in northwest Arkansas. She, her husband of twenty-three years, and three teenage sons now call the Pacific Northwest home.

Author's Note

The community of Mountain Springs, Arkansas, exists only in the mind of the author. However, other northwest Arkansas locations described in *Stranger on the Shore* are as real and as accurately portrayed as this writer's skill allows.

Monte Ne resort was built in 1901 by William "Coin" Harvey and garnered national fame as a health spa prior to World War I. The resort experienced a rebirth of notoriety in 1931, when the Liberty Party's national convention was held on the site and selected Harvey as its presidential candidate. Franklin D. Roosevelt won the election, Harvey became a footnote in American political history, and Monte Ne once again faded into obscurity.

By 1960, when dam locks on the White River were closed to create Beaver Lake, all that remained of the once-elegant resort were collections of sepia-toned photographs, yellowed news clippings and a few scattered architectural ruins. Today Monte Ne slumbers peacefully fifty feet beneath the surface of Beaver Lake, disturbed only when water levels fall low enough to expose a few of its secrets.

Chapter 1

"Cissie, Cissie. You gotta come quick. A man's about to catch ol' Scarface."

Sarah Wilson straightened from beneath the blackberry bramble growing along the shoreline of Beaver Lake and instinctively braced her back with her free hand. Moving cautiously over the slippery, moss-covered rocks, she waded across the shallows and set the berry bucket on the bank before turning her attention to the boy. "What are you talking about, Jimmy Joe? What man?"

"A big man," the excited eight-year-old boy answered, his face agitated beneath his shock of red hair. "Down by the deep hole. He's trying to catch Scarface. Please, Cissie. You gotta stop him."

"Slow down a minute, Jimmy Joe. Fishermen have tried that hole before. No one's caught him yet." Sarah's eyes danced with amusement and affection. She kept her voice calm and deliberate, trying to reassure the boy.

"But this one's different. He's got on those fancy rubber boots. He's fishing with a skinny little rod and he puts that plug right on the edge of the hole every time." His words tumbled out almost on top of each other.

Sarah repressed a smile. "Every time? Just how long were you watching him? I thought you were supposed to be helping me pick blackberries for Grandma."

"Ah, gee, Cissie, I got half a bucket already. And I didn't spy on him so long." The boy hung his head, guilt written all over his face. "But he always hits that same spot," he insisted. "Five or six times. I saw him. Didn't miss once. I tell you, he's different."

"He's a fly fisherman," Sarah explained patiently. "Scarface is in no danger. That old bass is too canny to be tricked by a bit of fluff or feathers."

Jimmy Joe's breathing slowed. "You're sure? You're honest-to-gosh sure?"

"As sure as I can be." Sarah brushed back the bangs hanging damply across her forehead, leaving a streak of blackberry juice on her skin. Seeing the skepticism still on the boy's face, she reached out impulsively and tousled his hair.

"Tell you what. I'll walk that way with you and take a look for myself. Only we have to be quiet." She inspected her threadbare jeans, rolled up almost to the knee, and her stained sneakers, still muddy and wet from wading in the lake. "I don't want to be seen. As Grandma would say, 'I ain't dressed to be seen by strangers.'"

Ten minutes later, as they left the trail, she cautioned the boy not to speak. Voices, even whispers, carried easily along the lake. Quietly she followed her young cousin into his hiding place, a sassafras thicket on the hillside overlooking the lake, then leaned forward to catch her first glimpse of the stranger.

The sight of the man shocked her. Jimmy Joe was right. He was big. And different. Sarah drew a shaky breath as an unexpected warmth curled through her.

She was close enough to see the sun-bleached hair on his arms. She couldn't get an exact perspective on his height. Nearly six foot, she guessed, and he was whipcord-lean and powerfully built.

Mesmerized by his lazy strength and unconscious grace, she watched the muscles ripple smoothly down his arm as he made an almost imperceptible flick of his wrist. His cast placed the fly exactly on the far edge of the pool.

Curiosity drew her forward until she felt the touch of Jimmy Joe's hand on her arm. She flushed, then closed her eyes, willing a return to sanity.

The boy's eyes met hers, an I-told-you-so look on his face. Sarah nodded her head to reassure him. She wasn't worried—at least not about the fish. An icy knot settled in her stomach.

The stranger's wading boots were top-quality. His jaunty canvas fisherman's hat—the uniform of a fly-fishing aficionado—had bits of polar-bear hair and pheasant feathers stuck into its band.

Sarah squeezed her eyes shut again, but his image refused to disappear. His face, all chiseled lines and planes, just missed being drop-dead handsome. Instead of softening his strong chin, a finger-deep cleft added to the impression of sculptured hardness. Tall and tanned, he could have stepped from the pages of any slick outdoor sporting magazine. But, instinctively, she knew fishing was not his reason for being here.

She had no real evidence for her suspicion. Everything was exactly as it should be, from the fancy wicker creel to the delicately balanced split-bamboo rod he handled so deftly. Yet she knew. This was the stranger who'd been asking questions about her up and down the valley. He'd come here, not to fish, but to find her.

Signaling to Jimmy Joe to be careful, Sarah began moving slowly and cautiously back into the thicket. She'd seen enough. A nonedible fly would never fool that old bass. Sarah was the one who was more likely to be caught.

She'd almost made it to the flank of the hill when the sound of the man's voice drew her back.

"If you want to watch me fish, sonny, you can see better if you come a little closer."

His resonant voice was raised to exactly the right decibel level to penetrate the thicket, transmitting sensations that made her quiver invisibly. Jimmy Joe's face blanched white. His freckles stood out like measles spots as he gave Sarah a frightened look.

"Come on down, son. I know you're back. I'm not going to hurt you." The man didn't even turn to look at the thicket.

Sarah forced a calmness into her expression that bore no relation to the turmoil she felt inside. She put a finger to her lips, cautioning Jimmy Joe to say nothing about her presence, then gave him a slight nod to indicate that it was all right to go.

As Jimmy Joe crawled to the edge of the bluff and slid down the red clay slope to the edge of the lake, Sarah shifted her position to the front of the thicket, determined to keep a close eye on her young charge.

Jordan Matthias forced himself to appear unconcerned as he waited for the boy to come out of his hiding place. Why was he being watched? He'd known he was under observation earlier in the day, and had known, too, when his secret watcher left the thicket. When he'd found the child-size footprints in the soft dirt he'd breathed a sigh of relief.

A child was no threat. He didn't think his questions about the whereabouts of Sarah Wilson had caused overt animosity in the community, but he couldn't be sure. They certainly hadn't produced results. He was no nearer to finding his quarry than when he'd arrived two weeks ago. Now that the boy was back, his original question remained unanswered. Was he being watched because of his search for the elusive Sarah Wilson or because of a child's curiosity?

Even under the circumstances, Jordan had enjoyed the two weeks he'd spent in the area of Mountain Springs, Arkansas. The countryside in this quiet Ozark backwater was raw and unmanicured, yet beautiful. Outcrops of red and yellow sandstone and gray granite marred the green perfection of rolling pastures. The people of the area matched their land—rugged individuals, their soft-spoken courtesy veiling a granite reserve.

Given the native's natural reticence, he shouldn't have been surprised that he was unable to turn up the slightest clue about the woman he'd come to find. No, it wasn't surprising, but it was frustrating. He'd traced her this far, and then she'd simply disappeared.

Jordan turned his attention to the young man who now stood beside him, dusting the red clay residue from the seat of his pants. He looked to be about eight years old, his red hair tousled—a Tom Sawyer in Technicolor.

"How'd you know I was there?" the boy asked. "I know I was real quiet. Grandpa says I'm quiet as a possum."

"You were very quiet," Jordan agreed. "In fact, the first time you were here I wasn't sure who was stalking me. But when you left I found your tracks."

"So how'd you know I was back?"

"My antenna picked you up."

The boy's eyes bulged. He walked cautiously around Jordan, examining him closely. "I don't see them."

"See what?"

"Your antenna."

Jordan laughed softly. "I don't really have an antenna, son. I just meant that I can usually sense when someone is watching me."

"Oh," Jimmy Joe answered, the confused look on his face now replaced by one of understanding. "You mean you've got the sight. Like Cissie."

Jordan's pulse jumped at the boy's matter-of-fact statement. He deliberately schooled his expression to hide his excitement. Was it possible that after two weeks of frustrating failure he was going to accidentally stumble across the trail of the missing Sarah Wilson?

It took a conscious effort for Sarah to swallow the groan caught in her throat. Jimmy Joe couldn't have picked a worse topic of conversation or a more disastrous time to speak of it. She watched the man's face go absolutely still. His body seemed to freeze.

"No, I don't believe so," he finally said.

Could any voice be that totally neutral? Was she imagining it? Sarah managed to stifle another low groan, thankful that Jimmy Joe still called her by the nickname he'd given her when he was a baby. Hopefully the man wouldn't make a connection between "Cissie" and Sarah Wilson, because the longer she watched the more convinced she was that this was the man who had been trying to locate her. As she waited for him to continue, she forgot to breathe.

"Just who is Cissie?" the stranger asked Jimmy Joe, "and what exactly is the 'sight'?"

"Cissie's my cousin," the boy told him patiently. "She knows things, too. Like the time Uncle Hiram's best coon dog got lost and she knew it was caught in a cave. Or when company's coming, only they ain't said so. Things like that. Grandpa says she's got the 'sight.'"

"I see," the man said.

Sarah recognized the tone of suppressed excitement in the man's voice, even if her young cousin didn't. Undaunted, Jimmy Joe continued his story.

"She knows when something's watching her, too. Like once when we was picking berries she knew a bear was coming and made us get up a tree. We sat there for a long time. Then this old mama bear and her cub came out of the woods and waded right into the thicket where we'd been."

If he had been a professional speaker, Jimmy Joe couldn't have timed his pause better. Sarah watched as the stranger encouraged the boy to continue. "What happened then?"

"We waited until the bears finished eating all the berries they wanted and went away. Then we got down and went home. Grandpa says God made enough berries for us all," he added, "but sometimes you have to wait your turn."

The man laughed appreciatively, the humor softening the harsh planes of his face. "I'd heard these hills were full of storytellers, but I didn't know they started training you so young," he said.

"What do you mean, mister?"

"Just that you tell a good story. What's your name, son?"

"Jimmy Joe. James Joseph Lutteral. What's yours?"

"I'm Jordan Matthias. I'm pleased to meet you, Jimmy Joe." The man offered his hand. Jimmy Joe quickly wiped his own on the back of his grimy jeans before manfully extending it toward the stranger.

Turned to face the boy, the stranger was also directly facing the thicket. Again Sarah held her breath, daring even a leaf to move. His eyes, surrounded by thick lashes, were dark and alert. Feeling as helpless as a moth pinned to a display board, she struggled to control a shiver of apprehension.

Dear heaven, what was wrong with her? This man was a stranger—and, she suspected, a threat. Yet all he had to do was look in her direction and her heart fluttered like a giddy teenager's.

She breathed a silent prayer of thanksgiving when he turned back toward the lake and once again, with just the barest flick of his wrist, cast the almost invisible line across the water.

"Do you like to fish?" she heard him ask.

"Sometimes," Jimmy Joe answered nonchalantly.

"Do any fly-fishing?"

"Nah. Just worms. Grandpa says the fish here like things natural."

Jordan Matthias chuckled again. The pleasant musical sound drifted into Sarah's hiding place on the warm humid air.

"Your grandfather may be right. I've tried every fly I have on the wily old bass hiding out in that hole. I don't think he's having any of it."

Now Jimmy Joe's grin spread from ear to ear. "That's what Cissie says," he said confidently.

"So, your cousin talks to the fish, too. What else does she say?"

"Just—just that old Scarface won't have nothing to do with a bit of fluff or feather," Jimmy Joe stammered. "Scarface likes worms."

"Well, I don't know about that, Jimmy Joe," the man said quietly. "That bass has been around awhile. He hasn't tangled with too many worms on too many hooks. Otherwise he wouldn't be so big and sassy." He grinned again, as if he'd just had an amusing thought. "Or do you just catch him, feed him the worms and then throw him back? Is that where he got his preference for worms?"

Jimmy Joe shook his head solemnly. "No, we don't catch him." He dropped his eyes and nervously dug the toe of one shoe into the soft ground.

Sarah could see the guarded look that flickered across the boy's face. Apparently Matthias did, too.

A teasing grin tugged at the corners of the man's mouth. "So you don't catch him, huh? What does that mean? That you just feed him worms?"

When Jimmy Joe gave a guilty start, Matthias hesitated, then laughed aloud. "You had me going there for a minute," he told the boy. "Feed a bass worms, indeed. That, young man, is quite a story."

"I ain't telling no story, mister."

"That's what makes you so good. You just spun me a tall tale about feeding a lake bass worms, and you didn't say a word. You are something else, Jimmy Joe Lutteral."

"But I didn't tell you I feed Scarface worms," the boy insisted, a proud, stubborn look on his face.

"If you don't," the man said, "then who am I supposed to believe does?"

"Cissie."

Jordan eyed the boy standing defiantly in front of him. If Jimmy Joe's face was to be believed, he meant every word he'd said, as well as a few he hadn't uttered. Under his penetrating gaze the boy shifted his weight again, but refused to lower his eyes.

"Tell me, why do you call the bass Scarface?"

"'Cause he's got a big scar across his snout."

"You've actually seen him that close? Close enough to see a scar?"

"Sure."

Jordan studied the boy a minute longer, then threw back his head and laughed again, his teeth a flash of white in his suntanned face.

"You still doubtin' my word, mister?" Jimmy Joe asked defiantly.

Jordan let his gaze drop to the redheaded youngster again. "Let's just say you tell a good story, Jimmy Joe."

"You *are* doubtin' my word."

Jordan saw the anger spark in the boy's eyes. "There's no need to get mad. I've admitted you tell one of the best yarns I've ever heard. It beats the usual one-that-got-away tale all to heck."

"I never said he got away."

"That's an expression, Jimmy Joe. It's a classification for a tall tale—fisherman-style."

"But you ain't believing me."

The man paused, uncertainty and a bit of regret registering plainly on his face. "Would it make you happier if I said I believed your story?" he asked softly.

"Not if you didn't."

"That's what I thought. So, what do we do now?"

Jimmy Joe gave a quick sideways glance at the thicket before moving his eyes toward the deep pool. Then he looked uneasily into the fisherman's face.

The boy's obvious dismay disturbed Jordan. Damn it. He hadn't meant to back him into a corner. Who would have thought the kid would defend a point of integrity so intensely? He watched as the youngster grappled with his dilemma and saw the boy's eyes clear as he came to a decision.

Jimmy Joe turned toward the thicket. "Cissie," he bellowed. "Cissie, you gotta come out now."

"Why are you calling your cousin, Jimmy Joe?"

"'Cause Grandpa says that if a man doubts your word there's only two things you can do."

"And what are they?"

"You can either beat him till he cries uncle or you can prove yourself to his face."

"So why are you calling Cissie?"

"'Cause you're too big for me to whup."

Jordan bit the inside of his cheek in his effort to keep from laughing in front of the boy and nodded his head in acknowledgment. He didn't dare betray his excitement. It wasn't likely that Jimmy Joe's cousin, the one with the "sight," was the missing schoolteacher. But there was always that slim chance.

Sarah had known she was going to have to go to the boy's aid even before Jimmy Joe's summons. She'd waited, resigned, for his call, knowing it was as inevitable as the fact that out of the hundreds of miles of shoreline around Beaver Lake, Jordan Matthias had chosen to fish on her doorstep.

Only when she was pushing her way through the thicket did inspiration strike. She looked down at her tattered, berry-stained shirt. Overly large, and long-sleeved for protection against the briars, it adequately disguised the curves of her slim figure. Her five-foot-nothing height was often the cause of her being mistaken for someone much younger than twenty-seven. If she allowed herself to slip into the colloquial speech of the area, she might be able to pull it off.

As a plan, it wasn't the best, but it was the only chance she had. She would keep her eyes downcast and her face averted as much as possible, help Jimmy Joe uphold his honor, then get out of there. The man asking questions about a schoolteacher from St. Louis wouldn't expect to find her disguised as an urchin wading along the edge of the lake.

Sarah hesitated again at the top of the bluff. Even protected by distance and the camouflage of the thicket, she was barely able to control her racing pulse. She took another deep breath. This was for Jimmy Joe, she reminded herself, and stepped out of the underbrush.

There was no ladylike way to get to the bottom of the slope, but she wasn't supposed to be a lady, anyway. She sat down with studied nonchalance and pushed off with her hands, giving a perfect imitation of Jimmy Joe's earlier descent on the seat of his pants. One small moan escaped her when she came to an abrupt halt at the bottom of the bank. Her head snapped back, allowing her eyes to connect for a quick moment with those of the fisherman.

His eyes were brown, the color of rich, newly turned earth. At the moment they were wide with surprise, locked with hers in a gaze that seemed to look into her soul. Again she controlled a shiver, lowering her lashes and scrambling hastily to her feet.

Jordan had waited in barely concealed anticipation for the mysterious cousin to emerge from her hiding place. The possibility that this cousin with the "sight" might be the woman he was looking for was more than he dared hope. No, he wasn't sure what he'd been expecting, but it certainly wasn't the slip of a girl now standing in front of him.

She was small—actually, not much taller than the boy. And shy. She was careful to keep her gaze lowered. From what he could see of her averted face, there wasn't a lot of family resemblance between them. Of course, both were sunburned, which suggested the same fair skin. And there was the matter of the red hair. Not that theirs was anything alike. Jimmy Joe's was that flame red often described by writers but rarely seen. The girl's wasn't really red. It was more of a sun-streaked ash blond.

Sarah shifted uneasily under his intense scrutiny and placed one foot slightly behind the other, copying a gesture she had seen Jimmy Joe make earlier, deliberately digging her toe into the dirt.

"I told you I weren't dressed for strangers," she said to Jimmy Joe, "and you weren't supposed to tell about Scarface." She tried to sound petulant, but not too angry. She couldn't overact, or the boy would give her away.

"I'm sorry, Cissie. I just . . . I just . . ."

He looked so woebegone, Sarah had to steel herself to keep from giving him a reassuring smile or hug. She wouldn't really have minded if it hadn't been this man. And that certainly wasn't Jimmy Joe's fault.

"It's all right," she said. "This one time, anyway. Go find some worms, and I'll help you prove it to his face."

Jimmy Joe's grin lit his face. "I'll find some," he called over his shoulder, already running down the shoreline.

"Well, Cissie," the man standing beside her said quietly, "what do we do now?" He addressed her directly, hoping he could coax her into looking at him again.

Sarah kept her lashes lowered. "Wait for Jimmy Joe to find some worms."

He tried again. "And then?"

This time the tactic worked. She glanced up. Again his gaze locked with hers, a heated probing look so intense it seemed to burn the air from her lungs. "And then," she answered in a soft, almost breathless voice, lowering her face again, "I'll feed that old fish."

Jordan was confused. Jimmy Joe's cousin looked to be about sixteen, small, and gawky to the point of studied awkwardness. But his second glimpse of those mysterious green-blue eyes had strengthened his first impression. They didn't belong on a sixteen-year-old girl. A wood nymph, perhaps. Or a Lorelie.

He shook his head to dispel his fanciful thoughts and studied the girl again. Her hair was parted in the middle and loosely tied with pieces of yarn on either side of her head, above her delicate ears, in a style reminiscent of pigtails but without the confinement of braids. The way she held her shoulders, her slender neck and her finely formed head said that she was young and shy.

Cissie was exactly what she seemed at first glance, he assured himself—a somewhat shy teenager, nervous around strangers and completely chagrined at being caught in her berry-picking clothes. But God help the male sex when she grew a little more. Those eyes would have to be classified as lethal weapons.

"I got 'em, Cissie," Jimmy Joe yelled, running toward them along the bank. "I got three good worms. Think they'll be enough?"

"They'll be enough," Sarah assured him, reaching out with one hand and accepting the squirming creatures from the boy.

"What's next?" Jordan asked.

This time Sarah didn't look up. She didn't dare. "Now I feed Scarface," she said matter-of-factly. Still holding the worms in one hand, she began wading carefully into the water, heading from shore toward deeper water.

"If you want to see him, you'll have to come closer," she called over her shoulder, still managing not to look Jordan in the face. "But you've got to stay behind me so he don't see your shadow."

She moved cautiously into the lake, not stopping until the water was swirling just below her knees. "It ought to be deep enough 'bout here." She hunkered down in the water, ignoring the wet backside of her jeans and her flapping shirttail. Both Jordan and Jimmy Joe followed her into the water.

"Be quiet now," she cautioned. With her free hand she picked up a rock and tapped it against a small underwater boulder. She sat quietly for a moment, then tapped the rocks together again.

Jordan almost held his breath as he stared down into the lake. The water was so clear, he could distinguish the individual rocks on the lake bottom. He found himself anticipating, but he was still not ready to believe his eyes when a shadow, and then the graceful swimming form of an eighteen-inch largemouth bass, brushed by the girl's legs.

Sarah stretched out her hand, dangling the end of one of the worms just below the surface of the water. In the sunlight Jordan could see the distinctive black stripe on the side of the old bass. His flexible body bore the marks and scars of many years. Most pronounced was a misshapen dorsal fin and a large scar across the snout, as if the bass had rammed his head into a jar, neatly removing skin and scales in a perfect arc.

The fish nudged the girl's leg again, then moved back toward her hand and took a dainty nibble of the worm dangling in the water. He nibbled again before pulling the rest of the worm from her hand.

As the bass repeated the sequence, the girl calmly fed it the other two earthworms. The fish nudged her empty hand once more before flipping his tail and gliding silently out of sight.

Deliberately keeping her back to Jordan, Sarah stood, wiping her hand on the front of her shirt. She turned slightly and spoke to the boy in a soft voice. "Okay, Jimmy Joe?"

Jimmy Joe's eyes seemed to grin as he nodded.

"Grandma's waiting on the berries," she reminded the boy. "We gotta go home now." Still not daring to look at Jordan, she waded carefully back to the shore, ignoring the water streaming off her wet jeans and down her legs.

Jordan watched her climb the clay bank, still not quite able to accept the evidence of his own eyes.

"Come along now, Jimmy Joe, you hear?" Sarah called down.

"Just a minute, Cissie. Please?"

"All right," she said, barely managing to disguise her urgent need to get away. "But hurry up. Grandma's waiting."

"You going to be fishing here anymore, mister?"

Jimmy Joe's question jerked Jordan's attention back to the boy standing beside him.

"I planned to spend another couple of days in the area. However, I think I need a new fishing spot." He grinned at the boy. "I don't believe I'll catch much here."

Jimmy Joe was beaming, unable to hide his look of satisfaction. "There's a good hole about half a mile up shore," he offered. "An old snag hangs out over the water."

"Would you mind if I tried it?"

Jimmy Joe shook his head.

"Then I might tomorrow. Want to fish with me?"

Jimmy Joe shook his head again. "Ain't Friday. But I might come by and visit a spell."

"Do you only fish on Fridays?"

This time Jimmy Joe nodded his head. "Grandma fixes fish on Fridays."

"Every Friday?"

"Uh-huh."

"What happens if you don't catch enough?"

"I always do," Jimmy Joe assured him.

Jordan grinned again, amused by his supreme confidence.

"I gotta go now," the boy told him.

Jordan nodded. "Maybe I'll see you tomorrow, then," he said. "And Jimmy Joe, thank you, and thank your cousin for showing me Scarface."

"That's okay." Jimmy Joe scrambled up the clay bank to where his cousin was waiting. He turned to wave before they both disappeared into the thicket.

Jordan began collecting his fishing gear, his mind busy sorting through his impressions. The children, the lake, the countryside, its people—everything about this place intrigued him. Rural settings weren't new to him. The small farms, nestled like green emeralds in tiny valleys, reminded him of the home he'd known as a boy. But something about this place was different. It called to him, fascinated him, seduced him.

Beaver Lake was another contradiction—behaving at times like a wild river as it moved north collecting waters from deep gorges, in other places softly, lazily lapping the shoreline, like a complacent lover.

Then there was the woman—the one he'd come to find. For a moment, when the boy had first mentioned his cousin with the "sight," he'd hoped his search was about to end. He should have known it wasn't going to be that easy. Three days ago he'd been almost ready to give up his hunt. Then he'd discovered Sarah Wilson's name in the county tax records. But even that was strange. The deeds were part of old Monte Ne—a resort now buried under the waters of Beaver Lake.

Jordan wondered if he should backtrack to St. Louis and try a new path. No, damn it. The woman was here. He'd keep looking. Eventually he'd find her.

Besides, he wasn't ready to leave. Something held him. This was a place of enchantment—a place where children tamed lake bass.

Jordan's eyes moved once again to the place where he'd last seen the boy and girl. Jimmy Joe was a lovable imp. It had taken a lot of character for the boy to refrain from telling him "I told you so." His thoughts switched then to the girl. Mysterious eyes and the ability to charm the fish in the lake. Absolutely unbelievable.

Chapter 2

Sarah wasn't really surprised at the message awaiting her when she and Jimmy Joe returned to her grandparents' farm.

"Your aunt Cinda wants to see you," her grandmother told her. "T.J. brought the message."

"Did he say why?"

Sarah's grandmother shook her head. "She said you would know."

Yes, she knew. She'd known it would come to this ever since the stranger had first appeared in the valley. She'd tried to avoid it—to avoid him—but the meeting by the lake had destroyed her last defense. It was too late to alter events now.

Sarah sighed. Then, when she saw the concerned look on her grandmother's face, she forced a smile to her lips. The strange ability she shared with her grandmother's older sis-ter was one that was accepted but never discussed by the family. Neither was it understood. Sarah wasn't sure she understood it herself, nor the bond it created between them.

Why hadn't Aunt Cinda's daughter or even her granddaughter received the gift? She knew it could skip a generation, and in her case, it had. Aunt Cinda was the only one of that generation, just as Sarah was the only one of all her cousins who possessed it. In the generation between, there had been no one. Perhaps that was just as well. The bond between the two of them was frightening at times. She wasn't sure she could cope with another such bond.

Sarah redirected her thoughts. "Don't worry so, Grandma. I'm sure it's nothing. Maybe she's just feeling lonely. I haven't been to Hogscald in several days."

"Maybe, Cissie," her grandmother said, obviously not convinced. "I wish you could talk her into moving to Mountain Springs. Lord knows I've tried often enough. She's so far away, and there's no phone up the hollow. She gets around all right inside the cabin and right around the house, but she couldn't see to come down the mountain, even if she was able."

"I'll see what I can do, Grandma. I think she knows she'll have to move down before winter. T.J. or one of the other boys stops in every day now, but when winter comes they might not be able to get up there every day."

She smiled gently at her grandmother's frown. "It will be all right. Really it will."

"Are you going now? Or will you wait until morning?"

Sarah hesitated. When Aunt Cinda went to the trouble to send a messenger, as well as— "I think I had better go after supper. There'll be plenty of daylight left. And if I don't, she might start fretting."

Her grandmother nodded.

Shortly before sundown Sarah stepped onto Aunt Cinda's front porch and peered in the open door. She'd parked

the car at the end of the road and hiked the last half mile up
the trail to the cabin high on the side of the mountain overlooking Hogscald Hollow. Despite the fact that the sun was
low on the horizon, she was hot and tired.

The gnarled old apple trees around the cabin, planted by
a great-great-grandfather nearly a century before, cast
shadows across the small windows, throwing the interior
into semidarkness. There were no lanterns lit. Sarah doubted
that her great-aunt even bothered to light them now, except
for the convenience of a guest. It would make no difference
to her nearly sightless eyes.

"Aunt Cinda? It's Sarah. You wanted to see me?"

She moved into the cabin, waiting for her eyes to adjust
to the darkness. Her great-aunt was sitting in a rocking chair
beside the unlit hearth, her shoulders covered, as always, by
a soft woolen shawl. Her once-luxurious hair stood in white
wisps like combed cotton around her lined face.

"I've been waitin' for you, child, but you already know
why I sent for you."

"Aunt Cinda—" Sarah began, protesting.

"Don't you 'Aunt Cinda' me, Sarah Jane Wilson. You
know good and well why I had to send for you. And don't
you be trying to tell me no different. You know you have to
see him."

The image of the stranger's face flashed through Sarah's
mind. Why was he looking for her? Not that it mattered.
Events were already out of her hands. For better or worse,
she and this stranger were entwined in some way—for some
reason. Sarah sighed, wishing she could see into her own
future the way she sometimes saw into others.

"Yes, you know," the old lady continued confidently.
"What makes you wait when you know it has to be done?"

"I thought— I'm afraid."

"Why, child? What makes you kick against it so hard? What comes, will come."

"I know, Aunt Cinda. But this time...this time I sense change. And I'm not sure I want it. I don't even know what it is. I can tell Grandpa where he left his reading glasses. I can warn Bobby Wade to check his left rear tire before it goes flat. I can tell Uncle Hiram he has time to hay the south pasture before it starts raining. But I can't tell you what I'll eat for breakfast tomorrow. I don't even know *if* I'll eat tomorrow."

Aunt Cinda smiled at her gently, her expression reflecting love and understanding. "If you knew what you'd be eating tomorrow, you might be tempted to change it. And might be that it was best you didn't. If you need to know, if you need to change it, you'll know. As for the other, just living's change. You know that. What comes, comes."

She paused, but Sarah knew she wasn't waiting for a comment.

"The last time...the little boy in St. Louis? It bothers you?"

"No. Yes. I mean... I don't know. I feel tomorrow's all mixed up with yesterday."

"Did you have trouble? Did someone find you out?"

"I don't think so. I called that sergeant friend of Sam Bascomb's. He acted like... Well, at least he didn't out-and-out disbelieve me. Not like the first time, anyway. It was all so muddled. I didn't see much. Just bits and pieces. I was afraid I didn't know enough. I had to call anyway, Aunt Cinda. I didn't have any choice."

"Of course you didn't."

"But I felt so vulnerable. So exposed," Sarah said, hoping the old woman couldn't see the tears in her eyes, then realizing she would know anyway. "There was so little time.

He was being so brave, and he was so scared. I was afraid I didn't know enough—that they wouldn't find him in time."

"But you did. They found him."

"Yes, they found him. Still, there's something in the past that isn't finished. Maybe it's something to do with the boy. This man may be part of it."

"Then you can't avoid it—or him."

"I came home for peace, Aunt Cinda. As long as I'm here, I'm fine. But out there... It's all some kind of bad joke. Even when I was talking to that sergeant... I told him everything I knew. Then I asked him if it was enough, if they could find the boy. Do you know what he said? He said, 'I don't know, miss. You're the one with a crystal ball.' And he's supposed to be a friend."

"He hasn't known you long. Give it a little time, honey. Folks 'round here have known you all your life, and some of them are still a bit skittish. That comes from being afraid of what they can't understand. You know that. You did your best. What you had to do. That's all anybody can do. Lots of times we can't see the whole design."

Sarah let her aunt's reassuring words wash over her, knowing that if anyone could understand what she was feeling it was Aunt Cinda.

"Sometimes there's no way of knowing what's going to happen," Aunt Cinda reminded her. "Then's when you have to take a chance and don't go worrying about it."

"You mean, follow my own instincts?"

"Instincts, heart—whatever you want to call it. Just be sure you listen to yourself. Life don't come with any guarantees, child. Just listen to your own self."

Aunt Cinda fell silent for a moment, staring into the open hearth. Sarah waited patiently.

"It's good you came home to rest. That's just fine. But now you have to see this stranger. It's important."

A tiny shiver of apprehension moved up Sarah's spine. This time there would be no hiding, no pretense. This time, when the man's eyes probed hers, he would know who she was. But she still wouldn't know the reason he was looking for her. And by the time she found out it might be too late.

"Do you know this stranger, Aunt Cinda? Why he's asking about me? Why he's so important?"

"I don't rightly know why jus' yet. But he's important. You know it, too. If I knew who he was, maybe I could see more...."

"How did you know he was looking for me?"

"I knowed it the same way you did, child. Though I don't reckon we needed any special help this time. The whole valley's buzzing with the news. You have to talk to him, Sarah. Best find out where he's staying."

Sarah laughed ruefully. "That shouldn't be too hard. His name isn't a common one—not around here, anyway. He'll be in one of the fishing camps along the lake."

The old woman went still, and Sarah waited for her to speak.

"You know his name?" Aunt Cinda frowned. "You've already seen him." This last was a statement, not a question.

"Jimmy Joe and I talked with him at the lake," Sarah admitted. "But he didn't know who I was. His name is Matthias, Jordan Matthias. At least that's what he said."

There was a sudden light in her aunt's eyes as she turned toward Sarah. "He is handsome, this Matthias?"

Although it was phrased as a question, Sarah recognized its rhetorical quality. "He's all that, Aunt Cinda," she said softly, as the image of his compelling face and his leashed strength again sent a rush of blood to her face.

"And young?"

"Mid-thirties, I'd say."

The old lady nodded. "He's a lone one. No hearth," she said, almost to herself. "Now I'm beginning to understand."

Sarah was puzzled. Her great-aunt had chosen to remain isolated all her life. She monitored the joys and burdens of kith and kin throughout the valley, but seldom read outsiders, and particularly not ones she'd never touched or spoken to. So how did she know? Unless she was reading him through her great-niece. But that was impossible. Sarah had sensed nothing of that.

"You know him, Aunt Cinda? You know what he wants?"

"Yes. I know what he wants now. Even he doesn't know that. Not yet. There be other reasons for him being here." She lapsed into silence again.

Sarah waited expectantly. It would do no good to prompt the old woman. She'd say only what she wanted to say. And only when she wanted to say it.

When Aunt Cinda broke her silence, her voice was quiet, almost detached. "Do you like him, Sarah Jane?"

Did she like him? It was a question she'd avoided thinking about. "I don't know. I think I might have, if I hadn't been so afraid. He was good with Jimmy Joe. Jimmy Joe liked him."

"Youngsters have a way of seeing the truth. They don't let other things get in the way. They learn from yesterday, but they don't drag it around with them. It's time you let go of some things, too."

"I know, Aunt Cinda. I tell myself the same thing every day. It's why I made myself take that job in St. Louis. But it's hard."

The old lady nodded, sympathy in every line of her face. "You did right. Can't let what's gone tell us what's going to be." She paused for a moment, then abruptly changed the subject. "He's got no roots, this Matthias. And he's looking for Monte Ne."

"Monte Ne?" Sarah couldn't keep the surprise from her voice. Why had a stranger come looking for Monte Ne? Only a few old-timers and local historians even remembered the turn-of-the-century resort. "Monte Ne's been gone over sixty years," she said finally.

"Yes, but that may be the reason he looks for you. That may be the part of the past you're worrying about."

"I'm afraid I still don't understand, Aunt Cinda."

"He looks for Monte Ne, Sarah. Before the lake, who owned Monte Ne?"

Sarah shook her head. "I did," she admitted. "At least I owned some of the land where Monte Ne once stood."

The old woman nodded. "You owned enough. Go see him, Sarah."

The image of the stranger's face swam before Sarah's eyes, so real that she clenched her fists to keep from reaching up and placing her finger in the deep cleft of his chin. She blinked and released a shuddering breath.

"All right, Aunt Cinda," she agreed, struggling to keep her voice from wavering. "If you think it's so important, I'll see him."

"When?"

"Thursday. I'll see him Thursday."

Once again Jordan Matthias's eyes intently searched the area around the town square. He could see one old farmer dressed in overalls leaning against the antique hitching post in front of the town hall. That was all. No sign of anyone who might be Sarah Wilson.

After all this time and effort, it looked as if Miss Sarah Wilson was going to be handed to him on a plate. He didn't bother to suppress the grin that turned the corners of his mouth upward. Today was the day—if the whole thing wasn't a joke. He doubted that anyone around this town would play that kind of joke on him, though. True, a lot of people knew he was asking questions about the woman, but not one of them had ever heard of her. At least that was the answer he always received. Then someone had pushed that note under his door at the fishing camp.

For the tenth time he glanced at his watch. The note had been specific. "If you wish to speak with Sarah Wilson, be in the second booth of the Mountain Springs Café at three o'clock." That was all. No signature. No indication of where the note had come from or how it had been delivered.

Jordan opened the screen door and stepped inside the café. Despite the heat of the Arkansas summer, there was no air conditioning. An old-fashioned blade fan hanging from the high ceiling turned lazily. Its efforts only slightly disturbed the humid air, which was filled with the odors of frying onions and stale cigarette smoke.

He looked anxiously toward the row of booths along one wall. Then he relaxed. Whoever had written the note—assuming it wasn't a joke—obviously knew the café. Several of the tables, those most directly in front of the screened front door, were occupied, but the side booths were all empty. All three of them. No mistaking which booth was the second one. It would be the same if you counted from front to rear or from rear to front. Jordan wondered if the designation was deliberate or simply a lucky coincidence.

He glanced at his watch again. Exactly three o'clock. Well, he could afford to wait a few minutes on the off chance that Sarah Wilson, or at least someone who knew her, would show up. She'd certainly led him on a wild-goose chase thus far. He could only hope that the capture was as interesting as the hunt.

A young dark-haired girl approached the booth from behind the counter, pad and pencil in hand.

"Only iced tea for now," he told her. "I'm supposed to meet someone here."

The girl nodded, slipped the pad and pencil into the pocket of her apron and turned back toward the counter. She returned in a moment with a tall glass of iced tea and, still, without saying a word, set it in front of him.

Jordan sipped the tea and waited, letting his mind drift back over the details of his search for Sarah Wilson. He'd first heard of her while visiting a former army buddy who was now a police officer in St. Louis. At the time, the police had been busy searching for a missing boy. Hoyston had taken the telephone call from the woman.

Jordan recalled that his buddy had been gruff, almost antagonistic, as he'd recorded her information. She'd described the missing boy perfectly, even to his torn T-shirt. She'd talked about an old house with boarded-up windows, an old-fashioned peony garden, country scenery, city sounds and the smell of old burned wood. She'd said the boy had been left alone but would be in danger when the sun's rays began shining through the cracks between the boards covering the west windows of the house.

A psychic! Jordan had tried to hide his excitement, but Hoyston knew him too well. "Don't say a word," his friend had growled. "You didn't hear anything. You aren't even here. Get out. Right now. I'll talk to you later."

Jordan knew Hoyston, too, and knew when he meant business. So he had left, depending on his friend to make good on his promise to talk to him later.

Even as a boy, Jordan had been intrigued by the unusual—magicians, the supernatural, the unexplained. Houdini had been an early hero. As he had grown older he had realized it was all show business. As a boy, he'd wanted to believe in magic. As a man, he knew it didn't exist, but one small part of him refused to accept that. He was still looking for the magic. In his travels he'd uncovered several truly remarkable stories, but none of them had stood up to close examination. Even the most promising had been frauds.

It was his pursuit of one story that had led to his present career. His investigation of a Wall Street soothsayer had turned up evidence not only of fraud but of misuse of insider information, and that had led to criminal charges and the conviction of the major participants. His coverage of the story had attracted the attention of the editor of a major newsmagazine, and although Jordan had refused to join the organization, not wanting to be tied to a desk, the editor had kept him busy, often using him as a free-lance correspondent to cover stories in remote places where the magazine did not maintain an office. In the last few years his investigative articles had been international in scope and far removed from the realm of crystal-ball gazers and fortunetellers.

But the subject still fascinated him, and each time he heard another psychic story he investigated it, hoping this would be the one, the one he couldn't explain away. These stories were his recreation, his way of taking a vacation after a rough assignment. This time, the timing was perfect. After eighteen months on assignment in the jungles of South America he'd been ready for a vacation. Investigating Hoyston's psychic connection had seemed to be the perfect way to spend it.

He'd waited expectantly for Hoyston to contact him following his abortive visit with his old friend. The next day the papers had been full of the story. The police had discovered the missing boy in an attic room of a decaying old mansion—a half-burned building isolated on a five-acre plot—that had once been one of St. Louis's most prestigious homes. There had been no mention of a telephone call or a tip to the police or a psychic.

Several days had passed before he was able to reestablish contact with Hoyston, but the wait had been worth it.

"Next to me, you're the last person in the world I would expect to be tied up with a soothsayer," Jordan had told his friend. "How come? Have you turned believer on me?"

Hoyston had been silent for a moment. "I don't know anymore," he admitted. "My head tells me it's a bunch of garbage, but— Look, Jordan, I've talked to the lady exactly three times. The first time was sort of a get-acquainted talk. The next two were business. You heard the last one. Both times she knew exactly what she was talking about. The first time I thought she was probably involved. She wasn't. Believe me. I checked it out every way from Sunday. There is no earthly way that woman could have known what she knew. This time, either. You read the papers. We found the boy where she said we would."

"The papers didn't mention her."

"No. That's one of the conditions. Nobody is to know who she is. No one is to know she's involved."

"That's unusual. In most of the cases I've investigated, the more publicity, the better."

"Not according to her. She says people with her skills are natural targets for notoriety, that the serious ones don't encourage publicity. Claims it interferes."

Jordan had been even more intrigued. Most of the psychics he'd investigated had been more than willing to court publicity. They'd been happy to cooperate with him— at least until he'd managed to expose them as frauds. This woman sounded different.

"How'd you make contact with her? Why did she pick you, of all people?"

"I worked on a case with the sheriff from her hometown a couple of years back. He called me. Said he had a friend moving here and wanted me to talk to her. Made me promise I'd listen to her, then give her one chance to prove herself. One chance, he said. Didn't tell me what she'd be proving, or I'd probably have laughed in his face. But I gave him my word. So when she called, I had to follow through."

"Do you think she's genuine?"

"I told you, I don't know what to think."

"What's her name? What's she look like?"

"I can't tell you that, Jordan. Geez. I just explained, we have an agreement."

"Come on, Hoyston. Give. You know you can trust me. Tell me her name. How am I going to find out if she's on the level if I don't know who she is?"

"Now, look," his friend had protested. "I made a sort of agreement with the lady. She helps me and I protect her identity. I don't know where she gets it, but it's good information. I don't want to blow the connection."

"And what if your first instinct was right? What if she is involved somehow?"

"You're not getting around me that way, Jordan. I know you use words until white sounds like black. But the lady's on the right side. Otherwise she wouldn't be feeding me the information she does."

"The other time she helped—was it a kidnapping, too?"

Hoyston shook his head. "Hell, no. A mugging. A plain, everyday mugging. The victim was an old man. He didn't even have anything worth stealing except his social security check. If it hadn't been for the lady's information, the report would have joined hundreds of others in the inactive, unsolved file. But, thanks to her, we not only found the mugger—with the goods still on him—we also stumbled over a fencing operation that cleared over a dozen commercial robberies. It was a good bust."

"Any links between the fencing operation and the kidnappers?"

"Not that we know of. 'Course, we haven't caught the dudes yet. But it doesn't seem likely."

"But you don't know," Jordan had said, pressing home his argument. "You probably didn't round up the entire fencing ring. And you don't know who kidnapped the boy. There is a definite connection between them. You just don't want to admit it. One woman squealed on both operations."

"I told you, I checked her out," Hoyston had protested. "She wasn't involved."

"Maybe," Jordan had said, "and maybe not. What harm would it do to run a double check? And you won't even have to use department hours. I'll do it."

"You're not interested in the fencing operation, or the kidnapping. Just the woman. And a story. I thought you'd finished chasing crystal-ball readers. Moved on to bigger and better things."

Jordan had grinned. "This one interests me. Besides, I'm between assignments. Nothing better to do."

In the end Jordan had finally worn down his friend's resistance. Hoyston had given him Sarah Wilson's name.

"Don't you ever let anyone know where you got it," Hoyston had told him. "Her friend—the sheriff in her hometown—his name's Sam Bascomb. He can be one tough hombre when he's riled. I'm warning you, Jordan, Sarah Wilson's a prima donna, and Bascomb's her private guard. I'll admit I don't know much about the lady, but I do know this—she doesn't want anyone to know who she is. Or what she is. Whatever she is."

Jordan had laid his plans accordingly. He'd discovered that Sarah Wilson was a history teacher in St. Louis. But before he could find her she'd left Missouri for summer vacation. He'd followed her into her home territory and continued his search. Remembering Hoyston's warning, he'd avoided Sheriff Bascomb, although he knew the man was probably well-informed about his movements and his questions. For that reason Jordan had been careful not to hide his search. He'd found the hunt exciting, if at times frustrating. Now the hunt was almost over. Maybe.

He checked his watch again. Five after three. He wasn't going to give up this early. He was still willing to wait.

Chapter 3

Sarah let herself in the back door of the café and silently waved to her cousin behind the counter. Betsy returned the wave with a grin, then continued filling the salt and pepper shakers lined up on the counter in front of her.

Standing at the end of the counter, Sarah had a clear view of the man waiting in the middle booth. He sat facing the front entrance of the café, his eyes intent on the empty doorway. Without the fisherman's hat his light brown hair fell forward in a boyish wave over one side of his forehead. His features were as strong and unyielding as she remembered. Despite his casual air, she sensed the same self-assurance in him that she had recognized by the lake. This was a determined man with the persistence not to give up a search easily.

She drew a deep breath and crossed the space between the counter and the booth, her sandals making no noise on the worn wooden floor. She stood silently at the side of the booth, her body tense, her hands clenched at her sides.

Even if Aunt Cinda was right, even if his reasons for looking for her were innocent, she was still in danger. She'd been unable to explain that to Aunt Cinda. Jordan Matthias disturbed her in a way no other man ever had. She was risking more than exposure. Still, she had promised. She waited for him to acknowledge her presence.

Jordan was watching the café entrance so intently that it took him several seconds to realize that someone was standing by the booth. He turned slightly, thinking it was the waitress. A moment later he forgot the front door completely.

The woman standing beside the booth was small and perfectly proportioned. Her slim, tanned legs looked long and willowy despite her lack of height. The tiny waist above the gently flaring hips and the small breasts swelling beneath the crisp sleeveless cotton blouse were all definitely feminine.

Jordan shifted in his seat, turning his body toward her. Their eyes locked then—his an unbelieving brown, hers shifting prisms of blue-green light.

He unconsciously grasped the table, his knuckles turning white as he stared openly at the woman. The world around him suddenly faded away. The wooden floor of the café became the mud of the lakeshore. The quiet hum of the overhead fan was the gentle buzzing of june bugs and honeybees, and the woman's eyes were the mysterious, shifting waters of the lake.

"Mr. Matthias? I'm Sarah Wilson. I understand you wish to speak with me?"

Her voice pulled Jordan from his time warp. Those were the same eyes he had seen by the lake. He was sure of it. But Cissie had been about sixteen. Sarah Wilson was definitely a full-grown woman. And he'd been right. Her eyes were lethal.

Still bemused, he made an effort to stand, to offer her a seat. She seemed to take his initial movement as an invitation, and without waiting for the words she slid into the seat on the opposite side of the booth.

"You're Sarah Wilson?" He heard the incredulous note in his own voice. "I expected someone else. I mean, I certainly didn't expect you!"

She must have recognized the accusation in his voice. Yes, she knew he was referring to their encounter by the lake. She had the grace to look slightly uncomfortable.

"You knew who I was, that I was looking for you," he charged.

"I knew a stranger was asking questions," she admitted. "I suspected it was you. There aren't too many strangers in the valley."

"Then why didn't you say something?"

"Two days ago I wasn't sure I wanted to meet you," she told him.

"What happened? I mean, what changed your mind? Why did you suddenly decide to talk with me?"

Sarah shrugged her shoulders. "Just a feeling," she finally said.

Jordan scrutinized her face again, looking for more of an explanation. He found none—only the same haunting sense of incredulity he had experienced by the lake. Until this moment he had refused to acknowledge how disturbing the encounter had been. Perhaps, he reasoned, it was because he had refused to accept the fact that he had been so intrigued by, so attracted to, a mere child. It was a relief to know that the child was in reality a flesh-and-blood woman, and it was exhilarating to realize that at this moment she sat facing him from across the same table.

Then he remembered why he was here. This was the lady who claimed to be a psychic, then took such pains to hide

herself. And she'd hidden herself like a true professional.
She was cleverer than most of the pseudopsychics he'd run
across. His friend Hoyston had given him some pretty con-
vincing arguments that she was what she claimed, although
Jordan knew the policeman wasn't absolutely convinced.
Well, Jordan had no explanations, either. Not yet.

Jordan let his eyes meet hers across the table, uncomfortable with the fact that he wasn't in control. He'd been
unable to turn up a clue to her whereabouts—nothing that
would have forced her out of hiding. It was she who'd broken the deadlock, who'd decided to meet him. Now she was
sitting in front of him, a look of innocence on her face. No,
not quite. Her eyes were mysterious, almost hypnotic, but
they weren't trusting. They were wary.

Something of his thoughts must have been reflected in his
face. He saw her tiny frown, saw the shadow of uncertainty
that flickered in her eyes. He quickly made his expression
blank. Damn! She was suspicious. Somehow he'd have to
disarm her.

"You realize, of course, that you're really a figment of my
imagination," he said in a joking tone. "I mean, you don't
really exist. Ask anyone in here. As a matter of fact, ask
anyone in town. Sarah Wilson simply doesn't exist. Never
did. No one has ever heard of you."

She smiled sympathetically. "Don't be too hard on
them," she replied. "They're kin."

"Kin. You mean like relatives?"

She nodded.

"The whole town?"

"It's a small town. Most of us are related one way or another. If not blood kin, or kissing kin, then shirttail kin. If
there's anyone in town I'm not related to, they're probably
related to some of my kin."

Jordan leaned against the back of the booth. Amazing. He'd been chasing this woman for weeks. If what she said was true, she could probably have remained hidden until he'd given up and left the area. But she'd decided to meet him. She'd known he was looking for her, yet she still hadn't questioned why. Instead, she sat in front of him, calmly discussing relatives. He knew his face echoed his confusion.

"Let me give you an example," Sarah said, obviously misreading his expression. "The old man who owns the fishing camp where you're staying, he's shirttail kin. Not really a blood relation of mine, but his brother is the father-in-law to my cousin Maybelle. Shirttail kin, see?"

So now he knew how the note had been delivered, Jordan thought. He would also have bet that his every movement had been reported back to her. "What you're saying is that this is really a closed community, right?" He tried to keep his voice neutral.

Sarah nodded.

"And everyone I asked about you probably knew you. They were protecting you as part of the family?"

"Protecting my privacy, anyway," Sarah said. "They let me know someone was asking for me. It was then my decision whether or not to contact you. You're an outsider, you see."

"Okay," Jordan said. "I think I understand. Now, since I know you, will they talk to me?"

"Oh, no. Except maybe about fishing or the weather."

"Why not? I mean, if they know you agreed to meet me..."

"You don't understand our ways," she said. "You were asking about me. It's precisely because I did meet you that they won't talk with you. And, what's more, before they were only curious about you. But if you keep asking questions, they'll become suspicious. You see, because you do know who I am now, if you have any questions, you should ask me to my face.''

Jordan laughed appreciatively, remembering Jimmy Joe's determination to prove his story. ''You're big on face-to-face relationships around here, aren't you?''

Sarah nodded.

''And,'' he added, as the thought occurred to him, ''you have just set me up. You deliberately selected our meeting place in the town's only café so that it would soon be known that you had chosen to meet me. Those three old men at the table in front of the door are probably unofficial town criers. If I want to find out anything about you, I have to ask you directly.''

''Something like that,'' she said, giving him a small, satisfied smile. ''So, Jordan Matthias, why are you looking for Sarah Wilson? What exactly do you want from me?''

Jordan couldn't help but admire her composure, just as he couldn't help but salute her strategy. He hadn't expected her to be so young, or so lovely. And he certainly hadn't expected to be so attracted to her. He'd have to watch that and focus on the real reason he was here.

Of one thing he was certain—it was going to be interesting to discover exactly who and what Sarah Wilson was. He was delighted with the terms she had set—face-to-face. Yes, he was going to enjoy this little game very much. Now it was his turn to smile.

''What do I want from you? Thirty minutes ago I could have told you exactly what I wanted. Now I'm not so sure....'' He paused, then deliberately allowed himself to look into the depths of those unusual eyes. ''But I think it's going to be fun finding out.''

For the first time since she had slipped into the booth opposite him he knew he'd caught her off balance.

"Mr. Matthias, I—"

"Call me Jordan."

Sarah appeared to consider that for a moment. "All right, Jordan, I—"

"Good. Then I can call you Sarah?"

She nodded again, her reluctance evident.

Jordan decided he'd pushed enough for the moment. He forced himself to relax. He'd keep it light, light and friendly.

"I'm sorry, Sarah. I'm forgetting my manners." He raised his arm to attract the waitress's attention. "Would you like something to drink? My tea was very refreshing. Or something to eat? We could go somewhere else."

"Oh, no, nothing," she told him. "I wouldn't care for anything, really, except— Well, you did ask to see me. At least you were asking about me. Everyone in the valley knows. I—I'd like to know why."

Jordan hesitated for a moment, mentally rehearsing his story. He'd given a lot of thought to what he would do once he found Sarah Wilson. Obviously he couldn't tell her why he'd begun looking for her. Not if Hoyston was right. Yet if he lied, and she really was psychic, she'd probably know. Would part of the truth suffice?

"It's something of a long story," he said, stalling for a little time. He had to stick as close to the truth as possible. Discovering her name on those old Monte Ne deeds had produced an unexpected bonus. They'd given him a lead on another story. The old resort fascinated him. Not as much as the woman, of course, but he had the feeling that the resort would also make a good story. Now all he had to do was convince Sarah Wilson. He'd tell her he was a writer researching a story on Monte Ne. She owned part of it. And she was a history teacher. Surely those two facts would be enough to convince her that she was the logical one for him to turn to for help.

"I'm looking for someone to help me with some historical research," he said at last. "I'm a writer, and I want to do a story on Monte Ne. I understand you own part of it."

Sarah laughed softly. "No, I don't own Monte Ne," she told him. "A man named William 'Coin' Harvey built Monte Ne. Both he and the resort were gone long before I was born. All I own is some of the land where Monte Ne once stood—a few scattered fragments, the remnants of Coin Harvey's dream."

"But according to the deed records—"

"My name's on some of the deeds," she said. "But there's not much of Monte Ne left. Nothing, actually." She paused. "You do know that most of Monte Ne is now under the waters of Beaver Lake, don't you?"

"Yes. But I'm more interested in what it was than in what it is." Jordan wasn't sure what he'd done, or how. But obviously, he'd made a right move. He watched her animated face—not a hint of distrust now. Monte Ne was the magic word.

"Monte Ne must have been unique," he said. "I read a pamphlet about railroad tycoons, maharajas, eastern millionaires, all coming to the Ozarks at a time when most of the country hardly knew the place existed, much less how to get here. I mean, in 1900 this part of the country was pretty isolated, wasn't it?"

"You've obviously done some homework, Mr. Matth—I mean Jordan."

Jordan nodded. "I can collect facts and figures," he told her. "But I think Monte Ne was more than a collection of buildings. I want to capture the feel of the place. I thought you might be able to help. Besides owning part of it, you're a history teacher, too, aren't you?"

Sarah's gasp of surprise was clearly audible. "How did you know I was a schoolteacher?" she asked in a tight voice, her expression tense and wary again.

Jordan knew he'd goofed even before he heard her sharp intake of breath. Now he struggled to keep his expression from betraying him. Damn it! Even in his days as a cub reporter he'd never fallen into such a trap. Why couldn't he keep his mind on his business? Talking to this woman was like negotiating an unmapped minefield. He braced himself to answer her question, hoping he could brazen it out.

"The tax records showed a St. Louis address," he said quickly. "When I tried to find you, I discovered you were a schoolteacher, but by that time you'd already left for the summer. So I came here." He was relieved to be able to tell her the truth—or at least a slightly edited version of the truth. He remembered how disappointed he'd been when the tax records had listed her St. Louis address rather than a local one. Sometimes the worst disasters were really blessings in disguise.

Sarah sat very still for a moment, considering Jordan's explanation. Had he discovered anything else about her while he'd been in St. Louis? When he'd first said he was a writer, she'd almost panicked. Did he really want to do an article on Monte Ne, or was he after another kind of story? But Aunt Cinda said he was looking for Monte Ne, and she was rarely wrong. Sarah was surprised at how much she wanted to believe him.

She could feel his eyes scouring her face. There was something intense and compelling about this man. Carefully she considered her options. She now recognized the flaws in her original strategy. Setting herself up as his primary source of information in the community had been a mistake. But it was too late for her to stay hidden. If she wanted to find out what or how much he knew she would have to continue talking to him.

"How long do you—I mean, how much time do you think it would take?"

"All I can get—but no more than you're willing to give me. You might enjoy it, you know."

"Oh, I know I would," she said. "There's nothing more exciting to a teacher than an interested student. But I have other obligations."

"A job? I'd be willing..."

"No. Nothing like that. Mostly family obligations. Jimmy Joe and—and some others."

"I know. The whole town. It might be small as towns go, but as a family..." Jordan shook his head. The laughter in his voice belied the frustration on his face. "No wonder I couldn't find out a damn thing."

Sarah stiffened, then relaxed as the warm tremors of his laughter wrapped around her. His flashes of good humor, the few moments when he relaxed, were as spellbinding as any vibrations she'd ever encountered, as intoxicating, as compelling, as any pied piper's music. It was just as well he didn't laugh all that often.

"That's just family," she said gently. "Families are protective of their own."

"I wouldn't know," he said harshly.

The rasp in his voice caught Sarah by surprise. She knew her reaction was obvious when Jordan smiled at her ruefully.

"I'm sorry," he said, his voice gentler now. "I didn't mean to sound so harsh. It's just, well I don't know much about families. Never gave it much thought one way or another. You don't miss what you never had—at least not until someone points it out to you."

Sarah's eyes softened. So Aunt Cinda was right again. He had no roots, no home. Even though she was surrounded by family, she understood what it meant to be alone.

Jordan appeared to be lost in thought, and Sarah took a moment to reexamine her choices—as if, she thought ruefully to herself, she had any. Tension formed a hard knot in her stomach. The heat inside the café was oppressive, but did she dare leave the protection of familiar ground? With this man? What kind of choice did she have? This time she'd simply have to trust her instincts—and Aunt Cinda's revelations.

"When would you want to start?" she asked.

"What?" he asked. Her question had obviously taken him by surprise.

"I said, when would you want to start?" she repeated. "The research, I mean. I've decided to help you—at least as much as I can. Monte Ne has always been a bit special to me, but not many people outside the area have ever heard of it. Your article could change that. Monte Ne was important, you know. And I'm not just talking about local pride. It has its place in the greater scheme of history."

"How?"

"Discovery is the excitement of research into the past," she told him teasingly. "I'd rather you discover it for yourself, but if you don't stumble onto it, I'll tell you later. In the interest of scholarship, of course."

"I'll hold you to that," he said. "As to when, how about now? Is there anything left to see?"

"Actually, you're here at a good time. Low water exposes a few skeletons. But I thought you were more interested in what was than what is."

"It's a good starting point. You can build on skeletons. Do you scuba? Could we get a closer look that way?"

Sarah shook her head. "Most of the Monte Ne land is under shallow water, at least when compared with the rest of the lake, but the currents are treacherous."

"Okay. You're the expert. What would you suggest?"

Sarah considered her next move carefully. She'd already agreed to help, but how far should she go? Could she trust this man? Could she trust herself with him? He was an outsider. She didn't get involved with outsiders, at least not any more than was necessary, and certainly not on her home turf.

Don't be ridiculous, she told herself. He was only interested in Monte Ne. That was a lie, of course. She could see it in his eyes. She couldn't even let herself think about trusting him. Was this what Eve had felt when first confronted with the forbidden fruit?

"What you need is a guided tour of what remains of Monte Ne and one of my hour lectures on local history." The words fell unbidden from her lips. Had she meant to say that? No matter. It was done. She was committed. "Do you have transportation?"

"Yes, but—"

"I mean a truck or a rough-terrain vehicle?"

"I've got a four-wheel-drive Blazer. Will that do?"

"It will do just fine," she said, anxious to leave now that her decision was made. "Let's go."

Thirty minutes later, following her instructions, Jordan shifted the Blazer into low gear and eased the vehicle off the road and onto a faintly marked trail between two twisted oaks. The vehicle tilted crazily as the wheels slid over boulders embedded in the dirt, then bounced out of a series of deep ruts.

Sarah sat as far away from Jordan as the seat belt and the jolting ride allowed. She was anxious to keep as much space between them as possible. But it was too little, too late. She should never have agreed to this, even if his motives were exactly what he said they were. She couldn't understand why this man affected her so, why she was so attracted to him when every instinct told her to run.

The quick look she sneaked at him from the corner of her eye did nothing to reassure her. In profile his features were strong and clean. High cheekbones, classic straight nose, well-defined mouth, chiseled cleft in a strong chin. Her eyes returned to his mouth. Would his lips demand or beguile? Seize or share? She shivered inwardly, astonished at the direction of her thoughts, and jerked her mind back to her surroundings.

"Pull in under those trees so it will be easier to turn around," Sarah said when they finally reached the crest of the ridge. "We're here."

She remained silent as Jordan looked around the flat ridgetop in disbelief. Jagged sandstone outcrops were only marginally softened by the tangle of weeds and wildflowers that grew around their bases or clung tenaciously to small hollows in the rock surface. The summer heat had dried the wild grasses to yellow straw. Even the glossy, saber-shaped leaves of the bamboolike Johnson grass were wilting in the hot afternoon sun.

"This is Monte Ne?" he asked, his skepticism evident in the tone of his voice.

"Of course not!" Sara laughed. "But we can see the original outlines of Monte Ne from the top of the bluff."

The trailing yellow dust kicked up by the wheels of the Blazer was still settling back to earth as she jumped unassisted from the vehicle's seat and waited for him to join her. "Come on," she said, moving across the small clearing. "But watch out for the poison ivy. It's especially bad in dry weather."

Sarah pushed her way through the tangled underbrush, Jordan following close behind. She heard his quick intake of breath when they arrived at the edge of a thicket and stepped out onto the rock bluff. With her feet firmly planted on the jagged sandstone outcropping, Sarah looked across the valley, paying no attention to the void that lay below her. In the distance was Beaver Lake's curving shoreline, and above it the steep, rugged slopes of the Ozarks.

"People around here say 'Our mountains ain't so high, but our valleys sure are deep,'" Sarah said quietly. "When you stand here, you know exactly what they mean."

Jordan said nothing, apparently completely absorbed by the scene that stretched out beneath his feet. Then when she moved her feet and a loosened pack of pebbles fell into the void below them, Sarah felt herself suddenly jerked into his arms and held firmly against his broad chest.

The touch of her body against his seared her consciousness. It was a feeling she didn't fully understand and couldn't have defined. She held herself rigid as his arms tightened around her, then allowed herself to relax slightly when he loosened his hold without releasing her from the confining circle of his arms.

"I'm sorry," he told her. "I'm not usually a grabber. I thought you were going over the edge."

Sarah was fighting a battle with the sensations evoked by his touch. In the dim recesses of her mind she recognized her reaction to this man's closeness. It was reminiscent of a time she had tried to bury. But this feeling was stronger, more compelling, more frightening. Even more puzzling, she found she was enjoying it.

She forced a small laugh and tried to remove herself from the protective circle of his arms. "I've been climbing these hills since I first learned to walk," she told him. "The edge of the bluff is stable. I was perfectly safe."

Jordan's arms finally released her. "I didn't mean to startle you," he explained. "It's just that after the time I had finding you I don't want to lose you so soon."

Sarah recognized his attempt to turn his reaction into a joke.

"I'm sorry I frightened you," she said, breathing easier now that she was no longer in his arms. "I'll be careful, I promise." She looked around for a moment, then selected a shelflike rock protrusion several feet from the edge of the overhanging bluff for a seat. She motioned to Jordan to join her, trying all the while to bring her emotions under control.

Determined to ignore the way she'd felt in his arms, she waited for him to sit down and draw a small notebook from his shirt pocket.

"If you look carefully toward the other side of the lake, you can see a crescent-shaped strip of darker water curving around the contours of that hillside," she said, carefully disciplining her voice. "Do you see it?"

Jordan bent forward, his head almost touching her shoulder, his breath fanning her cheek. "I don't . . ."

"Not right along the shoreline," she said, moving slightly away to escape his closeness. "Start at the water's edge, then move your eyes toward the center of the lake. About a third of the way out the water gets deeper. It's darker in color than the water along the shoreline."

Jordan followed her instructions, slowly moving his eyes across the surface of the lake. "Now I see it," he said.

Sarah nodded. "You are looking at the famous Monte Ne lagoon. Before the dam was built and the lake was filled, that crescent-shaped channel was the water that created Monte Ne."

"What's that tall concrete tower on the shore? Was it part of Monte Ne?"

"That's the south tower of Oklahoma Row," she explained. "There was another hotel called Missouri Row nearly like it. They were separated by a large landscaped lawn and were famous for their rustic exteriors and elegant interiors."

"I found a pamphlet in the library about that, but quite honestly I couldn't imagine it," Jordan said quietly. "Crystal chandeliers, string orchestras, singing gondoliers—it sounded like a Hollywood stage set. I don't see how anyone even found the place. It's hard enough now. There couldn't have been many paved roads back then."

"No, there weren't. Not many cars, either," she agreed. "But Harvey knew how isolated the area was. He planned his resort, then built a railroad spur into Monte Ne. Visitors arriving on the Monte Ne Railroad rode from the train station at the head of the lagoon to the hotels in a real Venice gondola decked with flowers and complete with a singing gondolier."

"It simply doesn't fit...."

Sarah laughed. "You're right. Monte Ne wasn't exactly the typical Ozark community. The name was borrowed from the Spanish and a tribe of area Indians. It means something like 'Mountain Waters.' The name may have been apt, but Monte Ne itself was out of time and place. In fact, today you would probably say it was ahead of its time."

"How's that?"

"That's your mystery to solve."

"Its place in the greater scheme of history?"

"That's right," Sarah told him. "It's not really hard to find, not if you're any kind of researcher. It's just that I've never seen the connection in print before. I don't think even Coin Harvey realized what he was doing."

Sarah lowered her eyes, watching as Jordan hurriedly scribbled in his notebook.

"You said Monte Ne was Harvey's dream. What kind of man was he?"

"You can find material on Harvey," she told him. "He was a published author and considered a financial expert of the times. That's where he got the nickname 'Coin.' He was also an associate and supporter of William Jennings Bryan. Campaigned for Bryan during the 1896 presidential campaign. In fact, Harvey always claimed he discovered the Ozarks on the campaign trail."

"So," Jordan said slowly, "Harvey built himself a resort hotel."

"Three hotels. Plus a bank, a newspaper and a golf course. There was also an indoor swimming pool called the 'plunge bath,' a casino, a dance pavilion, an auditorium, a bowling alley and an outdoor amphitheater." She grinned, her eyes flashing. "As I said, not exactly your typical Ozark mountain community."

Jordan returned her grin. She waited, anticipating his next question. He didn't disappoint her. "What happened? Why did Monte Ne die?"

"The world intruded," Sarah said sadly. "First, World War I. People weren't interested or able to travel halfway across the continent just for a vacation. The railroad shut down. The bank closed. The newspaper stopped publishing. Monte Ne, at least as a national attraction, was all but dead by the end of the war. The crash on Wall Street in 1929 finished the job."

Sarah turned to face him. "And that about concludes my first hour lecture on local history," she said.

Jordan tried to remember why he was here, but the reason escaped him. All he could see was the little smile on her lips and the sadness in her eyes. All he wanted to do was chase away the shadows.

He leaned forward, pulled like a string puppet. His notebook fell unobserved to the ground. He ignored the tiny voice in the back of his mind that was registering its dissent. He paused for a moment, saw her start to protest, but it was already too late. He gave way to the incredible temptation in front of him, and with a quiet groan he lowered his head until his lips found hers.

The kiss, which began as the mere brushing of his lips against hers, captured and held Jordan with a strength that was deceptive in its gentleness. He sensed the initial shock, then the melting resistance and finally the fluttering feminine response emerging under his touch. Without conscious direction, his arms moved to pull her closer, to feel the sweet heat of her body against his, to capture and hold the elusive scent of honeysuckle.

No longer fully in control, his body yielded to an unconscious knowledge that guided and directed its actions. His hands moved over her back, memorizing the shape of her body as his lips played over her mouth. His tongue gently traced her lips, teasing, testing, tasting, absorbing the promise they held.

In the split second before Jordan's lips touched hers, Sarah found herself anticipating the contact. Instinctively she lifted her face to meet his caress. Reality, she decided moments later, was even more delicious than fantasy. Fantasy could not have produced that gentle, shimmering heat, that warming fire suddenly igniting deep within her. Like a tender new plant opening its leaves to catch the warmth of the sun, Sarah moved closer to the source of this pleasure.

Find this man. He is important. Sarah remembered Aunt Cinda's words in the moment before her world spun out of control. As Jordan's lips moved over hers, conscious thought was lost in a whirlwind of sensation.

What manner of magic was this? The titillation of his touch erased all memory of previous kisses, previous caresses. This was a new pleasure, and it was fueled by the knowledge that it was hers to enjoy.

She fought the surprise and wonder of it—the touch of his hands, the feel of his lips, the sun-warmed smell of heat and woods and man—then accepted the turmoil of her senses.

Slowly, reluctantly, Sarah felt herself being drawn back into the real world—to the rasping call of the crow, to the drumming beat of her own pulse...to the persistent summons of a horn disturbing the drowsy complacency of the summer afternoon.

Jordan, too, must have heard it. "What the devil—?"

"It's a car horn," Sarah said, still reeling from the kiss. She moved away from him, bereft, knowing she might never again experience that particular brand of magic. The honking continued from the clearing behind them. "It's a horn," she repeated. "Someone followed us here."

Chapter 4

The horn continued blaring from the flat above them as Sarah scrambled through the underbrush to the edge of the clearing. She spotted the dust-covered pickup parked conspicuously on the flat and stopped abruptly. The brash beeping sound faded into silence.

"T.J.! What on earth are you doing?" she called to the young man lounging casually against the side of the truck, his arm still extended through the window to reach the horn.

"It's about time, Sarah. I've been signaling you forever. The sheriff's looking for you."

Sarah tensed, searching for a familiar stab of comprehension and finding nothing. Her concentration was so intense that she failed to realize that Jordan had entered the clearing and moved to her side. Finally she forced herself to ask, "What's wrong?"

"The young Shelton boy's gone missing."

She stood stiffly, her thoughts turned inward, her mind still searching but still finding nothing.

"Sarah?"

Jordan's voice shattered her concentration, shifting her awareness back to the man at her side. She felt her pulse jump in sudden fear. How much had he heard? Would he make a connection between the sheriff's summons and Jimmy Joe's talk about her "sight"? She dared a quick glance at his face, found it totally impassive and allowed herself to relax slightly. Hopefully, he'd dismissed Jimmy Joe's talk as a tall tale.

"I'm sorry, Jordan, but I have to go," she told him, trying to keep her voice and manner detached. "It's— Oh, I forgot. Jordan, this is T. J. Shields. T.J., Jordan Matthias. Mr. Matthias is doing some research on Monte Ne."

"Nice to meet you," T.J. said. Sarah didn't notice when T.J. draped his arm casually across her shoulder.

"It took me a while to catch up with you," T.J. told her. "We should be going."

Sarah nodded. She hated to leave, yet she knew she must.

"Why does the sheriff want you to help look for the boy?" Jordan asked. "And how did he find us? I don't understand...."

Sarah's shoulders tensed as T.J. shifted his weight from one foot to the other. She gave him a quick look and was rewarded by his tight-lipped silence. Despite T.J.'s welcomed closeness, fear consumed her. "I don't have time to explain," she told Jordan quickly. "There's a little boy missing...." She hesitated, searching for a possible explanation. "I'm a close friend of the boy's mother," she said finally. "I guess the sheriff thinks I can calm her down or something."

T.J. cleared his throat. "I'll turn the truck around," he said, backing toward the vehicle. "It was nice to meet you, Matthias. Maybe we'll see each other again."

"I'm sorry, Jordan, but I really do have to go."

Jordan nodded, his lips still in a tight line. "Is there anything I can do to help? I could come with you. Join the search team or... or whatever."

Sarah shook her head. "You don't know the territory. T.J. will drive me. But thank you for offering."

She walked toward the truck, her thoughts occupied with the child. She couldn't seem to sense anything unusual, and that made her uncomfortable.

"Sarah? When can I see you again?" Jordan asked.

Once again his voice scattered her thoughts. "What? Oh, see me again..." She wrinkled her forehead when she realized she wouldn't have a moment to herself until after the weekend. "I'm busy the rest of the week," she finally told him. "Why don't you check out the historical museum in Rogers for information on Monte Ne. The Shiloh Museum in Springdale has a good collection of old photos, too. Monday I'll give you a guided tour of the ruins. I'll meet you at your fishing camp about ten."

"It won't be any trouble? To meet me, I mean? I could come for you, if I knew where—"

"Trouble?" she repeated vaguely, still trying to concentrate on the missing boy. "Oh, no. It won't be any trouble. I'll meet you at ten o'clock." She continued toward the waiting pickup. When she reached for the door handle, Jordan was there ahead of her. Placing his hand under her elbow, he boosted her into the high seat.

The touch of his hand burned her bare skin. Sarah stifled the recurring yearning and ducked her head to keep him from seeing the turmoil in her eyes. The pickup began moving almost as soon as the door slammed shut.

Jordan stood, his hands on his hips, staring at the dust cloud raised by the retreating vehicle. He swallowed the disappointment in his throat, not sure whether to blame his frustration over the way she'd dismissed him without apparent thought or his missed opportunity to see her psychic talents in action. Not that he was convinced they existed, but at least some people did. And according to his friend Hoyston, the town sheriff was one of those. That must be the reason she'd been summoned. But she'd neatly sidestepped his question about the sheriff's message. She'd also refused to let him go with her.

Hoyston was right. Sarah Wilson guarded her privacy very carefully. He'd just spent several hours in her company and he knew only a little more about her than he had before the meeting. She was definitely in Mountain Springs, but she was so well protected by the community that she could have stayed hidden indefinitely if she'd chosen to do so. And, he realized, he had no idea where to find her again. He had to depend on her to contact him.

He kicked angrily at a dirt cloud, his thoughts turning to that interrupted kiss. That was a complication he hadn't expected. Admittedly, she was attractive. Yes, he was definitely attracted. And if he read the signs right, the feeling was mutual. But an involvement with schoolteacher-psychic Sarah Wilson would be no casual affair. Assuming the episode on the bluff was a barometer, it would be an exploding conflagration likely to burn them both. In retrospect, perhaps the cavalry had arrived just in time.

Jordan's thoughts shifted to the sheriff's messenger. T. J. Shield's proprietary attitude, the casual way he'd laid his arm across Sarah's shoulders, disturbed but didn't surprise him. He was the stranger here. He'd already had a taste of how the natives regarded outsiders. What he really wanted to know was how T.J. had located them in this out-of-the-way spot with so little apparent effort. Maybe he'd have a chance to find out when he saw Sarah again.

He had no choice. He'd have to wait until Monday for answers. In the meantime, perhaps he'd better do a little research on that old resort. She was a schoolteacher, after all, and as he recalled, schoolteachers loved surprise quizzes.

Sarah looked over her shoulder for a last glimpse of Jordan, unconsciously rubbing the spot where he'd held her arm. Frantically she tried to deny the reality of the last fifteen minutes. The fantasy of that kiss, those few moments when she'd felt her—

The lurching of the truck as it bounced out of a rut knocked her sideways, effectively jolting her into the present. She grabbed for the edge of the seat with one hand, bracing her other arm against the dashboard. She looked toward her cousin, saw that he was about to speak and interjected her question first.

"Okay, T.J., tell me what's happened to young Jerry."

"Heck, Sarah, if I knew that the sheriff wouldn't have called for you."

"T.J., I'm warning you...."

"All right, all right. I was teasing. Since you didn't ask immediately, I figured he's really all right."

Sarah nodded. "I think so. I don't see anything."

"Both Clyde and Sheriff Bascomb think he's just wandered out of hollering distance. He didn't come in for lunch. But there were a couple of strangers by this morning, and Millie's convinced they took him. So I guess the sheriff decided to call you, just in case...."

Sarah sat quietly for a moment. "I don't see anything. He's probably all right. But we'd better go on, just in case. Millie shouldn't be so jumpy. It's the summer season. The lake and Eureka Springs always attracts a lot of tourists. Now, if it were wintertime, that might be different." For all her logic, Sarah couldn't completely still the feeling that maybe she was afraid to see, afraid to know.

"That's about what I thought," T.J. said. "But I told the sheriff I'd see if I could find you. Do you want to go back into Mountain Springs and then out Highway 12 or take the old road across Bald Ridge? It's rough, but it'll be faster."

"Bald Ridge," Sarah said, bracing herself for another jolt. Neither of them spoke as T.J. steered the truck onto the seldom-used logging road up the side of the mountain.

It was her cousin who finally broke the silence. "What were you doing out on the bluff with that stranger anyway? You ought to be more careful, Sarah. That bluff's awful isolated. And he is a stranger."

A stranger, indeed. Sarah heard disapproval of Jordan in his voice and found herself defending him. "Being a stranger doesn't make him an ax murderer, either, T.J. How'd you know where we were, anyway?"

"Betsy heard you talking about Monte Ne. Then Luther saw the two of you take the south fork at the junction. I figured you were headed there. It's the best spot around to see what's left of the old place. But honest, Sarah, you've got to be more careful. You don't know beans about that man."

This time Sarah refused to voice a retort. When the rutted road demanded T.J.'s full attention, she allowed herself a few moments of reflection. She supposed it really wasn't the wisest move she'd ever made, but what harm had it done? She'd enjoyed being with Jordan Matthias, even if she had been a little nervous at first.

Then had come that moment on the bluff, the moment when she'd realized he was looking at her as something more than a research assistant. And she hadn't resisted.

The truck reached the top of the mountain, and T.J. sped up slightly as they started down the other side.

Sarah saw T.J. glance into the rearview mirror. "That fellow wouldn't try to follow us, would he?" he asked suddenly.

"I don't think so. Why?"

"There's someone else coming over the mountain. I caught a glimpse of his dust trail before we turned into that last switchback. From the looks of it, he's traveling pretty fast."

"We're not the only ones who know this shortcut."

"No, I guess not," T.J. said, but Sarah noticed that he kept checking the rearview mirror.

"Damn fool," he muttered a few minutes later. "He's coming off the mountain too fast."

Sarah glanced over her shoulder. She couldn't see anything, but the tension in her cousin's voice was making her nervous.

With another muttered oath, T.J. suddenly increased speed.

"What are you doing? Slow down, T.J."

"He's coming down too fast. He's going to come barreling around one of these blind curves in a minute and be up my tail pipe before he has a chance to brake. We've got to put some distance between us or get out of his way."

Sarah clung to her seat as T.J., gripping the steering wheel with grim determination, sent the truck careening down the mountain.

"Hang on," he yelled as he yanked the truck left across the narrow road and into a small clearing, then slammed on the brakes. The speeding vehicle following them, its silhouette blurred by a swirling cloud of dust, shot past them moments later.

Sarah heard T.J.'s gasp of relief before he turned to ask if she was all right.

"I'm fine," Sarah assured him, her voice shaking slightly. "But we could have been killed. If he'd hit us we would've gone right off the side of the mountain."

"I might have stayed ahead of him, but I'm glad I remembered this turnout. Damn fool tourist."

"Tourist? Did you recognize him, T.J.?"

"No. I can't even describe that vehicle. I'd guess it was an old pickup. Dark-colored. That's all I could see. But it had to be a tourist. No local would drive this road like that. I take it you didn't see much, either."

Sarah shook her head. "I had my eyes shut," she admitted.

They rested another few minutes, still shaken by the close encounter, then resumed the drive down the mountainside. Sarah couldn't help heaving a small sigh of relief when they crossed the last low water bridge and turned onto the highway leading to the cutoff for Shelton Valley. Her eyes searched in both directions for a glimpse of the reckless vehicle. Her cousin was doing the same. The road was deserted from horizon to horizon.

"Well, whoever it was made it off the mountain in one piece," she said. "As far as I'm concerned, I'd rather not see him again."

T.J. nodded his agreement, turning the pickup in the direction of Shelton Valley. They'd driven only a few miles when they met the sheriff's cruiser coming from the opposite direction. T.J. made a U-turn in the middle of the highway, and both vehicles pulled to the side of the road.

"Doesn't have his lights on," T.J. commented. "Everything must be all right."

Sarah scrambled out of the cab and waited as the sheriff's car came to a complete stop behind them. She clasped her hands behind her back in an effort to control their shaking. The gray-haired law officer walked toward her. The suspicion that she looked as washed-out as she felt was confirmed when she saw the smile on her old friend's face turn to a frown.

"The boy's fine, Sarah," he quickly assured her. "Sorry I gave you a scare."

Sarah nodded, attempting to smile. "I thought he was. Where was he?" she asked as the knot in her stomach eased. There was always the chance her sight was wrong.

"Fell asleep in the hayloft and didn't hear his mother callin'," the sheriff said. "I suspect he'll think twice about visiting those kittens for the next few days."

Sarah's eyes reflected her relief. "You know better than that, Sam. Kids and kittens go together."

"Guess so. Well, anyway, Millie'll look there first next time. I'm just sorry I sent out a call for you. But if it wasn't Jerry who got you so frazzled, what's the trouble?"

"Some damn fool of a tourist nearly ran us off the side of the mountain," T.J. said, joining them. "Came boiling off Old Baldy like it was a raceway."

"What happened? Anybody hurt?"

Sarah watched the frown on Sam's face grow fiercer as T.J. described the near-accident and told him that he couldn't identify the vehicle.

"How about you, Sarah? Can you add anything?"

"No. By that time I had my eyes shut."

"And that's another thing," T.J. said. "You know where she was when I finally found her? She was out at Indian Bluff, alone with that stranger who's been asking about her. Anything could have happened. I told her, but she won't listen to me. Maybe you can talk some sense into her."

"Now see here, T.J.," Sarah began, "you're not the boss of me."

"Simmer down, Sarah. He worries about you," Sam said, laying a restraining hand on her arm. He turned his attention to T.J. "Thanks for hunting her up. I appreciate it. You can go on now. I'll get her where she needs to go."

"Yeah, well…" T.J. gave her a sheepish look. "I'm sorry, Sarah."

"It's all right." She stood on tiptoe and gave him a peck on the cheek. "Thanks for caring, T.J. You can go on back to work. Sam'll take me back to town."

T.J. nodded and climbed into the pickup.

Minutes later Sarah and the sheriff were headed toward town. Sarah told him her car was parked behind the café, then waited for the lecture she was sure was coming. It didn't take long.

"I hate to sound like T.J.," Sam began, "but it really wasn't very smart to go out to the bluff with that stranger."

"Don't you start, Sam."

He cleared his throat. "Thing is…I checked around a bit when he started asking about you. He's a writer."

"I know."

The sheriff gave her a startled look. "You knew, and you went with him anyway?"

"It's okay, Sam. Really. He's doing an article on Monte Ne. That's all."

"You sure about that?"

"That's what he said. What Aunt Cinda said, too. At least she said he was looking for Monte Ne. Honest, Sam. Sometimes I think you're as paranoid as I am."

"Nothing crazy about being careful," he told her. "But I guess you know what you're doing. What kind of fellow is he? Did you like him?"

The last thing Sarah wanted to discuss at the moment was her reaction to Jordan Matthias. At the mention of his name her mind recreated the image of his face. She dropped her eyes in confusion, hoping her face was still sunburned enough to hide the blush she could feel creeping up her cheeks.

"He seems . . . like a nice enough person, I guess. I don't think I'd like to be on the wrong side of him, but he's polite enough. Mostly we talked about Monte Ne."

"Well, you just be careful. From what T.J. said, you've got enough of a problem with your aunt to keep you busy this summer. You don't need to go around importing new ones from outside."

She'd known, of course, that her efforts to get Aunt Cinda off her mountain were common knowledge in the valley. "If you've got any suggestions on that one, I'd appreciate them. Getting Aunt Cinda to move is going to be a tough one."

"I know," Sam agreed, "but she's lived there all her life. She's not going to want to move. Lord, I couldn't even get her out of there last fall when we had all that flooding."

Sarah grimaced. "How far did the water come up?"

"Right to the edge of that old sycamore. I went up the next day to make sure she was all right. There she was, sitting on the front porch, rocking, just like she hadn't come within fifteen feet of being completely flooded out. I tell you truly, I don't envy you that job. It's going to be like trying to move the Rock of Gibraltar."

"I'll think of something," Sarah told him. "I have to. No one else in the family can do anything with her."

The sheriff grunted and changed the subject, asking her how her contact with the policeman in St. Louis was working out.

"All right, I think. He's not particularly enthusiastic. But he's keeping his part of the bargain."

"I expected that," Sam told her. "Hoyston is one of those I-believe-what-I-can-see men."

Sarah couldn't help but laugh. "Don't be so hard on him. After all, not everyone has the advantage of having a Cherokee great-grandmother."

"Is that why you picked me to confide in? I always wondered. You were just a child, and there must have been half a dozen other adults standing around. How old were you that day? About thirteen?"

"Eleven. And yes, I guess that's why I picked you. Of course, I didn't know about the great-grandmother. Not then. I just knew that you were the only one who might believe me. And I had to tell someone besides family. Except I never had. I mean, no one else knew that I could..." Sarah let her voice trail off, reluctant even now to say it out loud. "Anyway, I looked around and knew you were the one I should tell. Now I realize why. Because of your grandmother's talents, you wouldn't automatically dismiss me. You were at least predisposed to accept the possibility of knowledge you couldn't prove or explain."

Sam nodded. "I remember at the time I thought I was just humoring a little girl with pigtails as soft as corn silk. Besides, I didn't have anything to lose. We had no idea where the kid was."

"Sometimes things work out right."

"Yes, they do, don't they?" The sheriff cleared his throat. "You'll end up making a believer out of Hoyston. Wait and see."

"I don't really care if he believes me or not. Just as long as he acts on my information and keeps the vultures away," Sarah said.

"Well, watch yourself. And be careful with that stranger fellow, too. Have any problems, you come to me."

"I will. I promise, Sam. Haven't I been running to you for years?"

"See that you keep on doing it, too," he told her gruffly. The sheriff pulled into the parking area behind the café and parked next to Sarah's Volkswagen.

"Thanks for coming when I called, Sarah. Remember, you take care now, you hear?"

"I will, Sam. Promise."

Despite her involvement with her grandparents' out-of-town family guests, for Sarah the weekend dragged. She moved automatically through the days, helping her grandmother prepare meals for the crowd of visitors. Yet she stood alone, acting and reacting, isolated by the endless churning of her thoughts.

Should she meet Jordan Matthias on Monday? She'd promised him a tour of the ruins, but she could deputize T.J. and Jimmy Joe for the task. Jimmy Joe would love it, and T.J. would be willing if he thought it would protect her from the stranger. Did she want protection? Why did she find Jordan Matthias so attractive? The answer came as swiftly as a summer thunderstorm rolling across the valley. She found him attractive because he made her feel like a woman.

It had been so long since she'd allowed herself to be Sarah, the woman. She was Jimmy Joe's playmate, T.J.'s cousin, Aunt Cinda's niece, daughter to her grandparents. She was friend and prodigy to Sam Bascomb, neighbor to the population of Mountain Springs and teacher to classrooms full of students. She was all those things, but to Jordan Matthias she was simply a woman, perhaps even a woman he found attractive.

Saturday dragged into Sunday. The house was still filled with relatives. Once more she participated automatically, a part of the activity around her, yet separate.

And all the time she kept remembering that he'd be gone soon. The leaving was intrinsic to the coming. He would collect the material he needed for his article, then go without making a ripple in the placid life of Mountain Springs. It would make no difference in the scheme of things if, for only a few hours, she stepped beyond the limits of her life in the valley. This one time she would pretend to be just Sarah, a woman no different from any other. This once she would be a woman attracted to and enjoying the casual companionship of a man. What harm could it do? Certainly none to him. Besides, she'd promised to meet him. She recognized the futility of thinking about a future for them, but to meet him one more time? That was a promise she could keep.

Chapter 5

Jordan allowed himself a small smile of satisfaction as his eyes strayed to the woman seated beside him. He'd been right. Sarah Wilson had arrived at the fishing camp at exactly ten o'clock. Despite his belief that she would appear as promised, he'd felt a rush of relief when he'd caught sight of her through the windshield of the dusty vehicle as it stopped in front of his cabin.

During the three days since she'd left the clearing without him, she'd invaded his thoughts continually. Jordan couldn't remember another occasion when he'd felt such an instant attraction to a woman. He couldn't remember another occasion when it had been less convenient. Wrong time. Wrong place. Wrong woman. Somehow he had to ignore the spell she cast with those mystic eyes and remember his reason for being here.

As she'd suggested, he had spent most of Friday and part of Saturday checking area sources for information on Monte Ne. He found the old resort a fascinating subject.

Sarah was right. It did deserve recognition for its place in history. He would do an article on Monte Ne, but he still wanted the story on Sarah. She certainly didn't fit the usual psychic subject profile, and that gave him more hope than anything. He had the feeling that this time he had found the magic.

Jordan ignored a twinge of guilt at not being completely open with her. After all, he only intended to tell the truth. If she proved to be psychic, she should have no objection to that. If she turned out to be another fake, well, she deserved no sympathy.

His vacation was shaping as both interesting and busy. He had two articles to work on—one on Monte Ne and one on Sarah. That, he reminded himself firmly, is assuming you keep your rampaging hormones under control and concentrate on your research.

He cast another quick glance in her direction. She'd already thrown him one curve this morning. After that interlude on the bluff he'd expected her to show up wearing her guarded reserve like a shield. Instead she'd bounced out of the car, eyes shining, like a child anticipating a special treat. He'd allowed himself a moment of chagrin—obviously she wasn't as affected by him as he'd imagined—then welcomed her friendly demeanor. It would make his job much easier.

"The missing boy—Jake said he was safe and sound." Jordan disciplined the tone of his voice to reflect casual interest. He didn't want her suspecting he'd guessed the reason she'd been summoned.

"He was visiting the barn cat's new family and fell asleep in the hay," Sarah said, welcoming the respite granted by his neutral comment. "He had no idea of the commotion he was causing."

"That sounds—" Jordan hesitated. A boy visiting a new batch of kittens sounded logical to him. Why hadn't the mother thought to look there before pushing the panic button? But he wasn't going to ask. The boy's mother was Sarah's friend. Criticizing her probably wouldn't earn him any brownie points.

"You're right, it was a logical place to look," Sarah said, just as if he had vocalized his unspoken question.

Jordan swallowed his sudden excitement. Did she realize what she was doing?

"I think Millie panicked because Jerry disappeared right after two strangers stopped by the farm house. The last time she saw him he was talking to them."

No, apparently not, Jordan decided, as Sarah continued responding to his unvoiced thoughts. Of course, it could be simple coincidence. "Well, I'm glad he wasn't hurt. But surely strangers aren't all that threatening—especially in the summertime, with the tourists and all...."

"That's true. Eureka Springs draws a lot of tourists during the spring and summer months," she went on. "So does Beaver Lake. But Shelton Valley is a bit off the beaten path."

Jordan forced himself to return his attention to the road. One look into the blue pools of her eyes and he found himself fighting for control of his senses. His hands tightened on the steering wheel. *Keep it light,* he told himself. *Keep her talking.*

"You know, Sarah, one thing puzzles me. How did you become owner of Monte Ne?" His voice was cautious as he probed the parameters of what she might consider either a fair question or an invasion into her private affairs.

He waited a moment. Then when he failed to detect any signs of resistance, he continued. "Even before you were born, all that remained of the old resort was its name on the

country plat. Yet your name was on practically every Monte
Ne deed I inspected.''

Sarah welcomed the question, glad to be on familiar
ground. She'd seen the barely concealed spark of personal
interest in his eyes and known she wasn't able to deal with
it. Keep him interested in Monte Ne, she told herself. After
all, that was the reason he was here.

''It was an inheritance, and it isn't that strange, not if you
understand hill folks,'' she explained, yielding to the skill of
his gentle questioning. ''I ended up owning Monte Ne because my great-grandfather Wilson didn't cotton to outsiders.''

Jordan's voice also echoed the results of the lightened atmosphere. ''Somehow I get the idea that 'cotton to' doesn't
exactly say it all.'' The tiny laugh lines around his eyes
creased as he grinned. ''Are you going to tell me the story?''

Sarah smiled back. It was a heart-stopping smile that
pulled the breath from his body.

''I knew you were perceptive. Of course I'm going to tell
you. I'm just trying to decide which story to give you, the
official account or the unexpurgated version?''

''Ah,'' Jordan said, still grinning. ''I'm willing to bet
your respect for the true and complete version of history will
win.''

Sarah's eyes widened in surprise. After such a short ac-
quaintance, could he really read her that completely? ''How
did you know?''

''Let's just say I hope you never play poker,'' he said in a
lighthearted voice that suddenly reflected his mood. When
she failed to respond immediately to his comment, he lifted
one hand from the steering wheel, reached across the seat
and touched her hand with a quick, light stroke of his fingers.

"So, what did Great-grandfather Wilson have to do with Monte Ne?"

"Nothing," Sarah said, striving to deny the effect his touch was having on her heartbeat. "Absolutely nothing. At least not at first. You see, he was one of those hill men who accepted change slowly. He didn't like strangers, and certainly not the idea of outsiders owning a part of his Ozarks.

"Over the years most of the locals were won over to the idea of Monte Ne. They enjoyed the entertainments it offered, and I guess they added local color to its activities. But the family says Great-grandfather never participated, not even in the annual fiddling contest. And he was supposed to have been one of the best fiddlers in these mountains.

"However," she added, laughing slightly to herself, "he also believed a man should take advantage of his opportunities. So he finally resigned himself to getting some good out of it."

"What did he do?" Jordan asked, silently congratulating himself on maintaining his pose as an enthusiastic student. The teacher facet of her personality was the easiest for him to deal with. He could enjoy her presence and still keep his mind on the business at hand. When she was playing her role as eager instructor he wasn't as tempted to wander down the other paths he so desperately wanted to explore.

"He cleared every field he owned and planted corn."

"Corn?"

"Corn," Sarah repeated.

"But what did corn have to do with Monte Ne?"

"Oh, come now, Jordan. You may not be a historian, but you should be able to figure that out. What can you do with corn?"

Jordan looked puzzled. "I guess you can cook it to eat or store it as food for livestock or as seed. You can dry it and grind it for cornmeal, too."

Sarah grinned. "You forgot one."

Feed, food, seed, meal. Jordan frowned as he mentally listed the options, trying to concentrate. Once again he found himself floundering in his effort to retain control of his thoughts as she turned the full power of those mysterious eyes on him.

"Food, meal, feed, seed." He shook his head. "I can't think of another thing," he admitted finally, recognizing that the surrender signified more than an inability to discover a fifth use for corn.

"You can also distill it."

"Distill it? You mean like moonshine?"

She nodded. "Around here we call it white lightning. Anyway, Great-grandfather had a ready market for his product right on his doorstep, so to speak. By the time the crash came he had saved quite a little nest egg. As the land came on the market, he bought it. He must have thought it poetic justice that the very outsiders he objected to gave a native the means to reclaim the land."

"That's the official account?"

"No, that's the true story. The official account says he found a cache of Confederate gold buried in one of the caves on his north section." She stopped, puzzled, when Jordan burst out laughing. "What's so funny?"

"It just seems strange to me that a story that shows such an entrepreneurial spirit would be hidden in favor of one that depended on luck."

"Not if you remember that Carrie Nation lived right down the road." Her grin flashed with the brilliance of the sun breaking over a high ridge line at dawn.

"You mean *the* Carrie Nation? The one with the hatchet?"

"The one and only," Sarah assured him. "In fact, Hatchet Hall, her last home, is quite a tourist attraction in Eureka Springs."

"Well, I'll be damned..."

"I don't know about that." Sarah laughed. "But Great-grandfather would have been—at least in some circles—if his business had been known."

As Jordan's appreciative laugh joined hers, Sarah allowed the warm tremors of his laughter to wrap around her. It was going to be all right. Her anxiety had been for nothing. Jordan Matthias was exactly as advertised—a man who was looking for information about Monte Ne. For those few moments when he'd looked straight into her eyes she had imagined something different. But that was all it was— imagination. Like the make-believe feelings she'd experienced when he'd kissed her on the bluff. Summer madness. A simple case of summer madness.

"I take it your family's been here for a long time."

"Every family in Mountain Springs has been here for a long time. The younger people are sometimes forced to leave because of the local economy, but the people who stay have been here forever. If there were room for newcomers, more of the younger generation would be able to remain."

"The young man who came after you the other day—is he a local farmer?"

"T.J.? He's helping on the family farm and trying to start his own quarter-horse spread. Why?"

"No particular reason," Jordan said, surprised at himself for wanting to know and at Sarah for not guessing why. "I just wondered if he was one of the younger generation who planned to stay."

"I don't think T.J. could survive away from here, not if he had to leave for good. For him, this is home."

As it is for you, Jordan thought silently. *You leave to teach, but always come back. You would never be at home any other place, either, would you, Sarah Wilson?* For some reason, the thought was depressing.

"What about you, Jordan? Where is home for you?"

Jordan shrugged his shoulders. "I don't have one. Haven't really had one since we left the farm after my dad died. My mother died a couple of years later. I was in the army for a while. Home was always the next assignment. When I left the military I kept right on roaming—wherever the next story took me. I've got a small apartment in St. Louis, a place to hang my hat between assignments. But you couldn't call it home. Sometimes I don't see it for a year at a time."

Sarah tried to understand. "And it doesn't bother you? Not having a place where you belong?"

"Never has," Jordan told her. "I've always felt I belonged in the place I happened to be at the moment."

That explained a lot, Sarah thought. And it certainly tallied. Aunt Cinda had said he had no roots. She didn't know whether she felt sorrier for him or for herself.

"Is this the road where we turn?"

His question forced her attention back to her surroundings. "This is it. Just follow the road until we run into the lake."

Minutes later Jordan parked the Blazer at the side of the road. The summer sun high overhead reflected brightly off the placid lake nestled at the bottom of the valley. Cracked, dried mud flats extended down the hillside from the lake's usual high-water mark to the present water level.

Sarah choked back a small gasp of surprise. "They said Beaver was down, but I didn't realize it was this low."

"But why? I mean, why is it so low this time of the year? It's only June."

"Beaver's a hydro-power lake," she told him. "Electric power generation demands determine how much water is released through the dam. But it's unusual for them to lower water levels this much."

Without waiting for Jordan's assistance, Sarah jumped from the high seat to the ground. The scene before her was eerie in its silence, a silence broken only by the buzzing drone of the few flying insects energetic enough to cavort in the hot summer air and the occasional call of a bird from the wooded thickets on the ridge above them.

"Look," she told him, emphasizing the command by pointing down the shoreline. "Even the amphitheater is exposed. We couldn't see that from the bluff."

But Jordan's attention was caught by the sight of a large concrete structure standing high on the bank overlooking the lake. The straight lines of its undressed concrete walls were relieved by three tiers of precisely spaced openings, bare of even the wooden casements necessary to support the missing windows.

"Is that the same tower we saw from the top of the bluff? The one you said was once part of Oklahoma Row?"

Sarah stumbled as she raised her eyes in the direction of the tower. As her step faltered, Jordan moved to catch her, his fingers wrapping securely around her elbow.

With the physical contact, Sarah could feel the heat of his hand on her bare skin, feel the surge of energy flowing between them. Her eyes shifted from the tower to his face. She saw the concern reflected in his eyes.

"Are you all right? Did you turn your ankle?"

"I'm fine. A misstep. Really, I'm okay." She moved restlessly under his touch, pulling her eyes away from his, shifting her gaze back down the shore toward the tower. She was unable to control the tremor that rippled through her body.

Reluctantly Jordan released his hold on her arm. He frowned, puzzled by her complete absorption in the ruins of the old tower. "It's impressive. Even more so than from the top of the bluff. It is the same tower I saw from the top of the bluff, isn't it?"

"Yes. It's the same one. The south tower of Oklahoma Row."

"Is it possible to see it up close? To actually go inside? I saw old photos of the hotel in the museum, but they didn't look real. Standing there, being physically present in the same place, might give me a better perspective."

Sarah tore her gaze from the old tower, turning her head to look out across the expanse of blue-green water. A whisper of a breeze moved across the surface of the lake, ruffling its mirror finish, blowing cool against her heated skin. She lifted her eyes, searching the sky for clouds, for any sign that would indicate an approaching storm. She found none, only the bright glare of sun on water.

"Sure, we can walk to the tower, if you like," she told him with determined cheerfulness. "But I'll warn you, there isn't much to see."

Jordan heard her reluctance. What was disturbing her? Was it him? He was willing to admit to feeling awed to find himself surrounded by the physical remains of Monte Ne, but she was already familiar with them, and something of a historian, besides.

"Let's walk by the lake's edge. There's usually a breeze on the water," she said as they began moving down the shore in the direction of the tower.

"The tower's never really underwater, is it? It seems a long way away from the edge of the lake."

"No. It's right inside the high-water line. The basement level gets water when the lake's at normal levels. But even when the lake's brim-full, water never reaches the first floor.

Of course, there's no first floor anymore. It's an empty shell—one of those skeletons you were talking about.'' She stopped suddenly and pointed up the bank, away from the lake.

"Oh, look. There's one of the arched footbridges I was telling you about. There were several exposed the last time the lake was this low, but I didn't know if any of them had survived another decade underwater."

"One of the bridges you had to cross if you didn't want a ride in a gondola?"

"That's right. They were small works of art in themselves. Probably built by local labor. And if there's anything an Ozark native knows, it's how to work with stone."

In unspoken agreement, they turned their backs on the lake and began walking in the direction of the small bridge.

"You're right," Jordan said as they drew close enough to make out the details of the picturesque bridge. "Native stonework, and beautifully laid. If this is a sample of the landscaping, Monte Ne must have been impressive."

"I think so, too. The historical society has old photographs of most of the buildings—the important ones, anyway—but I've never seen any of the gardens. Harvey was such a perfectionist, they must have been at least as picturesque as the rest.

Sarah grinned in spite of herself. She didn't know what was wrong with her this morning. The prospect of seeing Jordan again had made her afraid that he might consider that moment of summer madness on the bluff an invitation to continue—or, worse, that he might think she casually accepted such physical intimacies. Yes, that was the right word. Even though it had only been a kiss, there had been something intensely intimate about it.

But Jordan hadn't referred to the incident. He'd done nothing to make her uncomfortable, nothing to cause the queasy feeling she'd been trying to shake since arriving at the lake. Must be too much sun, she decided. She should have brought a hat. The sun's merciless rays were as potent for natives as for outsiders. She shaded her eyes with her hand and squinted up at the sky.

"Looks like we're not the only ones taking a trip into the past," Jordan said, pointing to several vehicles parked near the tower. "I didn't realize this was so well known to tourists. There's a station wagon from Tennessee, a car from Illinois and a pickup from Oklahoma. I don't see their passengers, though."

"The Oklahoma one doesn't count," Sarah said. "We're so close to the state line, we see them all the time—don't even consider them tourists. Everyone's probably on the other side of the tower. Part of the foundation slab is still there. It makes a nice level spot for picnicking."

Jordan hesitated for a moment. "Let's skip the tower for now and go on to the amphitheater. I'm not in the mood to share my personally guided tour with a group of strangers."

Sarah nodded without speaking and turned in the direction of the amphitheater. She was unable to repress her sudden pleasure. She didn't want to share these moments, either.

They arrived at the amphitheater near the location of the old stage. The ornamental concrete seats of the vast outdoor arena, their original splendor now eroded and stained, still stood in stately rows extending from the top of the hill to where the blue-green water of the lake lapped softly against the shore.

Jordan had seen old photographs in the files of the historical society. He'd studied the original plat map of Monte Ne in an old county atlas. He'd listened to Sarah's descriptions. But now, for the first time, he began to visualize the scope, the actual physical dimensions, of what had once been, and he found himself mourning the passage of a magnificence that could be recaptured only by the imagination.

As he turned to speak, Sarah, seemingly oblivious of his presence, began climbing through the stained, eroded benches, up the hillside and away from the water. Jordan followed. They moved along the original aisles when possible, when necessary climbing over or around the massive overturned benches that blocked their path. Sarah stopped to rest a little over halfway up the mountainside.

Jordan turned to look in awe toward the top of the amphitheater. He made a sweeping gesture with his arm. "Is all this usually underwater?"

"Yes, most of the time. In fact, the last time I remember the amphitheater being exposed was over ten years ago. Her voice was hushed, as if she were reluctant to allow the present to awaken what had once been.

He wondered if visitors to mausoleums felt the same unwillingness to awaken the resting past. When he spoke, his voice reflected a quiet reverence for this place of forgotten dreams. "I'm going on to the top. I want to see it in its entirety."

"Go ahead," Sarah answered quietly. "I'll wait here." She watched him begin the climb to the top, then sat down in the shade cast by one of the benches, leaning back to enjoy the coolness of the concrete.

The buzz of flying insects was occasionally joined by the raucous call of a pair of crows in the distance. Somewhere nearer she recognized the song of a bluebird. The sound of Jordan climbing through the ruins above her gradually faded away.

Sarah let her mind go free, thinking of nothing in particular, enjoying the solitude. Time slipped by unnoticed and unobserved. She wasn't sure how long she'd been resting when she realized that the birds were gone. No song of bluebirds, no call of crows—the quiet was disturbing, threatening.

Suddenly alert, she strained to hear and was rewarded by the ponderous sound of rolling stone. Instinctively, without looking, without hesitating, she flung herself under the nearest concrete bench. From a distance she thought she heard the sound of her name, but the thundering noise of falling rock made it impossible to be sure.

She rolled herself into a tight ball, resisting the urge to run from the rumbling sounds drawing nearer. Small rocks and chips of concrete rained down about her. The thunder came closer. Once more she thought she heard the sound of her name, but the thunder was now above her, around her. She coughed once, choking in a cloud of dust. It was the last thing she remembered.

Chapter 6

From high on the other side of the amphitheater Jordan watched in horror as a massive concrete slab tumbled end over end down the side of the hill. The falling slab gathered momentum as it fell, striking other bench seats, knocking loose chunks of concrete and stone, letting nothing deflect it from its destructive path.

"Sarah!" His call was both warning and petition as he scrambled over benches toward her. His only answer was his own voice, reverberating among the rows of deserted benches. "Sarah," he called again, the sound feeble in comparison to the thunderous roar of the tumbling debris.

With a speed that looked deceptive in its ponderous slow-motion movement, the tumbling concrete slab ricocheted its way down the hillside, finally coming to rest on the flat surface at the bottom of the shell. Only seconds later, Jordan reached the area where he'd last seen Sarah.

"Sarah," he called again as the echo of the falling rubble faded away, leaving only an eerie silence as answer. Then he saw her lying quiet and still beneath the bench. He dropped to his knees, reaching for her instinctively before caution could intervene. He ignored the trembling of his hands and felt for the pulse point on the side of her neck, breathing an audible sigh of relief when he located the steady beat with his fingers.

He unconsciously caressed her cheek with his hand as he pondered his next move. The massive bench above her had held, though the concrete now bore fresh scars from the falling debris. Cautiously he ran his hands through her hair, feeling for a bump, a cut, anything that would indicate a blow to the head. He found nothing.

He forced down the fear boiling up in his throat and tried to remember the rudiments of first aid. He shouldn't move her, not until he could identify injuries. Carefully, trying to recall the instructions he'd received in a first-aid class years before, he checked for broken bones, running his hands along her arms, down the slim length of her legs, gently probing her rib cage. Again he allowed himself a breath of relief when he found no indication of a break.

Should he move her? There was always the possibility of a neck or back injury, but instinct told him it was unlikely. She'd protected herself by ducking under the bench. Momentum had carried the rubble over the bench and on down the hillside. He reached for her, wanting her out of the dust and dirt.

"Sarah?" He called her name again and was rewarded by a flickering of her eyelashes. "Please, Sarah. Tell me you're all right."

His voice was her first reality—his voice calling her name, anxiety and concern in every word. Then she felt his hand against her forehead, soothing, comforting. She tried to open her eyes. Again she heard her name. This time she was able to respond. She opened her eyes.

"Sarah! Thank God you're awake. No, don't try to move. Not yet. You may be injured."

Sarah lay still, trying to remember. The last of the gray fog melted away. She turned her head to focus on his face. He was on his knees, halfway under the bench were she lay. When her eyes locked with his she saw the color begin to seep back into his white face.

"Were you hit?"

She shook her head slowly. "I don't think so. I don't remember being hit."

Jordan, moving awkwardly in the confined space, moved to help her from beneath the bench. "Careful now. Don't hit your head on the overhang."

"I'm all right, Jordan. Really. I'm sorry I fainted. I shouldn't be such a coward."

Jordan stood her on her feet. Then, as if to reassure himself that she was undamaged, he gently moved his hands down her body.

Sarah took a deep breath and willed her racing pulse to slow. He was only checking her for injuries, she told herself. It wasn't personal. Why, then, was the touch of his hands chasing coherent thought from her mind?

"I wouldn't call you a coward," Jordan said as he finished his inventory, his hands lingering for a moment at her waist. "If I'd seen that bench tumbling toward me I would probably have frozen. You had the presence of mind to instantly identify your best chance for safety."

Sarah's little laugh echoed in the quiet air. "That wasn't presence of mind. That was instinct. Faced with danger, I always hide one way or another. This time I fainted—just went away."

"Not before you'd protected yourself. Call it what you want—I call it pretty good instinct, lady."

Jordan let his eyes sweep the hillside as he speculated on the cause of the accident. The obvious reason hit him at the same time as the realization that more than one of the massive concrete slabs might be in the same condition. Years of immersion underwater had probably weakened the mortared joints that held the massive benches in place. He had to get Sarah out of here.

Before she realized his intention, he swept her into his arms, cradling her against his chest and burying his face against her neck.

"I'm all right, Jordan. I'm not hurt. I can walk. Jordan, put me down!"

"Please, Sarah, I need to—to hold you." He stopped and looked down into her eyes. "Humor me. Hurt or not, you've had a shock. So have I. I want to get us out of this sun. And touching you, holding you, is helping convince me that you're really all right."

She was helpless before the pleading light in his eyes. Slowly she nodded her agreement. Then she leaned her head against his reassuring strength. Her arm moved around his shoulder, her fingers unconsciously tangling in the clipped hair at the nape of his neck.

In an effort to redistribute her slight weight, Jordan shifted her position in his arms, trying to ignore the sensation of pleasure evoked by the softness of her body against the harder planes of his.

"Are you sure you're all right?" he asked, hoping that she wouldn't detect the slight husky note in his voice. "No pain? No headache?"

"I'm fine. Really I am, Jordan. I told you, I'm perfectly capable of walking." Sarah carefully schooled her voice, trying not to betray how much she was enjoying the feel of his arms around her. If she were sensible she'd insist on walking, she told herself, ignoring her own warning and snuggling closer against him.

"Spend the rest of the day with me, Sarah. Please?"

She looked up, her eyes wide with surprise. Jordan chose the moment to drop a quick peck of a kiss on her forehead.

"I think we've both had enough of ruins for the day," he rushed on. "But we can stop by the store at the junction and collect supplies for a picnic. You must know dozens of good picnic sites. Share one with me."

Sarah avoided looking at him as she turned the idea over in her mind. She could feel his gaze on her face as he waited for her answer.

"We can collect Jimmy Joe, if you like. He'd enjoy it. And I'd like to see the little scamp again," Jordan added, trying to lend additional force to his request.

Sarah shook her head. "Grandpa took Jimmy Joe to the auction barn in Bentonville today." The idea of a picnic, of an afternoon with Jordan, was inviting. She knew what she wanted. Hadn't she already decided there was no harm in spending the day with him? She had half a day to go.

"I'd like that," she said finally. "Do you have a pair of swimming trunks?"

Jordan nodded.

"Then I have a better idea. Let's collect your swimming gear and my car, then drive out to the farm. I'll pack us a picnic lunch and introduce you to my favorite swimming hole."

The sound of birds singing in the berry thicket on the side of the hill supplied a melody to the accompaniment of falling water as the river wound its way through the rocks and boulders at the top of the ravine. The waters slowed, spreading into a quiet pool at the bottom of the gorge, as if resting to gather strength before rushing on down the mountain.

Jordan rolled onto his stomach and propped his head on one hand. "It's beautiful," he said, watching Sarah pack the remains of their picnic lunch into the basket. "A perfect sylvan glen. No wonder you call it your favorite swimming hole."

"This has always been one of my favorite places." She set the basket to one side and lay back on the blanket spread beneath the twisted oak. Diamonds of sunlight filtered through the canopy of leaves, dancing across the blanket. "When I was a little girl I was going to live here always—in a house on that high flat next to the old orchard. Then, every morning, I could pick an apple for breakfast, run down the hill and jump into the river."

"Maybe you will someday."

A cloud passed over her face. "Probably not. My uncle has leased this property for years. There's about eighty acres of good pasture here. But the owners recently put it on the market. And Uncle Hiram's not in a position to buy it." She shrugged her shoulders, then grinned weakly. "Besides, when the apples are ripe, it's too late in the fall to swim."

Jordan's fingers feathered lightly along her cheekbone. "Thank you for bringing me here, for sharing it with me."

His touch was doing strange things to her heartbeat. Sarah tried to tell herself to ignore it even as she fought to prevent herself from turning her head into the caress. She sat up abruptly. "I've always thought beauty should be shared to be appreciated. That's why I brought you here." She reached down to tug off her shoes. "Let's go swimming. Last one in is a rotten egg."

She quickly stripped to the two-piece swimsuit she wore under her jeans and cotton shirt and entered the pool in a shallow dive. The shock of the cold water momentarily restored her equilibrium. She looked back toward the shore, laughing as she watched Jordan hopping up and down on one bare foot, trying to remove the boot from the other.

"That was an unfair advantage," he protested, and tugged the second boot free. He dropped it by the edge of the quilt. "I wasn't ready."

Sarah's musical laugh echoed in the glen. "All's fair in—" Her voice died. The sunlight danced across his broad shoulders and his tantalizing golden flesh as he quickly shed his shirt.

"So it's war." His eyes glittered wickedly as he took a menacing step toward the pool, his hands busy at the button flap of his jeans. "Just be warned. Rotten eggs don't play fair."

Sarah ducked her head under the water, hoping the cold water would reduce the heat in her face. She squeezed her eyes shut, trying to block out the image of his all-but-perfect male body clad in bright green boxer-style swim trunks.

She surfaced in time to see his sleek, trim body enter the pool in a graceful racing dive. He surfaced a few feet in front of her, scattering a shower of water droplets with a casual toss of his head. "Race you to the waterfall and back. And I'll be fair—this time. You can have a head start. Your arms are shorter."

"How much of a head start?"

Jordan answered her teasing grin with one of his own. "To the snag on the left bank. You can start from there."

Sarah looked at the dead tree, which was approximately a third of the way to the waterfall. "You're on." She moved toward her starting point in a leisurely crawl, then turned to look back at him. "Don't kick too deep. The center channel's only about four feet deep, except right in front of the fall."

Jordan acknowledged her warning. She positioned herself in the water opposite the dead tree. "Go," he hollered, watching for another second or so as Sarah took off toward the waterfall in a well-controlled, fast-paced crawl. Then he began, his powerful strokes unaffected by the slight upstream resistance as he followed her through the water, reducing the distance between them.

She was only a few strokes ahead of him when she reached the fall pool. He flipped out of his turn, pulled aside, slowed to give her a wicked wink, then pulled steadily ahead. He was standing at the starting point when Sarah, her chest heaving from her efforts, joined him, treading water while she tried to catch her breath.

"Somehow I knew you were the kind of person to finish a race, even when you know you've lost."

"I know I'm out of practice," she gasped, "but you're good."

Jordan pulled her against him. "Rest against me. I'm tall enough to stand."

"What are you? A former Olympian?"

He gave her a mischievous grin. "Hardly. But I will admit to competitive swimming years ago. I try to keep in shape."

"I should have known when you gave me a head start," she told him, letting her head fall forward and resting her cheek against his chest. The feel of his sun-warmed flesh against her skin further complicated her efforts to control her labored breathing.

She knew she should move away, but the steady beating of his heart beneath her ear was hypnotic. Slowly her breathing returned to normal as she relaxed in the comfort and support of his arms.

"Better now?" he asked, easing her slightly away from him.

Sarah nodded, afraid to trust her voice. His hand, casually stroking her back, seemed to be interfering with her vocal cords.

"Good. Then I can claim the victor's prize." Before she realized his intention, he lowered his head to claim her lips.

Sarah couldn't breathe, couldn't think. She found herself helpless, held fast, not by the arms that still cradled her gently but by the searing fire of his mouth. The heat of his touch spread through her body like a summer grass fire. She felt herself go limp in his embrace, unable to move when he broke the contact and lifted his head.

Jordan had intended only a brief kiss, a playful reward, a token of victory. But the moment his lips had touched hers he had known his impulse had gone awry. He lifted his head to find his vision filled with the sight of green flame burning in the depths of her eyes. With a moan, he recaptured her lips.

He gathered her in his arms then, one hand splaying over the side of her face, holding her firmly against him as he raised his head and moved toward the bank. His lips sought hers again as he climbed from the water, breaking contact briefly as he knelt to lay her in the center of the quilt. Leaning over her, still on his knees, he cradled her face, cupping it in his hands while his lips moved softly against hers. His breath fanned against her cheek as he traced the contours of her face with his mouth, touching her eyelids, feathering her cheekbone, returning with unerring accuracy to the sweetness of her lips.

Sarah felt his hands, so strong, so gentle, drift from her face. She gave an inarticulate cry and moved closer to him, wanting the caress of his fingers against her flesh. She released her hands from the back of his neck, running them, palms open, across his shoulders and down his bare back, glorying in the play of muscle and sinew beneath her touch.

His mouth moved along the sensitive skin at the side of her neck, teasing her earlobe, capturing her fluttering pulse. He shifted, stretching out full-length beside her while his hands lightly skimmed her body, igniting a burning spark deep inside her, sending wave after wave of molten liquid through her body.

She let her hands search his body, sliding along the strong column of his neck, tracing his collarbone with the tips of her fingers, caressing the hollow of his throat, moving downward to the fine hair that curled along his chest.

Jordan released a low sound from the back of his throat as, with a delicate touch, he molded the indentation at her waist, then brushed his fingers across her naked midriff. His palms moved upward until the weight of her breasts rested in them, his thumbs gently caressing her sensitized nipples through the silky material of her swimsuit.

His touch added fuel to the flames flickering through her veins. His mouth swallowed the small moans of pleasure escaping her softly parted lips. He groaned again, then dipped his head to nuzzle aside the soft fabric of her swimsuit.

Sarah gasped, arched closer and let her body float on the cushion of sensation created by his touch. She was held fast, like a leaf captured by the flow of the river, twisting, turning, on the currents of passion, being carried relentlessly downstream by forces beyond her control.

She was only vaguely aware of the shudder that rippled through Jordan's body when he pulled her against him, his arms trembling. For a moment he held her tightly, as a drowning man might grasp a buoy, the heat of his body scorching hers, branding her with an intensity she did not yet understand. Then he was gone, leaving her shaking, confused, bereft. Dazed, uncomprehending, she looked to where he sat on the far side of the quilt, his arms hugging his legs, his head resting on his knees.

Sarah's fingers fumbled awkwardly in their efforts to rearrange her halter. She and Jordan were strangers—more than strangers, they were opposites. Yet they had nearly— She had all but come apart in his arms. She shivered in spite of the heat, knowing she'd had no thoughts of caution or even survival in his arms—only melting sensations and insatiable need for his touch. Against all reason, she would have given herself to him—if he'd wanted her. But somehow, something had warned him that she was different. Even if he didn't know what or how, he'd sensed something, and he'd pulled away. Sarah felt a rush of shame and humiliation sweep over her.

"I'm sorry, Sarah," Jordan said. "I had no intention of letting that happen." His voice was as ragged as her own breathing. He turned his head toward her, saw the wariness in her eyes, saw the trembling of her passion-swollen lips, and forced himself to look away.

He drew a rasping breath, disgusted with himself. At first touch he'd forgotten everything but the fact that she was in his arms. He had no defenses against her, or against his desire for her. Never before had he felt so intense a desire for a woman. And yet, at the point of no return, he'd stopped. It wasn't a conscious decision. It wasn't—Jordan didn't know what it was, unless it was an inborn sense of survival. But for whom? Him or her?

"Don't blame yourself, Jordan. I wasn't exactly discouraging you."

They were brave words, but Jordan heard the vulnerability, the confusion, the shame, in her voice. Yet he sensed no blame toward him although he was the one who had instigated the scene.

Jordan frowned, trying to sort out his various impressions. No, she hadn't discouraged him. She'd melted under his touch, becoming a molten fire that consumed as it burned. And he'd willingly jumped into the caldron. He could understand her confusion. He, too, was confused. And he could accept and share her feeling of vulnerability. Never before had he felt so defenseless against the wants and needs of another, or against the demands of such a desire on his own body. But why shame?

It struck him then. Not shame. Humiliation. Startled, he turned to look at her. She met his gaze, then cast her eyes downward and averted her face. She couldn't possibly think he'd rejected her because he didn't want her, could she? But the answer was there—her wariness, her hesitation, the humiliation in her voice. He'd been the one to pull away.

There were lots of reasons for his actions, although he'd been thinking of none of them at the time. But not that one—not a lack of desire. He wanted her with an intensity that still throbbed in his veins, that still held his body on the threshold of pain. Somehow he knew it was important that she understand that.

"Sarah, listen to me," he said, unable to completely control the husky rasping of his voice. "I've never wanted anyone more than I wanted—want—you. I want to be with you, to make you part of me, me part of you, to lose myself in your incredible magic." His voice trailed off. He shook his head, like a prizefighter trying to clear his muddled senses. "There are reasons.... Don't you understand? With you, it wouldn't be enough...."

Sarah caught her breath. She wanted to believe him, but even if she could, it would make no difference. "Jordan, don't...." she pleaded.

He turned at the sound of pain in her voice, the golden flecks in his eyes shimmering.

"Do you understand, Sarah?" he said again, unable to hide the strain in the hushed tones of his voice. "Shared attraction, shared liking, mutual physical pleasures . . . it's always been enough before. But not this time."

He drew in a long, slow breath, consciously unclenching his fists in an attempt to unleash the tension in his body. "Damn it all, Sarah, I couldn't share that with you and then walk away. When it came time for me to move on, I'd leave bits and pieces of me here. I'd walk away wounded, unwhole." His voice turned bitter. "It's too high a price to pay for temporary pleasure."

Sarah took a ragged breath.

"You belong here," he added in a bleak, controlled voice. "You're a part of this place, its people—one of the native flowers, an unexpected blossom growing protected amid the rocks and hills. I belong to the wind, always restless, able only to pause and appreciate the beauty around me before moving on. I only travel through."

Sarah blinked in an effort to control the moisture threatening to escape her eyes. "I'm sorry." Her voice was still husky, but it was no longer trembling. When she raised her eyes to meet his, there was acceptance in their depths.

Jordan beat back the instincts that told him to take her in his arms again. She was so damned open. She wanted him. God knew he wanted her. But he was walking a tightwire with his conscience now. She didn't know why he was really here. If she did, she wouldn't have agreed to see him, and she certainly wouldn't come here with him. He would never have held her in his arms, never have kissed her, never have . . .

Jordan's body uncoiled from his seat on the blanket like a tense spring. He moved quickly toward the river, praying all the while that the water was as cold as he remembered.

He swam relentlessly toward the waterfall, flipping his body underwater in the deep pool at the bottom of the fall, surfacing to return without losing rhythm, stroking powerfully through the water to his starting point, then turning to repeat the process.

Sarah watched as he made the journey, twice, three times. Slowly the strength crept back into her own limbs. She pulled her jeans and shirt over her swimsuit.

By the time she'd tied her shoes, Jordan had abandoned the water and slipped into his own clothing. She shook out the quilt and folded it in her arms. Jordan reached for the picnic basket. With one last look at the quiet pool they began the climb out of the glen.

Sarah led the way through the woods, then across the pasture to the road, speaking only occasionally. Jordan followed close behind, careful not to touch her except once, when she tripped over an exposed root. He grasped her elbow only long enough for her to regain her balance, then jerked his hand away as if the touch had burned him.

They walked up the winding driveway to her grandparents' farmhouse, and Jordan stopped beside his Blazer. He handed her the basket.

"You're leaving now."

"Yes." His mouth twisted into a wry grin. "It's best I go."

Sarah nodded, her eyes searching his face. "I understand," she said quietly.

"Somehow I doubt that. I don't understand it myself," he told her, hoping the expression on his face belied the churning emotions beneath the surface. What in the hell was he doing walking away like this? He wasn't finished here. He'd never walked away from an investigation in his life. However, this time every instinct screamed for him to go.

"What about your article?"

Her question slammed into him like a left hook to the solar plexus as he grappled with the idea that she'd known what he was doing all the time. It took him a moment to realize that she was referring to the story on Monte Ne, not his investigation into her psychic abilities.

He saw the puzzled look on her face, saw her reach out to touch his arm, and realized that he'd flinched when she'd dropped her hand without completing the motion. Jordan tasted the bitter bile of regret in the back of his throat.

"Between the research I did over the weekend and today's tour, I think I can finish it," he said. "I'd like to thank you for the help. I'll make sure you receive a copy when it's published." Even to his own ears, he sounded callous.

Sarah stepped back, feeling as if she'd just been slapped. "I was glad to help," she said quietly, tilting her chin as pride came to her rescue. She stood for a moment, looking at him, asking herself why she should be surprised. She'd known from the beginning that he was a stranger—that he was just passing through.

Jordan returned her look, his expression hard, his eyes veiled. Then he turned abruptly, opened the car door and swung himself into position behind the steering wheel.

Sarah took another step backward. "Goodbye, Jordan," she said quietly.

The slight sound of her voice resounded like thunder in his ears. Jordan raised his head and tried to form his mouth into a smile. Defeated, he turned his attention to starting the motor.

He knew he was leaving here with his job only half finished. He didn't know how he was going to explain the defection to his agent, and he hoped the story on Sarah hadn't already been sold on speculation. He'd write other stories— even other stories about psychics. But not this one. Not one on Sarah. He had to go. The price of staying was simply too high.

He managed to raise his arm in a farewell gesture and turned the Blazer toward the highway. Unable to resist one last look, he let his eyes stray to the sideview mirror. She was standing as he'd left her, alone, her hands tightly clutching the picnic basket.

Chapter 7

Sarah's life slipped back into the pattern of Mountain Springs. If she was quieter, more withdrawn, than usual, the family didn't question it. They gave her space and silent but loving support. The first day passed, slipped unnoticed into the second, then the third. A week went by before Sarah stopped and allowed herself to think about Jordan Matthias.

Her first reaction was anger—anger with herself for ever believing one day couldn't make a difference. But mostly she felt alone. It seemed a familiar state of affairs. She'd always been alone—surrounded but apart. This was no different, except perhaps that now she knew the void in the center of her life would never be filled.

"What will come, comes," she reminded herself, and stoically moved through the motions of day-to-day living, coping with the exhausting energy of one small boy cousin, worrying about the future of one stubborn great-aunt and

assisting her family when and where she could. Almost unnoticed, the second week slipped by.

When she heard the rattling pickup pull into the yard,
Sarah dried her hands and stepped onto the screened back
porch to welcome her cousin.

"Got a glass of lemonade for a thirsty farmer?" T.J.
yelled, climbing out of the truck. "Can't remember it ever
being so hot in June. I'm already dreading August."

"Come on in, T.J.," Sarah told him. "I can probably
find a sandwich of some kind, too. What are you doing over
here this time of day? All the cows go on vacation?"

"Don't I wish!" T.J. pulled off his straw hat and plopped
it on the counter, then rinsed his hands under the kitchen
faucet. "I've been checking Dad's stock in Canfield's east
pasture. We may have to move them."

"So, they finally sold the place."

"Not yet. But if they do, we'll have to move fast. They
only let us run this summer on a week-to-week lease."

Sarah hesitated a moment. She hated to ask, but knew she
had to. "Is there any way you could make them an offer?"

T.J. shook his head. "No chance. Not until late fall,
probably not even then. If they'd held off one more year
before putting it on the market...but they didn't." He
pulled one of the straight-backed chairs out from under the
scarred harvest table and sat down.

"Oh, T.J., I'm sorry. What about your horses?"

He shrugged. "I'll find somewhere for them. There'll be
other places for sale come spring. Always somebody wanting to sell after winter. If I'm not able to buy, I can always
lease. For now I've shifted them back to Dad's. He said he
didn't feel up to nursing a bunch of calves through the winter anyway. We'll winter the horses there instead." T.J. took
a long, slow sip from the tall glass of iced lemonade Sarah
placed in front of him.

"It doesn't seem right. The place's been sitting there for years. And now, just before you're ready to move, they decide to sell." Sarah added a slice of tomato to the ham sandwich she was making, plopped the sandwich on a plate and set it in front of him.

"Buck up, Sarah. There's always the possibility nobody else wants it. If they do, it's not the end of the world. You just don't want to lose your favorite swimming hole."

Sarah ignored the sharp pain caused by his casual remark. Despite the unseasonably hot weather, she hadn't been there in two weeks. She made up her mind to go this afternoon. It was time to face the ghosts.

"You're right, I don't." She gave him a wry grin. "But I also hate to think of strangers buying it. With Grandpa on this side and Uncle Hiram on the other, it just seems it ought to be family."

"Cheer up, cousin. Things will work out one way or the other. Speaking of family, have you been able to make any progress getting my grandmother off the mountain?"

Sarah made a small grimace. "I thought you said cheer up. Thinking about moving Aunt Cinda is hardly a cheerful subject."

"That bad, huh? Haven't you made any progress at all?"

"None. You're more than welcome to try your luck. The last time I mentioned it, she told me there was only one way to get her off the mountain short of carrying her off feet first."

"One way? What is it?"

"She wouldn't say. And I can't read her." Sarah's voice reflected her frustration.

T.J. finished his sandwich, drained the last of the lemonade and pushed back his chair. "You'll figure it out. We can always count on you."

"I wish I had your confidence. I was thinking, T.J., if you could get your horse ranch established, find a place with a little house on it, maybe we could say you needed someone to look after you. I have a little in the bank, if that will help, and—"

"Hold it right there, Sarah Jane Wilson. I love Grandma dearly. But have her take care of me? She'd drive me crazy in a week. She'd drive you crazy in a week, too, and she's closer to you than anyone. It won't work. What we need is a small place near some of us so she can be independent and still close enough to somebody to get to her if she needs help."

T.J. rescued his hat from the countertop, and Sarah followed him out onto the porch. "You're right, of course," she told him. "Maybe I can find a small place for rent."

"I think your time would be better spent finding out what one reason will bring her off the mountain. Then the rest will fall into place."

Sarah made a face at him. "I could use a little help. Why don't you try to find out?"

T.J. laughed. "She's being mysterious. You know that's your department." He took the two porch steps in a single stride. "Thanks for the lunch." He started to climb into the truck cab, then turned to face her again.

"By the way, you want to see that writer fellow? You know, the one who was around here a while back?"

Sarah went very still. She opened her mouth to answer, closed it without uttering a sound, then tried again. "He's gone."

Her cousin shook his head. "He's back. Saw his Blazer in the square this morning."

"There's a lot of blue Blazers around," she finally managed to say. "If it is him, he's probably just double-checking a few facts for that article he's writing."

"Sometimes you can be awful dense, Sarah Jane. I saw the way he looked at you. Like an ice-cream cone on a hot day."

When Sarah started to protest, he quieted her with a gesture. "That's none of my business. Just tell me if you want to see him or not. I'm heading to the Co-op now. If he's still in town, I can manage to run into him. If he asks, I can tell him how to reach you. Otherwise you'll be top item on the valley grapevine again. He'll be asking all over town—like last time."

Sarah's thoughts tumbled. Was he really back? And was T.J. right? Would he want to see her again? When he'd said goodbye, it had sounded final to her.

T.J.'s drawl interrupted her thoughts. "Well, what's the answer? Do you or don't you?"

She took a deep breath. "If Mr. Matthias is back in town and he wants to see me, he knows where to find me. He came out to the farm once." Her voice was as cool and noncommittal as she could make it.

"I didn't know that, Sarah Jane. Guess you don't need my help after all. If I see him, I'll just say hi!" T.J.'s face broke into a wide grin.

"Don't you be volunteering anything. You hear me, Timothy James? You let things be."

T.J. just laughed and gave her a jaunty goodbye wave.

Sarah dumped the last of the green beans into the pan, then stretched to ease her stiff back. She'd sat on the porch for the last two hours, one ear listening for the phone, one eye on the driveway, while her hands automatically snapped the beans. Her busy hands had done little to distract her chaotic thoughts.

When the phone rang, she jumped like a scalded cat. It wasn't as if she were expecting a call, she told herself, then laughed at her foolishness. Not expecting, but hoping. And wondering. Considering the way he'd left, what could possibly bring him back? She forced herself to be calm and picked up the phone.

"Sarah? This is Jordan."

"Hi, Jordan," Sarah said lightly, only her white-knuckled grip on the receiver betraying her agitation. "T.J. said he thought he'd seen your Blazer in town." There was a momentary silence on the other end of the line and what sounded suspiciously like a slowly released breath.

"I saw him," Jordan told her. "He gave me the telephone number. I couldn't remember your grandparents' name."

Sarah waited, afraid to speak, determined not to betray the havoc the sound of his voice was wreaking on her carefully controlled emotions.

"I didn't know T.J. was your cousin," he added suddenly.

A tiny laugh escaped Sarah's lips. "You didn't? I told you the whole town was kin."

The voice on the other end of the phone relaxed. "Well, I didn't know. Tell me, is he blood kin or kissing kin?"

Sarah laughed again. This time it was not a laugh of nerves. "Blood kin. Second cousin, in fact. Our grandmothers are sisters. Does it matter?" she asked teasingly.

"It could," he answered, his voice suddenly solemn. "Sarah, I need to see you."

Anticipation battled with caution. Sarah took a long, slow breath to give herself a moment to collect her thoughts. She knew she shouldn't see him again. She admitted how much she wanted to. Inevitably she bowed to her desires. "Of course, Jordan. Are you having problems with the article?" She could only hope her voice sounded normal. With the hammering of her own pulse in her ears, she couldn't be sure.

"No, the article's fine. In fact, it's already sold and scheduled for publication in September."

"Then why...?"

"Don't be dense, Sarah. May I come out and talk to you?"

Although he phrased his request as a question, Sarah didn't fail to catch the determination in his voice. She was glad there was no one there to see the rush of blood to her cheeks.

"I'd like that. When?" The words were out of her mouth before she could stop them. She heard something that sounded like a relieved laugh on the other end of the line.

"Now. If that's all right. I have a proposition for you."

"A proposition?" She was caught completely off guard, and her voice all but squeaked.

This time she definitely heard the low rumble of his deep-throated laugh.

"Don't worry. It's not that kind of proposition," he told her. "I'll drive out now. All right?"

Sarah nodded, almost afraid to trust her voice, then realized he couldn't see her from the other end of the phone line. "Okay," she told him, a little breathlessly. "I'll see you in a little while."

Jordan put down the receiver, not sure whether he was facing judgment day or had just won a last-minute reprieve. In fact, at the moment he wasn't sure of anything—and especially not why he'd returned to Mountain Springs. But he was here. He'd found himself driving down the small town's main street at midmorning with only one thought in his mind. He had to see Sarah again.

He considered the feasibility of telling her why he'd come, then summarily dismissed the idea. Later, maybe. But not now. If she knew that the reason he'd come to Mountain Springs was to research a story on her psychic abilities she'd refuse to see him. Then he'd never know what she was or why he was so drawn to her.

It had to be this way, he told himself, refusing to give into the doubts created by his guilt over deceiving her. He had no other choice.

Sarah barely had time to wash the green-bean stains from her hands and change into a crisp cotton sundress before she heard Jordan's car in the driveway. Knowing her grandparents and Jimmy Joe were due back any minute, she met him at the door and suggested a walk.

She didn't want to revisit the glen by the creek—not with Jordan, not until she knew exactly why he'd returned. Instead, she led him behind the barn, across the pasture and up a small hill. The conversation was casual. It was as if they had both decided independently not to discuss anything personal until they reached a resting place.

She couldn't quite suppress her grin as she bent to unlatch the gate to the small picket-fence enclosure. She knew Jordan would be standing behind her, looking in amazement at the structure protected by the fence.

"What . . . what is it?" he managed to ask.

"Depends on who's talking. My grandparents call it 'Gertie's gazebo.' Everyone else calls it 'the folly.' Grandpa built it for my grandmother as a first-anniversary present. It's modeled after one they saw in New Orleans on their honeymoon."

"But why in the middle of a cow pasture?"

"The original, the one in New Orleans, was by the side of a small lake. According to Grandma, there were ducks and swans swimming back and forth and water lilies blooming in the water.''

She moved aside to allow Jordan through the narrow gate, stiffening when his hand casually brushed against her arm. His touch was as breath-stealing as she remembered. She walked to the corner of the enclosure and waited for him to join her.

"See that shallow ravine down the hill? Grandpa planned to put a stock pond in there. A gazebo by a stock pond wouldn't be too romantic. So he built it up here to overlook the pond, but he ran into a problem. Evidently there's a fault in the bedrock. The ravine won't hold water. So, here it sits, Gertie's gazebo, high and dry on the side of a hill pasture."

Jordan followed Sarah up the steps into the hexagon-shaped structure. The open-air building, enclosed with latticework to a four-foot height on the sides and covered by a cone-shaped roof, provided a circular view of the surrounding hillsides. "I don't think Grandma minded about the pond," Sarah said, her voice soft and hushed. "She and Grandpa still come out here often. They say it's the best place on the farm to see the Milky Way."

"No, I don't think she would," Jordan agreed. "This is one of those cases where it's the thought that counts."

Sarah took a seat on one of the cushioned benches built along five sides of the structure and silently gave a sigh of relief when Jordan selected a bench opposite her. "Anyway," she added, "I thought it would be a good place for us to talk. At the house we run the risk of being interrupted every five minutes."

Jordan nodded, shifted restlessly on the bench and unconsciously raked his hand through his hair. He looked across the small space separating them, wondering how to start. Sarah beat him to it.

"Why are you back?" she asked, her eyes meeting, probing his.

He fought to control his breathing. "I had to come." Although he knew his voice sounded brisk, matter-of-fact, he'd had no control over the words. How did she do that to him? A feeling of disquiet, something akin to anger, stirred in his body. He stood abruptly, took a quick step toward her, then stopped. Shoving his hands deep into his pockets, he turned away, looking out over the countryside.

"Look, Sarah, I don't know if I can explain it, but I need to try. I once told you I was like the wind, occasionally resting in strange places for a while, but eventually moving on. I've never found a place where I thought I could stay. But this time, when I left, it was different. It called me back. I couldn't get it out of my mind."

He turned toward her again and forced her to meet his eyes. "I couldn't get you out of my mind." He watched her face for a moment, as if waiting for a reaction.

Sarah clutched her hands together in her lap, forcing them to be still, hoping he hadn't noticed her agitation. Her mind swam dizzily, caught between separate reactions of hope and fear. She stared at him mutely, wondering if he was waiting for her to say something, wondering what she should say. But before she could gather her thoughts, he continued speaking.

"I got to thinking, what if I'm not like the wind? What if I'm not a leaf of a piece of flotsam, but a seed caught in the current, blown around, looking for a place to land? What if this is the place where I could settle, could grow? Do you understand, Sarah? I don't know if it is. All I know is, I want to find out."

Sarah tried to think. The implications of what he was saying and her own emotions mingled in a chaotic jumble of reason and desire. "What . . . what are you asking, Jordan? What do you want? What do you want from me?"

His response was immediate. "I want to stay here, for a while at least. I want a chance to taste life as one who might belong, as more than a passing visitor."

She didn't realize she was holding her breath until he paused. He took a step toward her, then abruptly stopped and thrust his hands into his pockets again.

"I don't want to hurt you, Sarah. And I'm not masochistic. I was being truthful before. We could hurt each other. It would only take a spark. I'm not asking for that. I want a chance to get to know you, you and this place. But under the circumstances, I won't stay if you don't want me to. Do you, Sarah? If I stay, can you be my friend?"

Sarah sat silently for a moment, almost afraid to believe what she'd heard. It was as perfect an answer to her problems as she could hope to find in an imperfect world. He was asking for time—time for him to get to know her and for her to get to know him. Could she give that to him? Could she not? First friendship, then, later, perhaps... *What will come, comes,* she reminded herself.

Jordan stood waiting, wondering if he should have approached her differently, if he could have won her agreement more easily. He held his breath as she finally raised her eyes from the floor and looked into his face. He began to hope when he saw her smile.

"How much of a purist are you?" she asked in a slightly breathless voice.

Her question threw him into total confusion again. "Purist?"

"I know you'd never personally bait a hook with a worm, but how do you feel about eating one someone else has caught that way?" Her eyes teased gently. "You can stay for supper tonight, if you like. But it's Friday. Jimmy Joe provides the fish.''

Over the next few days Sarah inserted Jordan into the midst of the summer farming activities, introducing him to members of her family, watching in fascination as her relatives' natural wariness of strangers was replaced by acceptance and friendship.

Although Jordan was house-sitting at a colleague's home near Eureka Springs, each day he drove through the throngs of tourists, arriving at the farm ready for the activities of the day. Sarah carefully arranged her schedule so that at least one member of her family of chaperons was always nearby.

But she couldn't prevent her eyes from following his tall, lean frame whenever he was in sight. Nor could she escape the fluttering sensations she felt each time his eyes purposely sought hers. Although she'd carefully avoided any physical contact between them, she knew that her obvious restraint was causing raised eyebrows and knowing grins from certain of her kinsmen.

It was only a matter of time until her well-meaning relatives intervened ''on her behalf'' and rearranged her carefully laid plans. But even with that knowledge she was unprepared to feel Jordan's hands at her waist, hands lifting her from her position in front of the suds-filled kitchen sink and gently depositing her to one side.

''It will be faster if I wash and you dry,'' he said. ''You know where things go.''

''You're going to wash dishes? But Grandma—''

''Your grandmother is taking a well-deserved rest in a rocking chair on the front porch. What's the matter? Don't you think I know how to wash dishes?'' His voice was a soft, teasing sound. He lifted a towel from the stack next to the sink and tied it around his waist. ''It's been a while, I'll admit, but I washed my first stack of dishes standing on an apple crate so I could reach the sink. It's like riding a bicycle. Once you learn, you never forget.''

Sarah watched, afraid to trust her voice, as he expertly washed and rinsed three plates, setting them on the drain board in front of her. The white suds clinging to his arms emphasized the golden hue of his skin.

"You couldn't keep avoiding me forever, you know. Your cousins are already taking bets—'' He grinned when she raised shocked eyes to his face. "Better grab a towel. You're getting behind.''

"They wouldn't dare—'' she protested as she automatically began drying the dishes. Then: "Yes, they would," she admitted in a resigned voice.

The grin turned into a full-fledged laugh. "I like your family," he said.

"Sometimes they can be a pain in the . . . the . . .''

"Derriere?''

"Well . . . yes.''

"As I remember, it's a very pretty derriere.''

"Jordan," she protested, looking quickly toward the open door between the kitchen and the dining room.

"It's all right. They've all adjourned to the front porch. Besides, I was choosing my words very carefully.''

Sarah found the teasing banter relaxing. "They like you, too. Grandpa says, for a city boy you do pretty well on a tractor seat. Believe me, that's high praise.''

"I was at home on a tractor seat long before I became a city boy, Sarah.''

"I didn't know that.''

Jordan regarded her with solemn eyes. "I think there's a lot about each other we don't know. I hope . . .''

"You hope what?''

Jordan caught his breath. *So many things,* he thought. *I hope you'll forgive me if you learn why I came back. I hope I'll discover what it is that draws me to you, to this place.* He refused to follow the thoughts any farther, afraid of what he might find. Instead, he smiled. "I hope we have a chance to learn about each other."

"Most of the time I think people help make their own chances," Sarah said.

Jordan's eyes met and held hers. It was too much to ask of any man. She'd avoided being alone with him for days. Didn't she realize that was like denying water to a man in the desert? Didn't she know it was part of the male psyche to accept a dare? Wasn't she aware that she was challenging him to make his own chance? He withdrew his hands from the dishwater, drying them on the towel around his waist, his gaze never wavering, never allowing hers to drop. Then he reached for her.

Sarah stood as she was, mesmerized by the compelling look in his eyes. She knew she should say something, do something. She saw him reach for her, tried to step back, discovered she couldn't move. She felt his hand warm on her shoulder, breathed the fresh smell of the lemon detergent mixing with the clean male scent of his skin. He bent his head, and his lips brushed, then claimed, hers with a gentle sweetness that spread through her limbs, weakening her knees.

This kiss was unlike the explosion on the riverbank, that searing blue-white blaze of wanting she'd been unable to forget. This was a carefully controlled flame, smoldering banked coals, no less intense in heat and no less compelling in nature. Sarah felt her resistance fading, felt her body swaying toward him, melting into his until only one small glimmer of reason remained. She knew that if she didn't move away she'd be lost, consumed in the fire of her own wanting. It was self-preservation that made her try to retreat.

Jordan felt her sudden resistance and reluctantly raised his mouth from hers. "Ah, Sarah," he whispered against her lips, "chance is sometimes a risky business." He continued to hold her for a second. Then, glancing toward the open doorway, he turned back to the sink, plunging his hands into the dishwater. If he was right, the kitchen was about to be invaded. "Start drying, Sarah," he hissed under his breath, "someone's coming."

His warning preceded T.J.'s entrance by seconds. Jordan turned toward the man, his movement blocking Sarah from sight, giving her another moment to collect herself.

"You here to help supervise or chaperon?" he asked, not bothering to disguise his good humor.

T.J. ignored him. "You'd better come, Sarah," he said. "Dad and Aunt Gertie are into it about Grandmother again."

"Not again," Sarah cried, throwing the towel at T.J. and all but running out the door.

"Well, I guess I know what she wants me to do," T.J. said cheerfully, reaching for a dish on the drain board.

Jordan eyed him curiously. "Family crisis? No, never mind. It's none of my business." He rinsed the last cup and set it in the drainer, then leaned against the counter as T.J. finished drying the few remaining items.

"It's no big secret," T.J. told him. "My grandmother is getting old. Her home's on the mountain above Hogscald Hollow. The family thinks she should move down to the valley, and everyone takes sides when they start talkin' about how they're going to get her off that mountain. And it don't amount to a hill of beans anyway, 'cause Grandma says she's fine where she is, and she don't plan to move."

Jordan tried not to smile at the look of disgust on T.J.'s face. "So why'd you run to Sarah?" Jordan asked, trying to untangle the complex family relationships. "If I understand it right, Sarah's grandmother and your grandmother are sisters. That makes Sarah a—what? Great-niece? Surely that's not as close a relationship as either her sister or your dad, who's her son. Right?"

"Yeah. But Sarah's the only one that can keep the peace, 'cause everyone knows she's the only one who has a chance of talking Grandma into leaving that mountain. They're both—I mean, Grandma and Sarah are special close. Always have been."

Both what? Jordan knew T.J. had started to say something else but had changed his mind. He didn't push. He didn't need to get involved in family affairs, but he was beginning to understand what Sarah meant when she talked about family obligations.

T.J. hung the damp dish towel on the back of the cabinet and moved toward the doorway, gesturing for Jordan to follow him. "I think we can go on out to the porch now. Sarah should have had time to calm everybody down."

Jordan grinned wryly as he followed. Sarah might be a calming influence on her family, but nothing about her had a calming effect on him.

Chapter 8

The sun dried Sarah's hair on their walk from the swimming hole. It lay in soft waves, framing her face with the same champagne cloud that had so intrigued Jordan during their first meeting.

As they turned off the road and into the long, winding driveway, Jordan allowed himself to drop a step or two behind. Sarah's slender hips, clad in the worn denim Levi's she'd pulled over her damp bathing suit, swayed under the tail of her outsize man's shirt. She moved with a natural grace, accepting her sensuality without thought.

How could he have believed he'd be able to maintain a platonic friendship with her? Every hormone in his body screamed in protest. In some ways the tension between them had eased since the night they'd shared dish duty and a kiss in the kitchen of her grandparents' farmhouse, but Jordan had been careful not to push the relationship too far or too fast. He forced himself to be content with an occasional caress, a quick kiss, a casual touch. Who was he kidding? I took every bit of his control to keep him from rushing his fences like one of T.J.'s amorous stallions. At times he convinced himself Sarah was completely unaware of how badly he wanted her. Then he'd catch her glancing at him and have to turn away to prevent himself from answering the unconscious promise reflected in her eyes.

Jordan clenched his hands, wanting to reach out and take her in his arms. He wanted to let his fingers twine through her silky hair, feel her smooth skin and her gently rounded hips tremble under his caressing hands. He wanted to feel her move beneath him, giving herself and accepting him in return.

As they neared the farmhouse, he quickened his pace, reached out and grabbed her hand, holding it in that casual way friends had. He hoped the physical contact would exorcise his erotic fantasies.

Hand in hand, they approached the porch steps, stopping abruptly when Sarah caught sight of the unhappy barefoot boy sitting on the top step.

"What's wrong, Jimmy Joe? Why so sad?" she asked gently.

"Grandma's mad. I can't find my tennies." Jimmy Joe's words were interspersed between barely disguised sniffles. "We were going to Billy Hawkins's house. Only I can't find my shoes, and Grandma says if I can't find my tennis shoes I can't go."

"Couldn't you wear your other shoes?"

Jimmy Joe shook his head, his eyes bright with barely controlled tears. "Grandma says we'd be sure to go wading in the creek, it being such a hot day and all. And if I have my Sunday shoes on, then I'll have to take them off. Then I'd probably cut my feet in the creek. So that's why I can't go if I can't find my tennis shoes." He paused for breath. A tear rolled unchecked down his freckled cheek. "I've looked everywhere, Cissie."

She smiled gently and tousled his red curls. "Not everywhere, I'll bet." Jordan watched as Sarah let her hand rest lightly on the top of his head for a moment. Then she frowned. "You went down to the springhouse yesterday afternoon, didn't you? Grandpa killed a copperhead there the other day. I thought he told you to stay away until he checked for a nest."

Jordan drew a quick breath. Sarah had been with him yesterday afternoon. How'd she know Jimmy Joe had gone to the springhouse? Coincidence? Or something else?

Jimmy Joe looked up, guilt written all over his face. "It was so hot. It's cool in the springhouse. I was only there for a little bit."

"I know it's cool there, Jimmy Joe. So do the snakes. That's why Grandpa told you not to go. You're not to go again. Understand?"

The boy's eyes filled with tears. "But—but that's where I left my tennies. I just remembered."

Sarah sighed. "I know. I'll get them. You're barefooted. You wait right here." She disappeared around the side of the house.

"Cissie's mad at me, ain't she?" Jimmy Joe asked.

"I think she's more worried than mad," Jordan told him. "Copperheads are nothing to laugh about. She doesn't want you to get hurt."

The boy hung his head.

Sarah returned minutes later, tennis shoes in hand.

"Are you going to tell Grandpa?" the boy asked.

"Not this time, if you'll promise me you won't go back until it's safe? Promise? No matter how hot it gets?"

"I promise. Honest Injun and hope to die." He threw his arms around her neck. "I'm sorry, Cissie. I didn't mean to scare you."

"I know," she told him, smiling. "Just remember your promise. Run along now. Grandma's probably waiting."

The boy's face cleared instantly. "Thanks, Cissie. I'm sure glad you see so good." He cleared the three porch steps in a single leap and raced toward the back of the house.

Still smiling, Sarah shook her head and turned toward Jordan. Her smile faded when she saw the expression on Jordan's face. How could she have forgotten? She took a quick breath, her smile faltering, her mind racing furiously. Could she bluff her way out of it? "All you have to do to keep track of an eight-year-old is figure out where he's not supposed to be..." she began. Then, defeated, she let her voice trail off into silence.

"You know, don't you?" She had to force the words. Their small sound clanged like a fire alarm in her own ears.

Jordan nodded, his expression becoming concerned when he saw how upset she was. "About the 'sight'? Jimmy Joe told me the first time we met. Remember? What I don't know is why you try so hard to hide it."

"There are reasons."

"Sarah..."

"You don't know...."

"No, I don't. And that's why I should." Jordan took a step toward her, stopping when she matched his movement by backing away. "Sarah, we were going to get to know each other better." He spread his hands helplessly. "How can I know you if I don't know about something that's so obviously a part of who you are?"

Sarah squared her shoulders and took a deep breath. "You're right," she said finally.

"Then why can't we talk about it? Can't you share it with me?"

She couldn't bring herself to look into his face. As much as she'd tried to hide from it, this was the moment she'd dreaded since Jordan's return. She'd known from the beginning that he'd never understand. No one ever had.

Jordan watched the conflicting emotions cross her face. Suddenly he wished he'd never started this. "I'm not the Inquisition, Sarah." Jordan spoke softly. "If it upsets you this much, maybe—" He stopped, not quite sure why he'd said that. This was the reason he'd come back to Mountain Springs. Now that she was finally ready to talk about it, why was he offering to let her off the hook? He wanted to know. Why, then, did he feel so rotten about it?

Sarah resisted his offer of escape. It would be so easy to pretend that nothing had changed, but it had. It didn't matter whether they talked about it now or later.

She blinked, attempting to banish the tears that threatened her vision. To stand by and let him leave would be the hard part. Every time she saw him, every hour she spent with him, made that parting harder. She'd wanted to pretend, to dream, a little longer, but as with so many other things in her life, she wasn't in control. Better to get it over with now.

"No," she told him softly, "you're right. We do need to talk about it, but I'm not sure where to start."

"Alice always says, 'Start at the beginning.'"

"Alice?"

"Alice in Wonderland."

Sarah turned abruptly, her eyes snapping green fire. "This is not a joke, Jordan. Not to me."

Jordan's face registered surprise at her attack. "I know that, Sarah. I didn't mean—"

Her shoulders immediately sagged in defeat. "No. That's all right. I know you didn't."

Jordan stood abruptly. "Let's go for a walk." As they moved off the porch, Jordan placed his arm around her waist. It was a casual gesture he'd indulged in many times in the last week. When Sarah stiffened, he refused to retreat. They walked across the yard, moving toward the woodlot and the high pasture beyond the barn. Gradually Jordan felt some of her tension dissolve under his touch.

"Do you know much about...about..." Her voice faltered.

"About the 'Sight,' or ESP, or whatever it's called?" Jordan shook his head, fighting his conscience, which was urging him to tell her the truth. Now wasn't the time, not when she was already upset. "I've read a bit about it, of course," he finally admitted. "But I've never known anyone with it before. In fact, the cases I've heard of have usually turned out to be fake." At least that statement was perfectly honest.

"A lot of them are. Especially the ones you hear about. But not always. Sometimes—" Sarah stopped again, allowing herself a second to gather her courage. She stepped away from his touch, turning to face him. "You have to understand, Jordan. I have 'it,' whatever 'it' is. I don't understand how it works. It just is. At times I know things without knowing how or why I know them. Most of the time I wish I didn't, but I wasn't asked. I don't have a choice."

"Why don't you begin by telling me what you do, besides tell little boys where they've left their shoes and sometimes answer questions that haven't been asked yet?"

"Did I do that to you? Mind-read your questions?"

Her startled expression surprised him. He'd known she hadn't realized what she was doing at the time, but he'd thought it was normal for her. "Is that unusual?"

"Yes and no," she said. "Occasionally I do it with people I'm close to, but I don't usually give answers without realizing the question wasn't asked."

"I think I'm flattered," he told her. "Especially the part about doing it with people you're close to." He saw a flicker of fear in her eyes. "So," he said, straining to keep a normal tone of voice, "you mind-read a little, and can see the past, like discovering where Jimmy Joe left his shoes. Anything else?'

"When I was at the university I did some research. I tried to match definitions with skills. Some of the definitions fit generally, but not exactly. For example, I seem to be clairvoyant, but usually not precognitive. Do you know what I mean?"

Jordan nodded. "You know or see things happening in other places, or things that have happened before, but you don't see things that have yet to happen."

"That's pretty close—at least according to the definitions. Sometimes I can force the clairvoyance, like I did with Jimmy Joe's shoes. Outside the community and family circles, where I'm exposed to more people, more things, I sometimes get flashes that have no meaning to me at all. I can't read the future on demand, although I can usually predict the weather and occasionally get glimpses of other things. Sometimes I get a warning, like when the bench was tumbling toward me."

"You knew *that* was going to happen?"

"No. At least not until it was seconds away. I didn't even have time to look at it. Only duck. Seeing my own future is one thing I can't do at all. Heavens knows, it would have saved me a lot of misery if I could. Sometimes I get vaguely uneasy, but I never know if it's a special warning or plain, ordinary fear."

Jordan saw her tremble. He gave her shoulder a reassuring squeeze. "I still don't understand why you work so hard to hide it, Sarah. After all, it's a pretty special gift. I suspect you help a lot of people. What makes you so afraid?"

"Exposure. Publicity. Threats. Public ridicule. If I'm careful, sometimes I can spare myself that pain, anyway."

Her voice was flat, not devoid of emotion but drained. He knew immediately that experience, not imagination, was the cause.

When Sarah turned and continued walking along the path through the woodlot, Jordan matched her pace. Neither of them spoke as they reached the edge of the woods. They stepped from under the trees into bright sunlight. The gently rolling pasture stretched green and silent in front of them, and the gazebo waited peacefully in the distance.

"I'm protected here in the valley," she said suddenly. "Outside, I'm vulnerable. When I left Mountain Springs to attend college on the other side of the state I discovered I could see things that had no connection with me or my family. They were things I couldn't keep to myself. I found I had no control over knowing them. And I also found that outside the valley people don't understand."

Jordan stopped, puzzled. "But didn't you know—before you went outside, I mean—that you were..."

Sarah's eyes filled with pain. "Oh, yes. I've known I was different since I was eight years old."

"Eight?"

She nodded. "That's when my parents were killed and I came to live with my grandparents. I'd used it before, but I didn't realize it. I was good at finding lost mittens. I always knew when it was going to rain, even if the sun was shining. I'd gather all my toys and bring them inside before there was a hint of a cloud in the sky."

When they reached the fenced enclosure, Jordan leaned over to unfasten the gate latch, then allowed her to lead the way. Inside the gazebo he seated himself on the cushioned bench next to her and reached out to take her hand. This time she didn't flinch at his touch.

Sarah leaned against one of the support posts and squeezed her eyes shut. Her hands still lay loosely in his.

"I remember Mother watching me gather my toys," she said quietly, straining to keep her voice detached. "Mother never questioned me. She'd watch for a minute, then take the wash off the clothesline, just as if it were the most natural thing in the world. I realize now that my parents knew I was different but were trying to treat it as something usual, natural. They were trying to let me be a normal little girl."

Her eyes misted over. "If—" Her voice trembled, then broke. She started again. "If I'd known I was different, that everyone didn't know the things I did, then maybe my parents wouldn't have died." This time she failed to stop the tears escaping from between her lids.

Jordan leaned forward and gently brushed the wet drops from her cheeks. He felt a dull ache, a churning grief deep inside. He wanted to hold her, comfort her, knowing it would also comfort him. "Sarah, don't..."

"I'm okay, Jordan. You were right. You need to know. You see, I'm psychic, or extrasensitive, or whatever you want to call it. But my parents weren't. When they left that night, I knew they wouldn't be coming back. I didn't know why. I only knew, as they went out the door, that I was alone. If I'd asked them why, maybe...maybe they wouldn't have gone. So in a way it was my fault. I knew and I didn't tell them."

"An eight-year-old trying to sort through that— Oh, Sarah, how did you survive?" Jordan could feel tears burning in his own eyes.

"Aunt Cinda."

"Aunt Cinda? The old lady who won't leave the mountain? Is she—"

Sarah nodded. "It seems to run in the family. Aunt Cinda didn't know about my parents. Neither of us predict the specific future very often, and never on demand. But she knew I was in trouble. She came running off her mountain in the dead of night to be with me."

She took another deep breath. "So Aunt Cinda took me under her wing. The rest of the family took over what my parents started, treating me as normal, protecting me, comforting me, and life went on. Little by little, with Aunt Cinda's help, I learned to cope. Or at least I thought I had, until I went outside. It was then I learned what a strange creature I am."

Jordan could hear the pain in her voice. Unable to resist any longer, he freed her hand and gathered her close in his arms. His touch was soothing, comforting. "What hurt you so badly, Sarah?"

She let her head rest against his shoulder while she tried to collect her thoughts.

"I had no idea of what it would be like, living outside the valley," she began in a tight voice. "I'd had no real reason to hide my skills, and I didn't fully realize how uncomfortable other people would be discovering them."

"Your aunt didn't warn you?"

Sarah shook her head. "She didn't know—not the worst of it, anyway. She's never lived outside this community. We know we're viewed as a little strange, a little different. There's a certain distance between us and other people, particularly outside the family circle. But we're accepted— at least believed—and to a certain extent shielded. Outside, it's completely different. I'm a freak."

Jordan wanted to say something—to offer reassurance—but was afraid to speak. He also heard what she didn't say. Some would consider her a freak, others a fake. He held her, offering comfort in the only way he dared—in the intimacy of his embrace.

Finally she stirred in his arms. The movement failed to completely disguise her trembling. Her eyes were clouded, like those of a child remembering a nightmare.

"Something happened." His voice was as calm and emotionless as he could make it.

Sarah looked up. "Yes," she said. "A private plane carrying a couple of state legislators crashed in the mountains near my school. There were newspapers and television people all over the place."

He could guess what happened next. "You got involved, and the story got out," he said, trying to make it easier for her.

"I had to. I recognized the crash site, but by then I'd learned a little. I thought I could protect myself. I tried to talk to the searchers, tried to suggest where the crash might be. They wouldn't listen. And they were searching the wrong mountain. In the end I had to go find them myself. I talked several friends into going on a hike, and we 'accidentally' stumbled across the crash. The pilot was dead, but the two passengers were still alive. We found them in time."

"I imagine the publicity was pretty heavy."

Sarah nodded. "It was bad enough when we were 'accidental heroes.' Then someone remembered the stories about me, and the searchers I'd tried to talk to remembered how I wanted them to search that mountain." She shuddered. "It was awful."

Jordan couldn't keep the sympathy from his eyes. He could imagine her as she had been then—young, unsure of herself, bewildered by it all and besieged from every side.

What was he supposed to do now? Despite the lack of what he would usually have considered proof, he had no doubt that Sarah was telling him the truth. She was real. If he'd been a fraud, like the others, it wouldn't have mattered, but this was a situation he hadn't considered. He'd given lip service to the idea that she might be psychic, but he'd never really thought about what he'd do if she was, because deep down he hadn't really believed it. His so-called search for the truth had been nothing but an excuse to bring him back to Mountain Springs. What was he going to tell his agent? Jack would expect a story one way or the other. But, more important, what was he going to tell Sarah? And how?

"I can imagine how it was," he said after a long moment. "Some of it, anyway. I wish I could say something to make it easier, but I can't. All I can say is I'm sorry."

Sarah shrugged. "I managed to survive—barely. I finished out the year, and then I came home. I transferred to the university at Fayetteville in the fall and finished there."

"Was Fayetteville better?"

"Much better. I'd learned a lot during that first year. And Fayetteville was closer to home. Then, too, there was Sheriff Bascomb. He knew some people in Fayetteville. So when anything happened, I had someone to tell."

She stood up abruptly, turned her back and walked across the gazebo. "There've been other times, Jordan. Some bad. Some only frustrating. But exposure, bad as it is, isn't the worst part of all this."

Jordan barely heard her last words, so softly were they spoken. "What is the worst of it, Sarah? Tell me. Let me help."

"No one can. That's part of the problem. I've learned that no one else can possibly understand. Sometimes they say they do, but then something happens, and he—they pull away as if they're afraid to be contaminated. It makes me feel so alone."

Anger sliced through him—anger directed at whoever had hurt her so deeply. He moved to her side. "Try me," he whispered softly in her ear. "Give me a chance."

Sarah took a deep breath, wondering if she dared. Would she be able to stand it when she saw that look in his eyes? She closed her eyes, determined that no matter what happened she would not see it this time. She'd know anyway, but she didn't have to see. She trembled. Then, resolute, she steadied her voice. "I'll give you an example," she said. "Right before I left St. Louis a little boy was kidnapped."

Jordan drew a quick breath, afraid to speak. Damn it. He should never have started this. He'd been almost ready to convince himself that he had no story, no concrete facts, just hearsay and possible coincidence. Now she was about to lay the story in his lap—an incident he was already familiar with, a case where facts could be verified. His arms tightened around her. She didn't seem to notice.

"The little boy was hurt, and alone and so afraid. For some reason, I read him. For a moment or so, I was him. I felt his pain and his fear, and I was hurting as much and was as afraid as he was. I didn't know where he was. I knew only what he knew. Then I knew one thing more. I knew what was going to happen to him if he didn't get help very quickly."

She turned in his arms, her body stiff. "Can you understand how I felt, Jordan? Do you know how afraid I was? Not just his fear. That was bad enough. But knowing what was going to happen to him if I wasn't able to get him help? If I hadn't seen enough to locate him in time?"

Jordan pulled her closer. She was reliving the experience. He could see it in her eyes. Before he could say anything, she sagged in his arms.

"It turned out all right. I called someone. They were able to find him in time. But those feelings, that's what no one understands. That's what I can't share. And it's even worse when things don't turn out right. The guilt haunts me. I feel helpless. Why should I have to feel things I can't do anything about? I don't want it. And there's nothing I can do about it."

For a moment, Jordan couldn't speak. Then, slowly, he searched for words.

"You're wrong, you know. At least partly wrong," he said finally. "It's true, I don't know what the boy was feeling. And I don't know what was going to happen to him. But I can feel the horror of it. That much I can share."

His hands moved up her back to her shoulders as he stepped far enough away to look down into her face. "People who know each other, who care about each other, share those kinds of feelings all the time. You're sometimes forced to share that kind of experience with strangers—with people you don't know. But even then it's not all that different. Not really."

Sarah's expression told him she didn't believe him, didn't understand what he was trying to say. He saw her start to protest and pulled her close again, muffling her words against his chest. He made another attempt to explain.

"I feel sorrow when sad things happen to people I don't know. I believe most people do. I don't believe any normal person can see or read about or hear about a tragic event and not feel something. When you feel those things there is a chance, at least sometimes, that you can help. It isn't your fault when you can't. At least you try. And that's more than the rest of us 'normal' people can do.

"I know the sorrow I feel when sad things happen isn't exactly the same thing as what you feel. But it's close. I think the difference is that you, being especially sensitive, feel more intensely. But those feelings, like grief, can be lightened by sharing.''

He rushed on, not wanting to give her an opportunity to protest. ''When something happens to someone I know, someone I care about, the sharing is more acute. If Jimmy Joe fell and broke his arm, my arm wouldn't ache in the same way his was aching, but I'd hurt for him anyway. When you were telling me about the last time you saw your parents, I ached for you, Sarah. There was a dull pain deep inside. That kind of pain can be shared, and the sharing makes it easier to bear.''

Jordan's voice died away. He stood waiting. He wondered if he'd managed to express what he was feeling, wondered if she understood what he was trying to say. Could she recognize the real meaning behind his words—a meaning so alien to his own self-image that he was barely able to recognize it himself?

Sarah wanted to believe his words, wanted to believe that the sharing he spoke of was more than words. She trembled as the echo of caring she'd heard in his voice washed over her. Unbidden came the memory of the last time she'd been held in his arms. She remembered the sense of oneness, even with the shadow of her secret between them. Never before that time had she been so touched by the sensation of completeness. She wanted it again.

Jordan caught his breath when he saw that her cheeks were wet with tears. Then he looked into her eyes. It was as if he could read her mind. Or perhaps she'd read his. He tried to move away. He was already too involved. He couldn't take anything else from her, not until she knew the truth. But he wasn't strong enough. He wanted her too much. His guilt quivered, faded, then disappeared, replaced by a desire too powerful to be ignored or controlled.

Sarah gave a soft sigh of contentment as he caught a tear with the tip of his finger. She felt the butterfly touch against her cheek and surrendered to the impulse that had tempted her since their first meeting. Her mouth curved into a smile, and her hand moved upward to lightly trace the outline of his mouth.

Jordan caught one of the wandering fingers with his lips, nibbled gently along its length, then captured her hand with his and pressed a kiss into her palm. The movement of his lips against her hand sent a familiar warmth rippling through her body.

She snuggled into him with neither thought nor reservation, giving herself up to the heady feelings of longing and expectation she'd repressed for a lifetime. Her hands went again to his face, then slid around his neck. She pulled his head down, raised herself up on tiptoe and caressed his mouth with a feather-light touch of her lips.

Jordan quivered under her touch, his body matching the trembling of her limbs. He braced himself, feet apart, holding her in the upright cradle of his body. As he felt the touch of her lips, he managed to resist for one second more.

"Sarah?" His voice was both protest and plea. "Do you know what you're doing to me?"

"I know," she whispered, stretching upward to reach his face once again. She planted a little kiss in the center of his chin, then once again returned to his mouth, her lips parting. He met her gentle explorations, opening his mouth to her.

Her hands slid from the back of his neck, caressing his shoulders, as she lowered her body to its natural five-foot height. Jordan bent with her like a tree swaying in a storm, his mouth clinging to the sweetness of hers.

He made a sound in the back of his throat as he shifted his hold and lifted her against him, fitting his mouth over hers again.

Sarah recognized the change in the texture of his kiss as it moved from exploration to passion. She wondered at the continued gentleness of his hands as she felt the hunger tighten his body. She answered with a quiver of pleasure and the unconscious melting of her own body.

The cushions that usually padded the wooden seats of the gazebo appeared magically beneath them. Sarah didn't know if Jordan had lowered her to the floor or if she had pulled him down to join her. Her only reality was the feel of his hands around her waist, the heat of his body warming that cold, desolate spot she'd carried in the center of her being for so many years.

She heard her name whispered against her cheek as his hands lovingly stroked her hair away from her forehead. He whispered her name again as she parted her lips for him, delighting in the slow movements of his tongue.

"Love me, Jordan," she murmured, knowing she was asking for more than relief from the need he had created in her, refusing to acknowledge that it might not be the same for him.

He answered by kissing her even more deeply, his body taut with passion and restraint, his hands gentle as they moved like a whispered promise over her body. She melted at this touch, her body responding to his hard need.

Enveloped by the sweet, wild fragrance of the honey-suckle growing around the gazebo, Jordan was lost in a world of sensation—a world made real by Sarah. She called to him with her gentle hands, with the music of her voice, with the magic of her eyes.

With shaking hands she unfastened the buttons of his shirt, allowing herself quick, light touches of her fingers against his skin.

Jordan's hand closed over hers. He took a deep breath and closed his eyes, willing a return to reason. As if she'd sensed his reservations, Sarah made a small sound of protest and moved her hands over his shoulders. Her need to be held, to be loved, his need to be the one holding her, loving her, conquered the last of his caution.

"Ah, Sarah," he whispered raggedly as he released her hand and unfastened the remaining shirt buttons. "Touch me again."

Sarah's fingertips lovingly traced the swells and ridges of muscle across his tanned chest. As her nails lightly raked over his nipples, she felt desire ripple through him. She echoed the same desire as his hands removed her clothing and his eyes moved over the feminine curves and silky firmness of her body.

For a long moment he touched her only with his eyes, fighting the raw need raging in his blood.

"Jordan?" she whispered, not sure what she was asking, but knowing only he could answer.

"It's all right, Sarah," he said, his voice husky and strained. "I won't hurt you." Finally he touched her, with a feather-light caress that moved from her moist lips to the soles of her slender feet.

Sarah's body arched beneath his touch, silently asking for more. His hand moved to her breast, caressing, teasing, until the sensation produced by his touch was indistinguishable from the desire curling in her veins. His lips touched her other breast, his tongue moving over the soft, firm flesh as she moved restlessly beneath him. At last he closed his mouth over her throbbing nipple. She moaned as the intimate touch of his mouth unfurled ribbons of passion deep within her.

His hand moved from her breast, lightly stroking downward to her soft, secret warmth. He touched her slowly, exploring the intimate secrets of her desire, learning the mysteries of her passion and savoring her response to his touch. As he lifted his head, he saw the look of awed wonder in her eyes and froze, tension coiling in his body as he tried to interpret the meaning of her astonishment.

"Sarah? Haven't you—" His voice faltered as he recognized the flicker of uncertainty deep in the blue-green mists of her eyes. He drew a deep, shuddering breath into his lungs.

"I'm sorry, Jordan." Her voice was a reedy whisper of pain. "Tell me what I did wrong."

"You did nothing wrong." His lips brushed a quick butterfly kiss against her brow.

"Then what happened? Why did you stop?"

The innocence of her question was almost his undoing. He pulled her into his arms, burying her head against his shoulder in an effort to hide the strain he knew was apparent on his face. His mind searched for the right words for the question he needed to ask. "Have you . . . haven't you made love with anyone before?"

"It wasn't like this. I didn't know . . . didn't feel . . ." Her voice faltered. "I'm sorry, Jordan."

With that he gathered her even closer, the strain of the last few moments, his own tumultuous hunger, evident in every taut line of his body. To realize that he had produced that look of awe and wonder in her eyes was a precious gift. "No, no, sweetheart. There's nothing to be sorry for. I needed to know. I didn't want to hurt you through ignorance. . . ."

He laid her back against the cushions, his own body following her down, stretching full length alongside of her. His lips teased the corner of her mouth, the freckles on the bridge of her nose, then swooped to capture her softly trembling mouth. Teeth and tongue moved lightly, probing the moist, secret recesses of her mouth. His hands stroked her small, perfectly formed body, delighting in the tactile sensations of her satin-soft skin, now gently heated with an inner warmth that had nothing to do with the hot air of the July afternoon.

He raised his head, golden lights dancing in his eyes, his breath coming in quick, shallow gasps. "I knew it would be this way with us. From the beginning, I knew. More than shared attraction, physical pleasure. Much, much more..." His voice trailed off into silence as once again he obeyed the call of the soft voice muttering low, musical sounds in the back of her throat.

Confident now in her ability to pleasure him as he pleasured her, Sarah let her hands, her lips, roam freely. She explored the different textures of his body, the smooth, heat-flushed skin, the wiry roughness of his cheek and chin, the soft sprinkling of hair running from his chest down the length of his torso.

As he raised himself above her, she welcomed him into her inner core of heat and need as she had already welcomed him into her heart.

He rested quietly for a moment, savoring the delicate sheathing that both satisfied and tantalized. He waited as she adjusted to him, then began to move slowly, creating undulating waves of passion, circles of sensation spreading like ripples from a pebble tossed into a quiet pool of water. The circles grew, spreading outward to encompass both as one.

Sarah's cry of wonder was swallowed in the heat of Jordan's mouth as together they reached the pinnacle and held fast to each other. They teetered for a moment, suspended in space, before triumphantly plunging over the top and into the pool at the bottom of the falls.

There they rested together, allowing the softer currents to wash away the turbulence they'd created, then shared.

Jordan rolled his weight to one side, carefully maintaining physical contact, a tangible assurance that the last few minutes had been more than a fantasy. He now knew that until now he'd been incomplete. He read the same secret in the sparkling depths of Sarah's eyes.

Sarah looked into his face and smiled. It was a fey, secret smile of satisfaction and contentment. She wasn't sure what tomorrow would bring, only that it would come, as it always did. But at least she would always have today to remember.

Chapter 9

Sarah removed the last two pieces of golden fried chicken from the hot frying pan and placed them on an already-heaping platter. She covered the dish with a clean white cloth and set it on the harvest table beside several similar platters.

The logistics necessary in preparing for the Lutteral clan's annual Fourth of July picnic would have horrified a professional caterer, but over the years the family had devised a system that functioned almost automatically. Each branch of the sprawling family made itself responsible for a particular favorite at the yearly feast. Sarah had mastered Grandmother Lutteral's specialty, a buttermilk-batter fried chicken, while still in her teens.

She and her grandmother had begun cooking as the first rooster had announced the morning. The sun was now at ten-o'clock high. When vehicles had begun arriving at the farm an hour before, Sarah had shooed her grandmother from the kitchen to meet their guests and finished the chicken herself.

She slipped her functional apron from around her neck and stepped onto the back porch for a moment of fresh air, lifting the damp hair from the back of her neck to let the slight breeze cool her. Her eyes scanned the large expanse of lawn, now mushrooming with picnic tables made from sawhorses and raw lumber. If the early-morning crowd was any indication, this year's family reunion would be one of the largest in years.

Her eyes shifted to the driveway, which was already lined with various parked vehicles. Jordan's blue Blazer was not yet among them. Her lips curved into a smile as she remembered the look on his face when she'd issued both invitation and warning. "Be prepared with evasive answers," she'd told him. "The great-aunts are notorious for considering the younger generation's love life, or lack of it, community property. Any unattached single is fair game."

Unbidden, her mind slipped back to their time in the gazebo the afternoon before. She couldn't be sorry it happened, although she realized that the significance of those magic moments was more hers than his. Jordan had been unusually pensive when they'd parted the night before.

Sarah drew a deep breath as a sudden dark thought crossed her mind. He didn't regret it, did he? Or blame himself? It had been her choice—her decision. From the moment she'd moved into his arms, she'd known that. They had been a fire about to happen ever since Jordan had returned to Mountain Springs, but Sarah had known, from the first time she'd taken him to the gazebo, that she was the one who held the match.

Yesterday she had wanted Jordan, needed him. She knew he'd wanted her. And the togetherness they'd shared was something she'd never believed was possible for her. Was it wrong of her to have taken, to have accepted, those few moments of magic? The family would have said so. Most of them, anyway. Would Aunt Cinda?

For some reason, despite all evidence to the contrary, Sarah didn't think so. She and Aunt Cinda were different in the same way. Sarah had known for years that the bonding between people like her grandparents, or the kind of love her parents had shared, was impossible for her. True, Aunt Cinda had married and raised a large family. Sarah didn't remember her great-uncle Udell at all. But families talked. Sarah knew that Aunt Cinda and her husband had never shared that kind of love.

No, she didn't think Aunt Cinda would criticize or condemn. For a short time Sarah had experienced a bonding that went beyond physical desire. Aunt Cinda wouldn't blame her for grabbing it while she could.

She told herself she wasn't building impossible fantasies. Not really. She knew that sometime soon Jordan would be ready to move on. And, she promised herself, she'd be strong enough to let him go.

She frowned at the thought and turned to go inside, regretting the fact that she and Jordan wouldn't have a moment alone today. Not with the family watching their every move. And they'd promised to take Jimmy Joe to the Springdale Rodeo tonight to watch T.J. compete. For this day, at least, they would again be friends, not lovers. Everything else would have to wait.

Jordan had traveled the distance between the cabin and Mountain Springs so often in the last few weeks that he now drove the road almost automatically. Today the scenery zipping past the windshield was noticed even less. His thoughts were elsewhere.

How had he allowed the intimacy of the previous afternoon to happen? He grinned ruefully to himself. Allowed? It had been beyond either of their control. He was not, after all, Superman. Sarah had haunted his dreams for weeks. The reality of her had exposed those dreams as pale shadows. Never before had he experienced such complete harmony of body and soul. Her natural, untutored responses to his caresses had enthralled, electrified, completely captivated him. He was no longer the same man who'd driven this road twenty-four hours before. Everything had changed. He was unsure about what happened next. He knew only that nothing could be the same as before.

His brow knit in concentration. Once again he felt vaguely uneasy as he tried to remember their strange parting. They'd been walking through the woodlot, and Sarah had said something that disturbed him. Then she'd walked ahead, giving him no chance to comment.

Jordan unconsciously tightened his hands on the steering wheel as he forced his mind to replay the walk from the farmhouse. She'd been trying to explain why she kept her talent secret. He'd seen her tremble, had touched her shoulder. He'd asked a question.

Her small, tired voice replayed in his mind. "Exposure. Publicity. Threats. Public ridicule. If I'm careful . . ."

Threats! The word she hadn't explained. Why threats? What threats? Those were the questions he hadn't asked.

Jordan was used to dealing with questions and answers. He wouldn't waste his time on idle speculation about what she'd meant now. Sometime today, despite the crush of people, he'd find the opportunity to ask his questions. He wasn't sure why, but he knew they were important.

Although Sarah had warned him that her family was a large one, when Jordan turned into the long, winding driveway leading to the farmhouse the number of vehicles already parked was a surprise. He stopped the Blazer behind the last of the cars and climbed to the ground. Jimmy Joe's tousled red head appeared beside him before he'd walked more than a dozen steps.

In one long breath the boy informed him that Sarah had told him to watch for Jordan, that she was waiting for him at the house, and would Jordan please be his partner in the three-legged race just before lunch.

Listening to the chattering boy, Jordan was aware of the curious glances cast their way as they walked past small clusters of people on their way up the driveway. He had met most of Sarah's close relatives—or at least he'd thought he had. The old joke about going home to meet the family suddenly took on new dimensions.

Jordan glanced uneasily around him. He couldn't help wondering if they would approve. He was amazed to discover that he cared. He tried to ignore the friendly but questioning looks being cast in his direction and turned his attention to the boy.

"I'll be glad to be your partner, but I might not be very good," he warned Jimmy Joe. "I don't think I've ever been in a three-legged race before."

"You gotta be better than Cissie," Jimmy Joe said. "Last year she got the giggles so hard we fell down."

"Sarah? Giggles?" He'd seen her gay and solemn, light-hearted and pensive, but in the weeks since they'd met he'd never once seen her giggle. Jordan looked at Jimmy Joe, one eyebrow cocked in disbelief.

"Honest," Jimmy Joe said defensively. "She was giggling so hard, we fell flat on our faces right in the middle of the race. We were beatin' T.J. and Sally, too. Till we fell."

"I believe you, partner. It's just—I've never seen Sarah giggle."

"Well, she don't do it much, not like a lot of girls," Jimmy Joe admitted. "But it weren't no time to start. Not in the middle of a race."

"Okay," Jordan told him, smiling. "If you want me to be your partner, I'll do my best. And I promise I'll try not to giggle."

"Then be careful not to get behind my cousin Mabel and her husband," Sarah's quiet voice whispered in his ear.

Jordan turned quickly, drinking in the sight of her. God, she was beautiful. Her smile was soft and welcoming, her eyes that deep blue-green that spoke of mystery and promise. Only a faint shadow of unease lurked in their depths. He stood there, just looking at her, unable to say what he wanted to say, not sure he could trust his voice if he opened his mouth. The space between them seemed alive with an energy, an electricity, that was probably obvious to anyone in sight.

It was Jimmy Joe who broke the spell.

"Here he is, Cissie. I found him like you said. And he says he'll be my partner in the race, so you won't have to." Jimmy Joe hesitated a moment, as if he were afraid of giving offense. "That's all right, isn't it, Cissie? I mean, you didn't want to race this year, did you?"

"It's perfect, Jimmy Joe." Sarah's voice and smile reassured him. "I'd much rather cheer you on."

"Okay." Relief was apparent in the boy's voice. "Aunt Cinda said she wanted to see you. She's under the big oak tree. I'm gonna go throw horseshoes with Bobby Wade now, if that's all right. You don't need me for nothin' else, do you?"

"Not until just before lunch. You go on and play." She stood watching for a moment as the boy disappeared in the direction of the farmhouse, then turned slowly toward Jordan.

"Good morning, Sarah," he said softly, and watched as a faint pink blush tinged her cheeks.

"Good morning, Jordan," she answered shyly, her eyes downcast. "How are you today?"

"I survived the gauntlet. It was worth it."

Sarah's eyes came up, wide and concerned. They reached over his shoulder, sweeping the groups of people clustered around the large yard. "Did anyone—?"

Jordan smiled and shook his head. "I haven't had time to speak to anyone yet. But I can see the questions in their eyes." He forced himself to remain still, retaining the distance between them, wanting to ignore the curious glances being cast in their direction. If he took two steps forward, two small steps, he would be able to sweep her into his arms.

She gave him an understanding look. "We don't usually bring outsiders to the picnic. Too intimidating. Nearly everyone here will be family, married to family or at least engaged. Once my cousin Sue brought a date. She didn't particularly like him, but she said he kept pestering her for a date, so she finally invited him to the picnic."

Jordan smiled wryly. He couldn't help feeling a little sympathy for the hapless fellow. "Did it work?"

Sarah nodded. "Sue said he never bothered her again."

"Is that why you invited me?"

The shocked look on Sarah's face was as eloquent a denial as her answer. "Oh, no, Jordan. I warned you."

"Yes, you did." The look in Jordan's eyes was at once tender and fierce. Ignoring the prying eyes, he moved to her side but managed to content himself with casually draping an arm around her waist. "And I meant what I said. It was worth it."

"I don't know, Jordan. You've hardly started," she warned him. Her hesitation was evident, but she didn't move away. "I have to take you to meet Aunt Cinda now."

"She really came down from her mountain?"

Sarah nodded. "This is the first time she's attended the picnic in years. I'm not sure why...."

"Don't be ridiculous. She wants to meet me." He took her hand in his and gave it a reassuring squeeze. "Don't worry so about it. I've been told I'm very good with sweet old ladies."

"Don't expect Aunt Cinda to be your typical sweet old lady," Sarah cautioned.

"I'm expecting a wise old woman who cares a great deal about you. How could I not like her? Now, which way to the royal oak?"

Jordan had seen the dried apple-head dolls in various native craft and tourist shops in the area and had always considered them whimsical caricature creations. His first sight of the old woman sitting regally in the shade of the spreading oak tree made him reevaluate his opinion.

She was small, even smaller than Sarah—so tiny, in fact, that the lawn chair she was sitting in seemed to dwarf her. Her crisp cotton dress, its high neck and long sleeves edged in white lace, gave the impression of coolness in spite of the heat of the day. White wisps of hair peeked from under the wide rim of her old-fashioned poke bonnet.

The heads of the people paying court around her turned in their direction, and all conversation ceased as Jordan and Sarah approached. It took Jordan a moment to realize that the bright eyes of the old lady, the ones that seemed to be looking straight into his soul, were all but sightless, at least in the conventional sense of the word. No wonder the family was so insistent that she move from her lonely mountaintop. In case of an accident, she'd be as helpless alone as a small wounded bird. In the silence around them he led the way to the space directly in front of the old lady's chair.

"Aunt Cinda, I'd like you to meet my friend Jordan Matthias. Jordan, this is my great-aunt, Mrs. Cinda Shields."

"I'm very happy to meet you, Mrs. Shields," Jordan said formally. He was completely unprepared for the strong, vibrant sound of her voice when she spoke.

"Might as well call me Aunt Cinda," she said imperiously, stretching out her right hand in his direction. "I'll call you Jordan."

Jordan hesitated for a moment, knowing that the women of the older generation had not adopted the business world's habit of shaking hands when greeting strangers. Gently he captured the small, wizened hand between the palms of his larger ones. He saw her smile at his touch and felt a rush of relief.

"Sarah, you can fetch me a glass of lemonade." Aunt Cinda waved her left hand in the direction of the farmhouse, allowing the right hand to remain cradled between Jordan's larger palms. "Jordan'll keep me company."

Sarah looked around uncertainly, only then noticing that the three of them were alone under the oak tree. The others had melted away when they'd arrived. She gave Jordan a desperate look. He answered with a reassuring smile and a small wink.

"I'll be back in a minute," she said in a resigned voice, and started toward the farmhouse.

"Have a seat," Aunt Cinda told him, gesturing with her free hand.

Jordan lowered himself into a chair, still retaining his gentle hold on her hand. She seemed content to let it remain there. "I'm very glad to meet you, Aunt Cinda," he told her by way of conversation. "Sarah's told me a lot about you."

Aunt Cinda's sudden stillness was almost tangible. Then her mouth curved into a knowing smile. "Has she now? Well, I reckon that saves a lot of time. And what do you think about my great-niece?"

Jordan realized that the old lady had read meanings he hadn't intended into his words, meanings that were unintentional but nonetheless true. He gave her a look of admiration. Did she always conduct her conversations on two levels? It would be difficult—no, probably impossible—to fool Aunt Cinda about most things.

"Sarah is a very special person," he told her.

Aunt Cinda gave a slight nod of her head and again lapsed into total stillness. For a moment Jordan was afraid she had stopped breathing. Then she spoke again. "And you, Jordan Matthias? Did you find what you were looking for?"

"I—I think so." His voice was hesitant.

"You don't sound too sure."

He straightened in his chair. When he spoke, his voice was clear and strong. "I am sure, Aunt Cinda. I think I'm still a little surprised. You see, for a long time I was looking for the wrong thing. Then, with the help of luck or fate or something, I found what I really wanted." This was the first time Jordan had put his thoughts into words. It was surprising that verbalizing them gave definition to the situation.

Aunt Cinda nodded her head knowingly. "So now that you've found it, what will you do?"

He hesitated. "I'm not sure yet, Aunt Cinda. It's all very new to me. The only thing I'm sure about is knowing what I have. And I don't want to let it go." His last words were almost a challenge—a challenge the old woman completely ignored. She turned instead to meet Sarah. Jordan hadn't even heard her approaching.

"Back already, child? Lawd's sake. You didn't have to run. Jordan's good company. We're gettin' along jus' fine."

Sarah looked questioningly from her aunt to Jordan, then relaxed under the tender, amused look in Jordan's eyes.

"Set yourself down, Sarah. This young man's big enough to take care of himself. Even from an ol' warhorse like me," Aunt Cinda told her sternly. "I weren't goin' to eat him."

The smile on Jordan's face reassured her. Sarah settled herself on the grass at Aunt Cinda's feet, close enough to reach out and touch Jordan.

"You're an old fraud," Jordan told Aunt Cinda quietly, knowing she understood his words. "You just pretend to be tough. Underneath you're a cream puff." He gave her tiny, frail hand a gentle squeeze.

Aunt Cinda's cackling laugh rolled into the summer air. "Your young man's got nothing to fear from me," she told Sarah. "We understand each other."

"He's not my...my..."

"Then you ain't as smart as I thought," Aunt Cinda snapped without letting her finish.

Sarah looked helplessly up at Jordan, who merely smiled and gave her another wink.

"Where'd everybody else go?" demanded the old lady suddenly. "After all the hoop-de-lah to get me here, you'd think a person could at least expect a bit of company."

"They were all a little squeamish. Didn't want to stay around and see the blood," T.J. said, appearing on the crest of the small hill in time to hear the last remark. He moved to the side of Aunt Cinda's chair, ducked his head under the wide brim of the poke bonnet and brushed her papery cheek with his lips.

"Good morning, Grandma. Did you let this stranger keep his head?"

"Hush now, Timothy James. You'll be scaring him off if you ain't careful."

T.J. laughed. "Believe me, Grandmother, it'll take more than me to scare him off if he doesn't want to go." He turned to Jordan, giving him a sympathetic grin. "So you decided to tackle the clan en masse? How's it going?"

Jordan returned his friendly smile. "I'm enjoying it. And I've survived so far, I think. If I can stay on my feet during the three-legged race, I might even be able to recruit some assistance."

Sarah squirmed uncomfortably, wishing she could think of something to divert the conversation. Whether by accident or design, her cousin came to the rescue.

"Well, Grandma, now that you're here, are you going to admit the valley isn't so bad? Going to let us settle you down here so Sarah can stop worrying about you?" T.J. was still smiling, but his voice held none of its usual bantering tone.

"You let things be, Timothy James. You ain't the boss of me," Aunt Cinda snapped.

"I don't want to badger you," T.J. protested. "But you can't stay on top of that mountain this winter. The family's dumped the problem in Sarah's lap, and she's so worried about you she doesn't know which way to turn." His voice softened. "You're the one taught me we can't always have exactly what we want. Give a little, Grandma. We only want what's best for you."

The old lady snorted, then let her stern expression soften. "I'll be off the mountain before the first snow flies. Now you-all stop worrying about me. It'll all work out jus' fine."

Sarah's relief was obvious in her expression. "I've been so worried, Aunt Cinda. You'll see. It won't be so bad. Uncle Hiram's planning a nice big room—"

"I ain't moving in with Hiram. I done raised him once. That's enough."

Jordan had to smile as the old lady's chin jutted forward stubbornly.

She shook her head furiously. "And I ain't moving in with my sister, either. Had enough of that when we was growin' up."

"But, Aunt Cinda," began Sarah, "where are—"

"I'm going to have me a nice new cabin," she continued, paying not the slightest attention to Sarah's interruption. "I seen it. A brand spanking new cabin, with nary a ghost, save the one I'll leave there someday." Her voice took on a dreamy quality. "It faces the east, so as to catch the morning sun. The porch stretches all the ways across the front. And there's a hanging swing, and a bright red front door. It's going to be one of those newfangled places, too. No more pail and a path. Yep. I think I'm going to like it. Even if it is in the valley."

Sarah looked helplessly at her cousin.

T.J.'s expression was as troubled as hers. "Grandma," he began, "where—"

"Never you mind," she said. "I jus' told you so's you'd stop worrying. I can still take care of my business. It'll be there when I need it. Now change the subject. Here comes your cousin and that skinny husband of hers. I don't need the whole valley tending my business."

Jordan's eyes widened at the sight of the ponderous middle-aged woman and the tall, thin man walking toward them. Hastily he laid Aunt Cinda's hand in her lap and stood to offer the chair to the large woman bearing down on them. He caught the twinkle in Sarah's eye but was unable to understand its meaning until Aunt Cinda began the introductions.

"Mabel, this is my friend Jordan Matthias," the old woman announced in a voice that set the seal of her approval on him. "Jordan, this here's Mabel and her husband, Harris. Set yourself down, Mabel, and visit a while."

Jordan avoided Sarah's dancing eyes, trying to keep from laughing as he solemnly acknowledged the introduction. Finally he risked a quick glance in Sarah's direction, the question in his eyes clearly asking if this was Cousin Mabel. As Sarah gave a slight nod of her head, Jordan was no longer able to control the smile hovering on his lips. The image of these two incongruous-looking people tied leg-to-leg in a race across the pasture was certainly adequate reason for an attack of the giggles.

Jordan could see the curiosity in the woman's eyes. He decided the wording of Aunt Cinda's greeting was deterring her questions. Cousin Mabel acknowledged his presence, then turned her attention to T.J.

"You going to let the Caldwell place get away from you, T.J.?"

Jordan saw the droop of Sarah's mouth and bent over to whisper in her ear. "Your swimming hole?"

Sarah nodded silently.

"Looks like it might, Cousin Mabel." T.J. shrugged helplessly. "I tried to arrange a lease-option, but they want an outright sale. I heard they'd turned down one offer, but if the buyers up their offering price, I'm afraid it's gone."

"Your great-grandpappy had no business trading it for that river bottom," Mabel said, turning on Sarah. "It should've stayed in the family."

Aunt Cinda's intervention saved Sarah from having to answer. "That was a long time ago," she reminded the woman. "And that creek bottom grew the best corn in three counties." She turned toward Jordan. "You young 'uns run along now. Mabel and me got some visiting to do."

Grateful for the opportunity to escape, the three of them said their goodbyes and started down the hill. They'd only gone a half a dozen steps when Aunt Cinda's voice stopped them.

"Jordan, you take good care of Sarah Jane, you hear?"

Jordan felt a chill at the back of his neck. He turned, blinking, as he imagined a dark shadow crossing Aunt Cinda's features. No, that was impossible, he told himself. It was only the shade thrown by the wide rim of her bonnet as she moved her head. "I'll do my best," he assured her.

As they continued down the hill, Jordan tried to shake off the sense of uneasiness caused by Aunt Cinda's parting words.

When they reached the farmhouse, Sarah turned to T.J. "Are you going to be around for a while?" she asked. "I've got to help in the kitchen."

"You go on. I'll keep an eye on Jordan," T.J. assured her.

"T.J.'ll introduce you around," she told Jordan. "I'll see you in a little while." She moved away, giving him no opportunity to protest. As Jordan watched her go, his clenched fists hidden deep in his pockets, she turned her head. She gave him a wishful smile over her shoulder, then disappeared inside the house.

"So, Jordan, how about a game of horseshoes?"

"I haven't tossed shoes in years," Jordan answered automatically, his mind still whirling with the implications of Aunt Cinda's last words, his eyes still on the door where Sarah had disappeared.

"She'll be back," T.J. assured him. He clamped a hand on his shoulder and nudged him toward the side of the house. "In the meantime, sounds like you could use a bit of practice. 'Round here boys start tossing shoes soon as they're big enough to pick them up."

Resigned, Jordan followed T.J. toward the horseshoe pits at the side of the house, knowing his questions would have to wait a little longer. Surely, he told himself, he would be able to find a minute alone with Sarah sometime today.

Chapter 10

When darkness finally overpowered the lingering twilight, it went unnoticed by the audience sitting under the artificial lights of the Springdale Rodeo Arena.

For Jordan the day had been an endless repeat of food and faces. But all and all, he considered it a success. He and Jimmy Joe had managed to stay well away from the sharp-tongued Cousin Mabel during the three-legged race—a move that had contributed to their third-place finish. Sarah had cheered them enthusiastically from the sidelines, then bashfully given him a quick kiss on the cheek as a reward. Jimmy Joe, silly boy, had preferred another slice of home-made peach pie.

Jordan gave Sarah's shoulder a squeeze and pulled her closer to his side, taking a deep whiff of the honeysuckle fragrance wafting from her hair. They hadn't had a moment alone all day, and somehow sitting here with one wiggling boy, surrounded by hundreds of spectators, didn't count. Perhaps after they took Jimmy Joe home...

Sarah leaned her head against Jordan's shoulder, ignoring the crowd around them.

Jimmy Joe settled back in his seat, still laughing at the antics of the rodeo clown who'd skipped nonchalantly around the arena, enticing an enraged Brahma bull toward the exit chute. As funny and fun as it looked, Sarah knew, it was dangerous business. She was thankful T.J. limited his rodeoing activities to the steer-wrestling and calf-roping events.

The announcer's voice blared over the loudspeakers. "Getting settled now in chute number four is Jack Perkins, our last bull rider of the evening. Jack'll be aboard Devil Boy. A lot of you folks know Jack. He's from Oklahoma, almost a hometown boy. For those of you who weren't with us last night, Jack was scheduled to ride Thunder in the third-night competition, but rodeo officials scratched the ride when his bull had to be tranquilized after a little fracas in the stock pens. Jack's number five in the national standings right now, and he always gives the crowd a good show. We're ready when you are, Jack."

T.J. slid into the empty seat on the other side of Jimmy Joe. "And you can bet he's thanking his lucky stars he's not aboard Thunder," he added as the announcer's voice faded. "That's one mean bull."

"Did you win, T.J.?" the boy asked, dividing his attention between the newcomer and the action in the arena.

T.J. grinned. "Looks like I might have scraped into the day money in the calf-roping," he said. "That'll pay the entry fee. And—" he paused dramatically "—I sold three horses."

"Three? That's great, T.J.," Sarah told him. "As good as you hoped?"

"I'll say. At best I had hopes of unloading two."

Puzzled, Jordan looked from Sarah to her cousin.

"That's why I compete," T.J. said in answer to Jordan's questioning look. "The bucking stock is furnished by rodeo contractors, but in the calf-roping and steer-wrestling the contestants furnish their own mounts. A pro is always looking for a well-trained mount for his string. So I ride my horses and let them see how good they are."

Pride crept into T.J.'s voice. "If a real pro had been on my horse tonight he'd have taken top money. And every one of them knows it. Doesn't matter how good a rider is if he doesn't have a good horse, especially in the calf-roping. It's the horse that does most of the work. My horses are the best."

"That's innovative marketing," Jordan told him.

T.J. grinned, accepting his praise, and turned his attention to Jimmy Joe. "And I've got a treat for you, kid. The contractor said we could tour the back lots after the rodeo."

The boy let out a whoop. "Will I get to see Thunder?"

T.J. hesitated before answering. "Only from a safe distance. I don't trust that bull. He's always been the meanest on the circuit. Now I think he's gone rogue."

Sarah leaned back again, content to let T.J. try answering the boy's never-ending questions. Using the brisk breeze that suddenly began whipping through the stands as an excuse, she snuggled closer to Jordan's side and felt his welcoming touch around her waist.

They waited in their seats until the stands were almost empty before T.J. led the way to the stock pens. The stock and staging area seemed almost as busy after the rodeo as the arena had been during the performance. Rodeo rowdies moved cattle and horses along the narrow aisles. The clank of metal against metal, gates opening and closing to form and reform chutes and pens, mixed with the calls of cowboys hollering instructions across the stockyards.

A wrangler leading two prancing horses forced them into a single file against the far side of the aisle formed by the movable metal rails. Jordan and T.J. made certain Jimmy Joe remained between them, neither of them trusting the inquisitive boy to stay out of trouble on his own. Sarah followed behind.

"Where're the bucking broncos," Jimmy Joe wanted to know as he skipped back into position beside T.J.

"You just passed two of the best," his cousin told him.

"But they weren't—"

"They're bucking stock, not wild horses," T.J. explained patiently. "Most rodeo stock, even the bucking broncos, are halterbroke. They just don't like anyone to ride them."

Jimmy Joe gave him a disappointed look. "Where's the bulls? I wanna see Thunder."

"They'll be at the very end of the yard, as far from the rest of the excitement as the rowdies can get them," T.J. said. "Before I take you over there, Jimmy Joe, I want your promise. No foolishness. The bulls are the most dangerous animals in the rodeo, in or out of the arena. Promise you'll do exactly as I say." He watched as Jimmy Joe gave a solemn nod of agreement.

The noise and activity level increased as the foursome neared the far pens. They were already loading the bulls onto the giant stock trucks, preparing to move on to the next rodeo. T.J. took a firm grip on Jimmy Joe's hand. Jordan and Sarah trailed behind them.

"Hurry up, T.J. I want to see Thunder." The boy tugged against his cousin's hold.

"You got plenty of time, young fellow," a cowboy told them. "That bull'll be the last they load. Then they'll probably have to tranquilize him and hoist him aboard.

Meanest damn critter God ever made. 'Scuse me, ma'am,''
he added when he noticed Sarah's presence behind the boy.

"Still acting up, is he?" T.J. asked. "Where're they
holding him?''

"He's in the middle pen. And actin' up ain't quite the way
I'd describe it. You mark my words. Butler's going to have
to turn that one out to pasture. Ain't no damn fool crazy
enough to try eight seconds on the back of hell. Not after
what he did to Pete Johnson. 'Scuse me again, ma'am, but
there ain't no polite words for that critter.''

Sarah nodded, choking back a laugh at the cowboy's
unorthodox politeness. They stood aside as the man pushed
his way on down the narrow aisle.

Jimmy Joe obviously wasn't the only one who wanted to
see the bull. The aisle side of the metal enclosure was thick
with people straining against the rails to get a look at the
creature. Still tugging against T.J.'s hold, Jimmy Joe pushed
his way to the front of the crowd, the other three trailing
behind.

In the large center pen, arranged to accommodate a half-
dozen animals his size, the bull stood alone, his eyes gleam-
ing a malevolent red in the glare of the lights. As the crowd
of people pressed forward, he snorted, lowered his head and
made a run toward the rails. Moving as one, the crowd of
people stepped back. The bull stopped short of the metal
fence, planting all four feet stiffly in the sawdust-covered
dirt. Then he raised his head and trotted slowly along the
fence, dewlap and back hump swinging in time with his gait.

He returned to his previous position in the center of the
pen and faced the crowd again. As he lowered his head for
another charge, someone in the crowd let loose with a wild
cowboy yell.

"Stupid jerk," T.J. murmured. "That bull's strung tighter than a drum now. Come on, Jimmy Joe. You've seen Thunder."

"What damn fool slipped the gate locks?" a voice yelled as the crowd once again moved back. All but Jimmy Joe. Determined to see what was happening, he wriggled out of T.J.'s hold and dived for the front of the crowd. Both Jordan and T.J. dived after him.

Jordan heard the sound of metal clanging against metal above the noise of the crowd and prayed it was the gate locks being securely refastened into place.

The mass of people swirled around Sarah, pushing her from side to side, then forward. She felt hands grasp her securely around the waist and gave a little sigh of relief. For a moment she thought Jordan had her safe. Then she felt herself being lifted up and thrown forward.

Jordan made a frantic grab for Jimmy Joe, felt his hand make contact with the squirming boy's shoulder, tightened his grip and held on.

A woman's scream suddenly shattered the air, quickly followed by a collective gasp from the crowd. Then came a hushed silence.

Jordan felt his blood turn to ice water as he whirled around, dragging Jimmy Joe with him. A small, crumpled figure lay facedown in the dirt and sawdust inside the enclosure. Seven feet away, a ton of quivering bull nervously pawed the ground.

Sarah! Jordan's mind screamed. Dear God, no!

He thrust Jimmy Joe into a bystander's arms and raced along the fence, grabbing a jacket from the unsuspecting hands of a stranger as he ran.

When he reached the far end of the pen he vaulted the fence into the pen with the bull, snapping the jacket and yelling as he landed. "Over here, you mangy creature. I'm over here."

The bull swung his ponderous head in Jordan's direction, then slowly returned his attention to the girl on the ground in front of him.

Jordan yelled again, taking one, two, three steps toward the bull. Again the bull swung his head in Jordan's direction.

"That's right, fellow. That's the way. I'm over here." He snapped the jacket again. The cracking noise sounded like a gunshot in the silence.

The bull's head came up. Slowly he shifted his feet, re-aligning his hindquarters with the rest of his massive body.

Jordan snapped the jacket once more. "That's it, big boy. Keep on turning." He kept his eyes locked on the slowly moving beast. "Sarah, don't move. If you can hear me, please, don't move."

Now the bull was almost facing Jordan. He stopped, swinging his head back in the direction of Sarah's still body. Jordan yelled. Again the bull's head turned toward him.

Jordan sensed rather than saw another man's presence near him. He waited, not daring to take his eyes off the bull.

"Jordan, it's me," T.J. said softly.

"Get Sarah out."

Both men stopped speaking as the bull lowered his head. Thunder took a step backward, pawed the ground once, then raised his head again.

"You get Sarah, Jordan. I'll tackle the bull. I've been around them more."

"Damn it, T.J., this is no time to argue. Get Sarah. I think she's unconscious. If she comes to she may moan, or move. He could still charge her. He'd rather take the target on the ground."

Jordan heard T.J.'s sigh of resignation.

"All right. You sound like you know what you're doing."

"I do," Jordan said tersely, his eyes never leaving the bull. "Go on. Get in position. I'll make sure he comes this way."

"For God's sake, man. Be careful. The bull riders say he hooks to the right."

Jordan nodded, then listened intently for the sounds that would tell him T.J. had reached the fence. The staredown between man and beast continued, with neither shifting eyes from the other. Jordan mentally calculated the time he thought it would take T.J. to move around the side of the pen to Sarah. An unnatural stillness settled over the backlots. The crowd clustered along the fence shuffled nervously but remained quiet.

That's it, Jordan thought. No noise. No sudden movements. Nothing to cause the bull to look back in Sarah's direction.

The bull moved nervously, his hindquarters dancing up and down as he shifted his weight from side to side. Jordan readjusted his stance. Droplets of sweat beaded on his forehead, then rolled unchecked down his face. He blinked quickly to clear his vision, never taking his eyes off the beast, fighting the urge to look at Sarah.

He took a cautious step backward, trying to lure the bull a step farther away from Sarah. As he moved, Thunder imitated him, taking a stride forward. The bull snorted, pawed the ground with his front hooves, then slowly lowered his elongated head.

Jordan's body tensed. He clutched the jacket in his right hand and shifted his weight to the balls of his feet. He had to entice the bull to charge, and he had to stand his ground as the animal moved toward him. The only way he could be sure the bull wouldn't change its mind and swing toward Sarah was to make sure the massive beast was already moving full tilt in his direction. Despite his massive size, once running, the bull would cover the distance between them in seconds. Jordan could only hope he correctly remembered the distance to the safety of the fence.

"All right, you son of Satan. Come and get me." Jordan punctuated his sudden wild yell by waving the jacket in front of him.

The bull stood stock-still, then began to quiver, bunching his muscles and readying himself for the attack.

"Come on, you miserable—" Jordan yelled as the bull lowered his head and charged. Eyes narrowed, Jordan stood his ground, shifting his weight from foot to foot as the creature's hooves chewed up the ground between them.

It seemed as if the bull was less than an arm's length away when Jordan finally moved. He threw the jacket into Thunder's face, at the same time throwing his body to the bull's left. He was on the ground, rolling in the direction of the fence and safety. Clutching hands grabbed at his shoulders, his legs, then pulled him out of the pen. For a second he lay still, flat on his back, gulping deep breaths of night air and allowing the adrenaline to drain from his tight muscles. His mind cleared. Sarah!

He called her name aloud as he jackknifed into a sitting position. Once again he felt helping hands, this time assisting him to his feet.

"The lady's okay," he heard someone say. "The other fellow got her out."

"Where is she?"

"I think someone said they took her to one of the trailers."

A small, dark cowboy pushed his way through the crowd to Jordan's side. He was dressed in the usual wrangler gear, with the addition of a bright orange vest boldly emblazoned with Butler, the name of the rodeo's stock contractor.

"Sarah?" he asked again.

"The lady's fine, mister. She's at the boss's caravan with the other man and the boy. I'll show you the way."

Jordan let the cowboy lead him through the throng of people, acknowledging their gestures of congratulation as he moved.

"Been in the arena a couple of times, haven't you?" the cowboy said as they reached a pasture where the lights of several travel trailers blazed in the dark night.

"Lord, no," Jordan told him. "I played with the bull calves once or twice when I was in South America. You know, the little fellows. Seven or eight hundred pounds. But no horns. Tonight was the first time I ever had to face a real bull—and I hope it's the last."

The cowboy nodded. "Must have been good calves. You did it just right."

"I was lucky."

They stopped by the door of the second trailer. "Here you are. Your lady's inside."

His lady! Jordan gave a quick knock on the door. Then, without waiting for an answer, he jerked it open and stepped inside. He absorbed the scene in a single all-encompassing glance.

Sarah sat behind a table on the end of a built-in bench, her hands closed around a cup of liquid that had steam rising from its rim. Wisps of sawdust were still stuck in her hair. Her face was white and strained, and her eyes were large and scared. Jimmy Joe was tucked in close to her side, his face also blanched except for his freckles. His cheeks were smudged with dirt and streaked from recent tears. T.J. stood by Sarah's side, one hand resting on her shoulder.

"*Sarah.*" Jordan breathed her name, took a step forward, saw the sudden light in her eyes. Then she was in his arms.

They were at once surrounded by a group of people, most of whom he hadn't even noticed in the room. Hands reached out to deliver pats on the back. The rumble of unfamiliar voices rose and fell around them. Jordan ignored them all, his full attention, his entire being, centered on the fact that Sarah was safe in his arms.

Jordan held her securely, his arms tight around her, felt the tension drain from her body, felt her relax against him. Slowly he loosened his hold and looked down into her up-turned face. "Are you all right? You weren't hurt?"

"Oh, Jordan, I was so afraid for you."

Jordan's arms automatically tightened around her. "Ssh...everything's all right now. You're safe and I'm fine." Suddenly conscious of the eyes watching them, he reluctantly let her go and moved with her back to the table. Jimmy Joe wiggled into the corner of the booth, and after Sarah slid in Jordan took a position on the end. Someone thrust a cold beer into his hand.

A large older man wearing a vest like the cowboy's slid into the seat opposite them. "Lord, Mr. Matthias, that was some—"

Jordan shook his head, warning him not to discuss the subject. He didn't want to upset Sarah any more. The man's voice faltered.

"I just wanted you to know we'll take care of the bull."

"Take him home and turn him out to pasture. He'll be fine in a while," Jordan said.

The man hesitated. "You mean you don't want—I thought you'd want him destroyed."

"Why?" Jordan asked. "He was just being a bull. We invaded his territory." He turned his attention to the woman sitting by his side.

"What happened, Sarah? How did you get inside the pen?"

Sarah shook her head. Her eyes were dazed. "I don't know. One minute I was being pushed in the crowd. I felt hands on my waist. Then, suddenly, I was flying through the air. I don't remember anything else. Not until T.J. grabbed hold of me. Then I saw that bull almost on top of you." The little color that had returned to her face since Jordan entered the trailer now drained away.

Jordan drew a sharp breath. "Someone threw you in-to—" He bit off the words, turning, his eyes searching for T.J., trying to ignore the nausea rising in his stomach. Aunt Cinda had warned him to take care, and he'd almost failed.

"They had to have, Jordan. Up and over." T.J.'s voice spoke quietly in his ear. "The gate locks were slipped, but the enclosure was never opened."

"I don't know how it happened, but it had to be an accident," Sarah said, not hearing the exchange.

The two men exchanged meaningful looks. Then, as if they had come to a mutual decision, they moved as one.

"Come on, Jimmy Joe. I think you've had your share of excitement for the day. Let's get you home." T.J. stood to one side, waiting for Jordan and Sarah to release the boy from his corner in the booth. "You can help load the horses," he added.

"And you, Sarah," Jordan said quietly, "are coming with me." He placed his arm protectively around her shoulder, and they moved toward the doorway. Before he and Sarah could follow her cousins out the door, the opening was filled by the tall, lean frame of Sam Bascomb.

Jordan had seen the gray-haired man around Mountain Springs on several occasions and had exchanged greetings with him in passing once or twice. But he'd never really had the opportunity to meet him or study him. He knew this was the man who had first brought Sarah and Hoyston to-gether. The sheriff's eyes quickly swept the room, obviously ignoring the fact that he was out of his home jurisdiction. They came to rest on Sarah, who was still white-faced and leaning against Jordan.

"What the hell? Sarah, are you all right?"

"I'm fine, Sam. Just a little shaky."

The sound of Sarah's voice reinforced Jordan's belief that this man was a special friend. He met the angry look in the sheriff's eyes with one of friendliness. Jordan too, felt indignant on her behalf. Indignant and scared to death. Something was going on here that he didn't understand. For some reason someone had tried to harm Sarah.

T.J. quickly filled Sam in with an edited version of the evening's events as Jordan stood by quietly, still supporting Sarah's wilting form.

"And no one saw what happened? How she got inside the pen?" The sheriff looked directly at each person in the room, waiting for an answer but getting only negative shakes of the head.

"Who else was there?" he demanded. "Somebody had to see something."

"Good Lord, man. There were probably twenty, thirty people milling around outside that pen," said an unfamiliar voice. "I guess some of them will still be around the pens."

"Then that's where I'm going."

Jordan couldn't help smiling to himself. If the local authorities resented the sheriff's intrusion in their affairs, it would make no difference to Sam.

"As for you, missy," the sheriff added, "you get on home. I'll talk to you tomorrow."

"Yes, Sam," Sarah answered meekly. "I think I'm ready. Come on, Jordan, let's go home."

With his arm still around her, Sarah let Jordan lead her out the door of the trailer. Sam, T.J. and Jimmy Joe all turned toward the back lots. She and Jordan moved in the opposite direction, toward the rodeo grounds parking lot.

They walked in silence, Sarah reassured by the pressure of Jordan's arm around her waist. He was safe! The chilling, paralyzing fear she'd felt when she'd seen that bull charging him had been just that—fear. Not a psychic glimpse into the future.

On the heels of her relief came the realization of how much this man had come to mean to her. She had never meant to let it go so far, never meant to allow him to become such a vital part of her life. If she'd been lonely before he'd entered her life, how much worse would it be when he left? Before she'd known only a nebulous feeling of incompleteness. Now she knew with a devastating clarity the missing ingredient of her existence.

She must have given some indication of her disturbing train of thought, because Jordan stopped in the shadow of the grandstand and moved in front of her. The moonlight played over his features as his eyes probed hers.

"Is something wrong? Are you sure you're all right? You weren't hurt?" His voice was soft, concern apparent in every tone. The sound settled around her, giving warmth and protection, like the comfort of a thick quilt against the chill of a winter wind.

"I'm fine. Really. It's just that my knees are still a little shaky."

Jordan gave her a tender smile, the corners of his mouth tilting upward. "I think that's allowed." He shook his head as if trying to clear his thoughts. "When I think what—" His voice stopped abruptly.

"Think what, Jordan?"

"Never mind now. You've had enough for the day. We'll talk about that tomorrow." He paused, then gave her another one of his little smiles, the kind that revealed so little and promised so much. "Do you realize this is the first time we've been alone all day?"

Sarah looked quickly around her. The lights in the arena had been turned out. The pasture that served as a parking area for the rodeo grounds stretched before them, now almost empty of vehicles. In the distance she could hear the sounds of livestock and rodeo personnel. But in their immediate vicinity nothing disturbed their quiet isolation.

"So we are," she said, giving him a shuttered look from beneath her lashes. "What do you think we should do about it?"

"This," he said, his voice as soft as the butterfly touch of his lips on hers. He pulled her tightly into his arms and rested a cheek on the top of her head. He held her for a long moment, as if trying to convince himself she was real, then slowly relaxed his hold.

"I think it's time to get you home," he said, looking into her tired face. "All in all, it's been quite a Fourth of July."

Reluctantly Sarah moved from his arms. She couldn't help wondering if he, too, experienced the same fireworks she did each time they touched.

Chapter 11

Sarah set her cup carefully on the saucer and stared in astonishment at the man on the other side of the kitchen table. T.J. had already been and gone this morning, after grilling her over and over about last night's events. That Sam had also showed up on her doorstep before she'd had a chance to drink her first cup of coffee was disturbing enough, but what he'd just said was unbelievable.

"You're wrong, Sam. Why would anyone want to hurt me? Last night was an accident. It had to be."

"I'm not so sure, missy. You've had a few too many accidents lately to suit me." Worry lines creased the sheriff's forehead. "And every one of them's happened since that stranger showed up lookin' for you. Damn it all, anyhow, warned you to be careful."

"Come on now, Sam," Sarah smiled indulgently. " know you don't warm up to strangers, but you can't suspect Jordan. He saved my life. T.J. says that if he hadn' gotten inside the pen as fast as he did Thunder would have charged."

"What if you're wrong? You know you never see what's in front of your face. What's he doing still hanging around here, anyway? Supposed to be writin' a story on Monte Ne. Hell, he's been here long enough to rebuild the place."

"He finished his article, Sam. It's going to be published in September. Now he's just on vacation."

"Man like that don't just go on vacation. He's here for something, girl. Can't you see that? And I'm betting it's for no good reason."

Exasperated, Sarah threw up her hands. "You just won't listen. It doesn't matter why he's still here. Jordan isn't trying to hurt me. Nobody is. Don't you think I'd know it if someone was?"

"Don't try arguing that with me, missy. I know good and well you can't see what's going to happen to you. When it comes to that, you stumble along like the rest of us."

"I might not know, Sam, but I get a warning."

"Only when you can do something about it. And then half the time you don't pay attention anyway."

"This whole conversation is ridiculous, Sam. Just because Jordan's an outsider... You're too distrustful. No one has any reason to harm me. No one. And especially not the man who risked his life to save mine."

"Maybe it weren't that much of a risk—him going into that corral that way. You ever think of that? As a matter of fact, it weren't hardly no risk at all."

"No risk? To enter a pen with a rogue bull?"

"Aha. So you do realize that being in that pen last night was dangerous."

"Of course it was dangerous. It was dangerous for me. And that was an accident. It was dangerous for Jordan, too. Only he chose to go in—to help me. Even if you do believe someone put me in that pen on purpose, I don't see how you can possibly think it was Jordan. That makes no sense at all." The look on Sam's face told Sarah that somehow she'd played right into his hands.

"From everything I hear, that writer fellow knew what he was doing in that pen. In fact, he admitted to one of the rodeo workers that he's worked the bulls in South America. As I said, for him—used to working with bullfight stock—it weren't that much of a risk. All he had to do was make it look good. Then no would suspect a thing."

"Sam..."

The tone of Sarah's voice must have warned him he was trespassing on dangerous ground. "I'm sorry, Sarah love. I don't mean to make you mad. But something's going on. I might not have your sight, but I've got better than thirty years chasing the bad guys. I know when something ain't right. Last night was the third time this summer you've been at your last prayers. First there was Bald Mountain, second the accident at the ruins. Then last night at the rodeo. One time I might believe. Maybe even two. But not three. And that writer fellow's been close by every time."

"T.J. was with me at Bald Mountain."

"But you'd just left that fellow at Indian Bluff. And he was with you both of the other times."

"I wish I'd never told you about the accident at the ruins," Sarah said heatedly.

"I'd have found out anyway."

Sarah studied the face of her friend. It was easy to see that he was really worried, and it was more than his usual suspicion of outsiders. But he was wrong. It was a little unusual, three accidents so close together. She'd admit that. But her warning system had warned her at Monte Ne. And the others had worked out all right.

"We both know lightning can strike twice in the same place, Sam, regardless of old wives' tales," she told him gently. "A tourist who didn't realize the dangers coming down a mountain too fast. A piece of concrete underwater for ten years breaking loose from its supports and tumbling down the hill. Being accidentally tipped over a rail when a shoving crowd suddenly panics. All those are understandable accidents."

"Or deliberately made to look like accidents," the sheriff said stubbornly. "The tourist picked the one day in the last year you happened to be crossing Bald Mountain. The bench that broke loose just happened to be the one directly above where you were resting. And of thirty or so people milling around that bull pen, you happened to be the one who ends up inside. All inside of six weeks or so. Damn it, girl, that ain't lightnin'. Lightning don't pick favorites. Somebody's watching you and picking his times."

Sarah sighed. "I've got no special protection against random accidents, but I'm not going to convince you, am I?"

"Not by a long shot. And I know you can't see a thing about yourself. That's what got me so worried. I tell you right now, I'm going to be checking out that writer fellow."

Sarah started to protest, but Sam ignored her sputtered remark.

"Now, I ain't saying he's the one, mind you, even if he is the best horse in the race right now. I'll be checking on the whereabouts of all the Ewell clan, too, although we ain't had any problems out of them in years. And everything else I can scratch up. But I want you to be very careful, Sarah. You hear me? You spend time with that fellow, you let someone know. And I'm going to let him know I'm suspicious. That way, if I'm right, he won't dare pull anything."

Sarah stared down at her coffee cup. She knew that nothing she could say would change Sam's mind. A native distrust of outsiders was bred into his being. If it hadn't been for her support of Jordan in the community circle, he would have been frozen out a long time before.

She watched the sheriff drain the last swig of coffee from his cup. Sam didn't really have to worry about Jordan, and particularly not if he carried out his plan and told him what he suspected. Jordan wouldn't be around much longer. He'd already stayed longer than she'd expected him to. Sam's accusations would give him good reason to move on.

Sam pushed his chair away from the table. As Sarah moved to follow him, he waved her back. "Finish your coffee. I reckon I can let myself out. You just remember what I told you. You take care."

Perhaps, Sarah reluctantly admitted as she watched Sam leave, it was best. She'd known from the beginning that, much like Monte Ne, Jordan was out of time and place in her life. Her hands tightened around the coffee cup as her mind came to grips with the inevitable. Intellectually she could accept it. Her heart was going to be more difficult to convince.

Jordan parked the car in front of the farmhouse a short time later and sat for a moment, examining his options. His talk with the sheriff had been encouraging in a perverse sort of way. Sam, too, recognized patterns. He, too, was convinced that Sarah's so-called accidents were more than coincidence. So did T.J. But according to them both Sarah was unconcerned. Jordan found his position at the top of the sheriff's list of suspects uncomfortable but understandable. He was the stranger in town. At least the man was looking for answers.

So what was he going to do now? The need to confess to Sarah why he'd come here grew greater with each minute he spent in her company. But if he told her now she'd be angry and hurt. Mostly hurt. And she'd send him away. Send him away! Her family would probably ride him out of town on a rail. He was violating their face-to-face philosophy. So he couldn't tell her because he couldn't leave. He didn't even try to convince himself that it was because he wanted to find out what was going on. He knew it was because he had to make sure she was safe. The story no longer mattered, although that problem still had to be resolved with his agent.

Keeping Sarah safe wouldn't be simple, either, not if she kept insisting she was in no danger. Sam didn't realize how much Jordan knew about Sarah's sight, but T.J. did. And her cousin insisted that Sarah had no talent for self-preservation. But even under Jordan's probing, T.J. had been unable to suggest any reason for Sarah being in danger. The fact that Sam was convinced Jordan was the villain suggested that the sheriff, too, had few ideas.

That left Jordan with only one choice. He was going to have to question Sarah about the threats. He was going to have to poke and probe, to lay bare even more of her secrets while still hiding his own. Even though he knew how painful it would be for her, he had no choice.

Slowly he opened the car door. Take it in order, he told himself. First step, uncover the danger. Second step, confess and hope she understands. Third—for now he refused to think about step number three. He wasn't yet sure if accommodations could be made to adjust his life to hers or hers to his. Number three would have to wait the outcome of the first two.

As Jordan approached the farmhouse, he deliberately forced himself to relax. If neither T.J. nor his old friend the sheriff were able to convince Sarah that someone was threatening her, it was unlikely that he would be able to do so. Perhaps he could accomplish his purpose more easily by taking a more casual approach.

He took one look at Sarah's tense face and at the pain reflected in the shadows of her eyes and immediately abandoned that strategy.

"What's wrong, Sarah?" he asked, at the same time drawing her into his arms. "Has something else happened?"

Sarah burrowed into his arms, relishing his reassuring presence, determined to savor these last few moments before she told him of Sam's suspicions and watched him walk away.

"Talk to me," he said. "Please—tell me what's wrong."

Reluctantly Sarah freed herself from his embrace and walked across the room. She stood, her back to him, looking out the window, her mind oblivious of the scene outside.

"It's Sam," she finally said. "He insists last night's accident wasn't an accident."

"I agree. I'm afraid I can't imagine a scenario that could have put you in a pen with that bull accidentally."

Sarah whirled around. "But you don't understand, Jordan. He—he suspects you."

"I know. I've already talked to him this morning."

As a look of complete confusion crossed her face, Jordan moved swiftly across the room toward her. "Is that what's bothering you? That your friend has named me top suspect on his list of possible villains? If I were in his shoes I would probably do the same. I'm the outsider, the unknown factor in the community right now. I'm just thankful he recognizes that someone may be trying to harm you. We need answers. I'm hoping the sheriff will be able to find them."

Sarah sighed. "You're as bad as he is. It was just an accident. There's no reason for anyone to want to harm me."

Jordan shook his head. "I wish I could think you're right, Sarah. But I can't. The bench breaking loose could have been an accident. Last night—that throws a new perspective on the whole thing. That had to be deliberate."

Sarah hesitated, bewildered by both Sam's and Jordan's insistence that she was in danger. T.J., too. It was true that she probably wouldn't know if she was, not until the last minute, anyway. But there should have been a vague uneasiness. And there wasn't. There hadn't been last night, either. Besides, Aunt Cinda would have picked up something, even if she hadn't.

Jordan had mentioned only two of the three incidents that had Sam and T.J. so worried. Obviously he didn't know about the narrow escape on Bald Mountain. Well, she wasn't going to be the one to tell him. It would simply reinforce his opinions. But he wasn't upset about Sam's accusations, either. So let the three of them run around looking for villains who weren't there. The important thing was, Jordan wasn't leaving. Suddenly Sarah felt much better.

"I thought you'd be upset . . . about Sam and . . ."

Jordan shook his head. "Not about that. I'll admit I don't like being suspected by people who care about you, but it's understandable. It's always best to eliminate the obvious first. That's what Sam's doing. He'll check me out, then move on to other possibilities. Is that really what has you so upset? That your friend suspects me?"

Timidly Sarah nodded.

Jordan shook his head. "We still have a lot to learn about each other yet, don't we?" He took another step forward, erasing the remaining distance between them, and enfolded her in his arms. He lowered his head to rest his cheek on top of her shining hair and once again gave thanks that she was safe. For a few minutes last night he'd been afraid he'd never hold her like this again.

Sarah gave herself up to the heady feeling of complete rightness she'd come to know in his arms. Jordan had come into her life such a short time before, but now it seemed as if he'd always been a part of her. In the dim recesses of her mind she knew that one day she'd be alone again. But for now she refused to think of it. She'd enjoy what she had today. Tomorrow would come soon enough.

She felt his embrace tighten around her, felt his lips brush her forehead. Then his hold on her eased.

"For a moment I forgot this kitchen is Grand Central Station," Jordan said. "If you've noticed, I have a tendency to forget where I am when you're with me."

Sarah understood perfectly. She found herself suffering from the same malady. There was no doubt in her mind that her family knew what was going on between them—at least most of it. But for some reason they'd remained strangely quiet on the subject. She appreciated their restraint, but today she wanted more than that. She couldn't help the giddy feeling that washed over her. He wasn't leaving. Not yet, anyway. She suddenly had the most incredible feeling. She wanted to grab hold of him and hang on tight. They'd had so little time alone. She wanted to be with him—just the two of them.

"Let's take a picnic lunch to the creek," she said impulsively. "I feel like being lazy today."

"Sarah..."

She caught the note of hesitation in his voice. "You have something else to do," she said, unable to hide her disappointment.

"No. I mean yes." Jordan sighed. "A picnic by the creek sounds wonderful...but I—we—need to talk about something else first."

Sarah needed none of her special talents to detect his uneasiness. "I'm not going to like this, am I?"

"Probably not. But I have to ask. It's something you said the other day when we were talking about your talent—and your past."

Sarah turned away. "You're right. I don't like it."

Jordan tried to think of a way to ease into the subject. Unable to come up with any ideas, he finally decided simply to plunge ahead. "I'm sorry, Sarah, but I have to know. The other day you said your sight sometimes caused threats. Who's threatened you?"

"It's nothing. Just goes with the territory." She tried to sound flippant and knew she'd failed when she saw his frown.

"Sarah, it is something, or you wouldn't have mentioned it in the first place. I'm sorry I have to ask. But it could be important."

"Because of this silly idea you and Sam and T.J. have? I keep telling you, they were just accidents."

"I hope to God you're right and we're wrong, but until we know for sure, humor me. I don't like to play devil's advocate, but if the threats were really unimportant you wouldn't have mentioned them. Now tell me who and when."

She whirled around to face him, the euphoria she'd felt earlier completely destroyed. "Most of the time I don't know who," she said bitterly. "As to when, every time I get my name in the paper. Why do you think I hide? Some call me a witch, or the devil's spawn. Some get mad because I didn't see enough or didn't see it soon enough. Or because I don't see anything and they think I'm deliberately not telling. Don't you see? There's no way I can win."

Jordan felt the color drain from his face. Her words hammered at him, each one a separate and distinct body blow. He fought back nausea, realizing for the first time how much harm he could do her. "I didn't know," he protested, knowing he was defending himself, as well as apologizing for putting her through this.

"I told you. No one really understands. And I don't want to talk about it anymore."

Jordan gritted his teeth, partly in frustration, partly in disgust at himself. But he couldn't stop now. He had to push her, had to make her tell him—for her own sake. He could only hope she wouldn't hate him.

"Sarah, I'm sorry. But we have to talk about it. You must know something about some of them?"

"Why are you doing this?" she cried, her voice breaking.

"I know you don't want to believe it, but someone's trying to hurt you. And it must be tied in with who and what you are. Sarah, you have to tell me. It's for your protection."

Sarah sank into a chair, defeated. "Can't you understand, Jordan? Most of the time I don't have the slightest idea where the threats come from. Unsigned notes, anonymous phone calls."

"You said most of the time. Tell me about the others, the ones you do know."

"You won't give up, will you?" she said bitterly.

"Not when you might be in danger. Sarah, I care about you. Please tell me. Let me help."

"There's only one...maybe two.... Most of the times when I've known who it was it was the Ewells. But Sam's already said he was going to check on them."

Finally he was beginning to get somewhere. "Who are the Ewells, Sarah?" he asked quietly.

The Ewells live—lived—over in the next county. There's been bad blood between them and my family for generations. I don't know why the trouble started, but it's been going on since before Aunt Cinda was born. Trouble is, there was a blood connection back there somewhere, so the Ewells know what we are—what some of us are, anyway. And they'd come over to ask about things. Only Aunt Cinda could never see anything, and neither could I.

"I don't know if the trouble started because we couldn't see, or if we can't see because of the trouble. But anyway, they always blame us—Aunt Cinda and me, anyway— whenever anything goes wrong for them. Some say we caused it. And the others blame us for not warning them that something bad's going to happen. It's another one of those no-win situations."

"Sounds like the Hatfields and McCoys," Jordan said under his breath.

"Something like that," Sarah agreed. "Anyway, the last trouble was nearly ten years ago. I was still a kid. Over the years the family dwindled down in size. I think the last of them moved to California several years ago."

"And Sam told you he was going to check on them?"

Sarah nodded.

"Okay. Now, what about the other one? You said you knew about 'maybe two.'"

"I'm not sure...."

"Tell me anyway."

Sarah gave in. "I was teaching in Tulsa about three years ago. I was able to give police some information about a hit-and-run driver. Their only witness wasn't able to tell them much until they put her under hypnosis. Then she gave them the same license number. The story got out—"

"What happened, Sarah?"

"They caught him, tried and convicted him and sent him to jail—despite his attempts to make them believe his car had been stolen."

"And the threats?" he asked quietly.

"They started after the newspaper story, of course," she said bitterly. "Just ugly things. Warnings to keep my devil's work away from decent people. That kind of thing."

Jordan flinched, forced himself to stay calm. "But who do you think was behind them?"

"I thought . . . some of them might have come from the man or his family. They were religious fanatics, you see. And most of the threats were the devil's-spawn variety."

"What did the police say? Did they think there was a connection between the threats and the driver?"

"I didn't tell them."

"Didn't tell— Dear God, Sarah, you need a keeper. Someone threatens you and you don't even report it. Why ever not?"

"There was nothing they could do. No way to prove who it was. And all I needed right then was more . . . more notoriety."

She hung her head, but not quick enough to prevent Jordan from seeing the tears shimmering on her lashes. Instantly Jordan knew—it was the man who'd hurt her so cruelly, so deeply, that thereafter she'd carefully channeled her emotions away from the possibility of being hurt again. The bastard! He had a lot to answer for. And yet Jordan could almost feel sorry for the man—to have won Sarah's love, then thrown it away.

"Sarah—?"

"Are you through now?"

"Almost. What was the man's name? And his sentence? Is he still in jail?"

"I don't remember his name. And, yes, he should still be in jail. So you see, there can't be any connection."

"I suppose your friend the sheriff could—"

"No! Sam doesn't know anything about it. And you're not to tell him."

"Sarah—"

"There's no reason for Sam to know. He'll just be off on another wild-goose chase. And I'll have to listen to another lecture." Tears welled up in her eyes. "I mean it, Jordan. There's no reason to tell Sam. I don't want him to find out about— I answered your questions. Promise me you won't tell him, or I'll . . . I'll . . ."

Jordan's mind raced through the possibilities. He had a friend in Tulsa he could get to do a little checking. Sarah was probably right. The feuding family sounded like a better prospect. He'd check out Tulsa and let Sam concentrate on the Ewells. At least they'd be covering different territory.

"All right, Sarah. I won't tell Sam, if that's what you want. But I am going to do a little checking myself."

"You'll just be wasting your time."

"It's my time. What were you doing in Tulsa, anyway? I thought you liked staying closer to home."

"I was teaching. They offered me a position, and I took it. The university in Fayetteville graduates teachers every year. And a lot of experienced teachers return to work on advanced degrees part-time, or to work while their spouses do graduate work. There are usually more teachers than jobs around here. Besides, even though it's too far to commute, Tulsa was close enough to come home on weekends if I wanted to."

"Is that why you're teaching in St. Louis? The local positions were all filled?"

Sarah relaxed a little, thankful he'd finally stopped grilling her about Tulsa. "Actually, no. I took the job in St. Louis because I wanted to try my wings a little. I think I'm getting braver—as long as I can run back here if I need to. St. Louis is only about two hundred and fifty miles away."

Try my wings. Jordan's mind captured the phrase and held on tenaciously. Did his little homebody have a secret dollop of wanderlust in her soul after all? The thought was a ray of sunshine penetrating the clouds after a long, dark night. Unconsciously his lips curved upward in a smile.

Sarah watched the myriad of emotions cross his face. "What are you thinking now?" she asked.

"Wicked thoughts," he said. Then, unable to resist, he gave her a teasing wink and dropped a quick kiss on her forehead.

Sarah's breath caught. "I don't think we should—" The touch of his mouth against hers cut off her words. He kissed her gently, his lips lightly caressing hers, but before she could fully appreciate the contact he raised his head.

"Don't get me off the subject. You distract me too easily," he growled in mock seriousness, and moved a few inches away, still retaining her hand in his. His eyes lingered on her face.

Sarah shivered. His gaze, the soft, expectant look in his eyes, was short-circuiting her thought processes. And yet, behind his look of exquisite wanting—a look that she suspected was echoed in her own eyes—she could see something else.

"I have an idea," he said suddenly. "Let's go away."

She gave him a startled look, then shook her head.

Jordan had spoken impulsively, but he knew immediately it was a good idea. Whoever was after her knew where she was and knew how to either blend in or stay out of sight. But until now no one had been looking. He needed to get Sarah out of the way for a while, to break her routine. It might give Sam and T.J. the time they needed.

"Why not?" he asked. "Just for a day or so. Come away with me, Sarah. Please. Three days. A long weekend. We can come back on Monday."

"But where . . . why?"

"We can go to Eureka Springs. As to why—I can think of several reasons." He bent over her, his lips brushing her cheek.

"Jordan, I can't just..."

"Don't you trust me?"

"No— I mean yes— I—" she stammered, her confusion battling with embarrassment.

His low, rumbling laugh interrupted her disjointed dialogue. "I shouldn't tease you, but sometimes it's hard not to," he told her. "You make such a delightful teasee."

She freed her arm from his grasp and stepped back. Jordan let her go.

"The summer home where I'm staying has three bedrooms, with a lock on every one," he said quickly. "You can have your pick—and your choice of single or double accommodations. This isn't a plan for a weekend orgy. I really think it would do you good to get away for a few days. And I—I would enjoy your company."

He'd enjoy her company! she thought to herself. Oh, Jordan! To be with him for three uninterrupted days—without worries, without family. The thought was an unexpected glimpse of heaven. Did she dare?

She looked up quickly as a low growling sound escaped his lips. "Jordan? What's wrong?"

"It would be easier on a man if you'd learn to play poker," he said in a shaky voice.

"I don't understand."

"I know," he said, turning to face her. With a deliberate nonchalance, he held out a hand. "So, how about it? Dinner tonight at Basin Park? I promise, Sarah, you won't regret it. We'll have a glorious time."

Chapter 12

Jordan couldn't be sure when he first suspected he and Sarah were being watched. He'd developed his ability to recognize that he was under observation along with his skills as a journalist. It was not an uncommon accomplishment in a field that sometimes called for a reporter to remain inconspicuous. However, he was usually alert to the possibility of detection before the warning phenomena triggered alarm. This time the sensation was unanticipated.

Their arrival in Eureka Springs shortly before noon had begun as planned. Sarah led the way through the downtown area, Jordan automatically taking the side along the curb, placing himself as a buffer between her and the traffic-clogged streets. They wandered hand in hand past the turn-of-the-century buildings that clung tenaciously to the side of the mountain.

When they stopped in front of a display of wood carvings in a gallery window, Jordan unconsciously moved himself directly behind her. Half a block later, at a gallery specializing in stained glass, he found himself intently watching the reflection of the street scene behind them in the polished glass of the shop window. By the time they reached a small sidewalk park he was consciously searching faces in the crowds for anything out of the ordinary.

"What's wrong, Jordan?" Sarah asked unexpectedly. "What are you looking for?"

"Nothing's wrong," he said. But the smile accompanying his words was unconvincing.

Sarah frowned, her skepticism apparent in her eyes.

Jordan let his gaze move beyond the crowd to the street. Bumper-to-bumper traffic traveled slowly along the winding roadway. None of the vehicles seemed particularly noticeable—mostly a collection of station wagons, pickup trucks and family-size sedans, with an occasional small sporty model sandwiched in between the larger vehicles. His gaze rested for a moment on a rusty, battered pickup.

Beside him, Sarah tugged at his arm, drawing his attention back to her. "What is it?" she demanded again.

"I thought I saw someone I knew," he told her, wishing she hadn't noticed his preoccupation. Hunches were supposed to be her field, not his. Still, he couldn't shake the feeling that someone was watching them.

He stole another quick look at the street. The pickup caught his attention again as it moved out of sight. Had he seen it before? Probably, he thought answering his own question and managing to produce a small laugh at his own expense. Eureka Springs's main thoroughfare meandered up and down the steep hillsides, never crossing another street. Most of the traffic in the downtown area seemed to be moving in circles—probably looking for a nonexistent parking place.

He turned to Sarah again. "I was just thinking, I'm glad you suggested parking on the outskirts and catching the trolley downtown. Sure is nice to have a personal tour guide.'' He pulled her to her feet, bent to deliver a quick kiss to her cheek, then tucked her hand securely in the crook of his elbow.

Sarah smiled up into his face, breathing easier, relieved that his earlier good humor had reestablished itself.

''Where now?'' he asked, trying to control his voice under the onslaught of emotions triggered by her smile.

''Did you know the Basin Park Hotel was built into the side of the mountain, so that each story has a street entrance?'' she asked. ''I've always wanted to go in the first floor, out the second, in the third...all the way to the top.''

Jordan grinned. ''Sounds like fun. You lead the way.'' And besides that, he thought, we'll finish up halfway up the mountainside. Though he was half convinced he'd been imagining things a few minutes before, he still wasn't ready to completely let go of the idea. Moving up the mountain inside a building was a good diversionary tactic.

They came out onto the street from the seventh floor in time for Jordan to see a rusty pickup moving slowly past the entrance. Was it the same one he'd seen earlier? Had he seen it before today? And if so, where? Jordan frowned speculatively as the vehicle disappeared, registering in his mind the fact that it carried Oklahoma plates. Unconsciously he placed a protective arm around Sarah's shoulders. He suddenly wished they'd never come to Eureka Springs.

Vainly Jordan tried to recapture the lighthearted mood they'd enjoyed earlier in the day. They inspected the town's quaint craft shops, toured the Gay Nineties Museum and the Queen Anne mansion and mingled with the tourists enjoying impromptu sidewalk concerts. Only at Hatchet Hall did the shadows seem to fade, and that was because the tour of temperance leader Carrie Nation's last home reminded them both of the story of Great-grandfather Wilson and his cornfields.

Even the elegant surroundings of the Basin Park Hotel, where they shared a late dinner, failed to diminish the restrained atmosphere between them. It was completely dark before they began the journey to Jordan's cabin.

In the moonlight the cabin's weathered logs gave the impression of having been part of the landscape since time began. On closer inspection, Sarah recognized it as one of the prefabricated log houses popular in the area as vacation homes. It blended unobtrusively into the wooded surroundings on a hill overlooking a quiet stretch of the Kings River.

Jordan unlocked the door, reached inside and flipped a light switch, then stood aside as Sarah stepped into the mountain hideaway. The soft glow from the single burning lamp bathed the interior of the cabin in a warm golden hue. Country-casual furniture formed a conversation grouping in front of a freestanding fireplace at one end of the room. Cotton rag rugs covered the wood-pegged floors. The room radiated a sense of peace.

Sarah collapsed into the nearest cushioned chair, pulled her sandals from her feet and began massaging an instep. "I should have worn hiking boots," she said wearily. "Now you know why they call Eureka Springs Little Switzerland."

"Sarah—" Jordan began.

She shook her head and, refusing to look at him, leaned back in the chair, her eyes closed. "Give me a minute," she begged. "Right now I'm too tired even to talk." Even with her eyes closed, she knew his eyes were on her. She could feel his gaze. She forced her breathing to remain slow and steady while her mind raced in confusing circles.

Sarah had welcomed the plans for a weekend away with hat-over-the-moon expectations. It was the forbidden apple, the brass ring, the ultimate fantasy getaway. But now, faced with the reality of her and Jordan alone without the restraining presence of others around them, she felt her euphoria dissolving. The beginning of their tour of Eureka Springs had been perfect. They'd been like two kids unexpectedly let out of school. Then something had happened. Sarah didn't know what. But slowly, steadily, Jordan had withdrawn into himself. Had she made a mistake in coming here with him? What did he expect of her now?

Jordan watched her from across the room, his gut twisting in response to the look he now saw on her face. Quietly he picked up her overnight case and went down the hall, knowing that if he didn't leave in another moment he'd be carrying her to his bed. She needed time, peace and safety. Most of all safety.

And he needed her. He felt his body tense at the thought. It was going to be like walking a tightrope—giving her what she needed while denying himself. But that was the way it would have to be—until she was safe, and until he could figure out a way to extricate himself from the mess he'd made. At least he had her close.

"Sarah, are you awake?" he asked softly when he returned to the front room. As far as he could tell, she hadn't moved since he'd left.

"I'm awake," she muttered, her eyes still closed. "Just tired." *And hiding,* she added silently. As long as she could keep her eyes closed she could pretend nothing was wrong.

"I put your overnight case in the back bedroom. It's farther down the hall from the bath than the other guest room, but it has a bed instead of bunks."

Sarah's eyes fluttered open. The back bedroom? Relief mingled with disappointment. Just what had she expected?

Jordan had made it plain he didn't expect her to share his bed before she'd agreed to this trip. So she shouldn't have been surprised. Especially after he'd become so quiet and pensive this evening. Why, then, did she feel so discontented? She was confused by his attack-and-withdraw tactics, bewildered by her own seesawing emotions. She knew something of her thoughts must have showed on her face when she heard Jordan groan under his breath.

"Damn it, Sarah, don't look at me like that."

She flinched, pressing herself back into the cushions of the chair.

"Oh, hell," Jordan muttered. "I'm sorry. Look, it's been a long day—a long two days. You're exhausted, and I guess I am, too. I didn't mean to scare you."

"It's all right. I think I was just startled—half asleep. You didn't scare me. Not really."

Jordan stuffed his hands deep in his pants pockets and turned away from her, staring blindly out the window into the darkness outside.

"Jordan? What's wrong?"

"Nothing's wrong," he said quietly. "We're both tired, and it's late. I think we should say good-night. Go to bed, Sarah. We'll talk tomorrow." He listened for the sound of movement behind him, allowing himself to relax slightly when he heard her walk across the room. He sensed she'd paused by the door to the hallway, and with the length of the room between them he allowed himself to turn and face her, the muscles in his jaw tightening when he saw the shadowed wariness in her eyes.

"Bathroom's first door on the left, your bedroom's at the end of the hall. I turned on the lights."

She stood for a moment, then finally nodded. "I'll find them. Good night, Jordan."

"Good night, Sarah. Sleep well," he said. He watched her disappear down the hallway, then quietly eased open the door and went out onto the front porch.

Shafts of silver moonlight slanted through the open window, relieving the darkness of the room. In the quiet dark hours the plaintive call of a whippoorwill echoed across the hills. Sarah stirred, gripped by a restlessness that nudged her from sleep into a state of awareness. She forced herself to relax, waiting for the expected insight that would dispel the mists of uncertainty swirling behind her closed eyelids.

The veils moved, shadowed and indistinct, silhouettes of light and dark too vague to interpret. She remained still, waiting. The mists moved again, turning, swirling into an unwavering curtain of gray. The past was unfinished, and the future as yet undetermined. And the present? It was as nebulous as the intersecting patterns of yesterday and tomorrow—a stage awaiting a performance by the players who would complete the designs of the past and determine the future.

A slight breeze carrying a trace of moisture from the nearby river ruffled the curtains at the open window. Outside, a chorus of tree frogs added their shrill voices to the symphony of night sounds.

Sarah forced herself to take slow, deep breaths as she tried to interpret the meaning of the dream—if dream it was. She'd been uncertain before, not always knowing if her waking nightmares were imaginary visions, subconscious fears or experiences of her special gift.

The incidents of sight often appeared unheralded and unexpected. But the images were usually precise and clear—sometimes a single scene, a moment frozen in time like an album snapshot. Sometimes pictures unfolded in sequence, the action caught on slow-motion film. There was never any commentary. What came before or after or even when was always open to interpretation. And Sarah was always part of the scene—not as herself, but as one of the participants.

She drew another breath, tense and disturbed. This one was different. The images were unclear, as if she were watching a screen obscured by a veil of gauze. She was also definitely a part of it, but as herself—not as someone else. Jordan was there, too, his features shadowed, half in darkness, half in light, but the reality of his being as clearly defined as her own. And just as definite was the absence of signposts for her to follow. This time she was on her own.

Sarah's eyes focused on the shaft of moonlight streaming through her window. She deliberately tried to clear her tumbling thoughts of the vague images and jumbled sounds that offered no help and made little sense. Instead, she heard the strong voice of Aunt Cinda echoing in her mind. *Times come when you don't know. Then's when you have to take a chance and don't go worrying about it.... Just listen to your own self....*

The moonbeam shimmered in the air, disturbed by a night breeze ruffling the curtain and shifting the leaves outside the window. The room was suddenly too close, too confining.

Sarah pulled her white terry-cloth robe over her shortie nightgown and quietly opened the bedroom door. She tiptoed past Jordan's bedroom, her bare feet making no noise on the polished wood floor, then eased the latch from the front door and stepped onto the porch.

Fireflies, each provided by nature with a luminescent signal, danced across the clearing, their silent mating calls flickering like tiny jewels in the night. From the distant ridge behind the cabin, the whippoorwill's wistful song sounded again. A second call floated on the night air, this time from the far side of the river.

A soft sigh escaped Sarah's lips. Nature's order. How simple and uncomplicated. She signals, he responds; he calls, she answers—natural selection, uncluttered by reason or doubt. The fireflies, the birds of the night, all knowing instinctively how to identify their mates. If only she could be as sure—

"Sarah?"

The sound of her name came from the darkness behind her. Sarah turned slowly, not sure if she'd heard or imagined the call. Jordan stepped from the deep shadows at the end of the porch into the moonlight. Still caught in her thoughts, she took a step toward him.

Jordan closed the distance, his arms reaching automatically to pull her close. Instead he forced himself to rest his hands lightly on her shoulders.

"Sarah, is something wrong?"

She trembled under his touch, trying to deny the enchantment of the moment—to ignore the call drawing her relentlessly forward. Silently she shook her head. "No," she said softly. "Nothing's wrong. I just came out for a breath of fresh air. I didn't mean to disturb you."

"You didn't," he said automatically, wishing it was true. The sight of Sarah in the moonlight was the fulfillment of all his fantasies. *Disturbing* was too weak a word to describe the havoc she played with his emotions. He'd been sitting on the porch for the last hour, waiting until he was sure she was asleep, not trusting his willpower if he went inside earlier. It took a herculean effort to hold her away now instead of crushing her to him. He dropped his hands from her shoulders and moved back.

She stood straight and stiff, braced against the feeling of desolation as he stepped away. "Did you hear the whippoorwill?" she asked suddenly. "He's down by the river. Listen."

The three-note birdcall reverberated across the clearing, a triumphant warble that was immediately answered by a similar call. The two calls came again—this time closer together.

"Yes," Jordan said, his voice a husky whisper. "He heard her. He's going to her. All she had to do was answer."

Sarah turned to him again, her face bathed in the soft iridescence of the moonlight, blue-green shadows in the depths of her eyes. Jordan hesitated, not wanting to push her, yet unable and unwilling to deny the inevitable. "Sarah...?"

Listen to your own self. Sarah blinked, remembering Aunt Cinda's advice. She held herself upright, wanting nothing more than to burrow into the strength and comfort offered by the man in front of her. He had come as a stranger into the land, mistrusted and misunderstood only because he was alien. He'd demanded nothing, asked little—only the opportunity to learn, to understand and to become a part of the peace he'd found here. He knew this place now. He also knew her, knew her secrets, knew her fears. He'd become a part of her—a part she could no longer gainsay. But for some reason, he no longer seemed to want her.

Jordan drew a quiet, deep breath, forcing himself to remain still. The whippoorwill called again and was answered so quickly that Jordan could envision the two birds, perched side by side, offering their three-note duet to the night sky. Without thinking he pursed his lips and softly imitated the three notes.

For a split second Sarah hesitated. Regardless of whether he would admit it or not, Jordan wanted her. He had called to her. And she wanted to respond.

Jordan read the answer to his invitation in Sarah's eyes. For a long moment he battled against himself. This wasn't the right time. He should protect her—from him, from herself, from the unknown forces that threatened her. But she'd breached all his defenses, destroyed his reason, overwhelmed his senses. With a low moan of surrender, he pulled her into his arms.

His mouth touched hers lightly, his lips sliding across her cheek, savoring the honey of her skin. The pulse point on the side of her neck fluttered under his touch, its rhythm erratic, an echo of the clamoring need coursing through his body. His hands moved across her back, molding her soft body to the hard, muscular length of his. He wanted her with an intensity that shook him. He touched the tip of his tongue to hers, tasted her sweetness as she returned the caress, felt her shiver under his touch.

"Jordan...I feel..."

He recognized her helplessness, her surrender, in the melting of her body. "I'm here, Sarah. I'm here. You can lean on me." He kissed her again, and this time it was an urgent, burning touching of the lips only partly tempered by the careful control he exerted over himself.

She cuddled into him, her head resting against his chest, and raised her eyes to look into his. Her lips curved, and her eyes shimmered with a silvery blue-green light. Her arms crept around his neck. The solid feel of his flesh was an affirmation that he was real. In Jordan's arms she discovered a new part of herself. With him she was complete. Without him she was only half an equation, only part of a whole. She needed him to fill a part of her that could not exist alone— that part that was woman, with knowledge and needs and gifts to share.

She spoke again, her voice a tiny lilt reverberating with the wonder of discovery. "Jordan, let's go inside."

Her words were an echo of his own thoughts. Jordan nodded, one arm tightening around her, afraid that if he relinquished his grasp she'd disappear, and led the way inside.

He touched her face, his fingers tracing the curve of her cheek, the contour of her jaw, the shape and promise of her lips. Then his hands moved to the tie at her waist, opening the robe to reveal the short lace-trimmed gown. Slowly he pushed the robe off her shoulders and down her arms, letting it fall to the floor, and took one step back so that he could see her.

"So beautiful," he said softly, his eyes holding hers as he efficiently discarded his shirt and jeans and stood before her clad only in his white briefs.

Sarah dragged her gaze from his, her eyes sweeping from his broad shoulders across his chest, following the silken line of dark hair across his flat stomach to where it swirled around his navel, then downward— Her head jerked up, her eyes wide.

Jordan's gentle laugh rumbled low in his chest as he reached for her. "And that doesn't even begin to say how much I want you," he whispered against her cheek. "You're both fever and balm in my blood."

Carefully he eased her onto the softness of the bed. "I've been searching for you all my life." He breathed the words into her ear as his lips nibbled at the sensitive lobe. "And I didn't even know it."

Sarah's arms went around him as he lowered his mouth to hers, tenderly claiming her lips and her heart. With low, musical endearments he slid the narrow straps of her gown off her shoulders and down her arms, caressing her body through the silken material. His fingers traced the border of lace draped low across her small breasts, their dusty-rose centers peeking seductively through the open mesh trim. Her nipples grew instantly taut and firm under his touch, as waves of pleasure, like the undulating surface currents of a lake, rippled through her body.

Sarah raised her mouth to his, her tongue probing delicately between his lips, at first teasing the sensitive skin inside, then burrowing deeper and deeper in a hungry kiss that imprisoned them both in a web of escalating arousal.

Jordan moaned, the sound escaping from low in his throat. "Oh, Sarah, what am I going to do with you?"

"Love me. Please, just love me," she whispered, her words both command and plea. She shifted, lifting her body as his hands skimmed the gown and her bikini panties over her hips. Her hands feathered down his chest to the elastic waistband of his briefs and tugged, no longer able to tolerate even that barrier between them.

Jordan groaned again, the low sound escaping unbidden as his lips reclaimed the sweet fire of hers. His muscles strained against the relentless surge propelling them toward their destination. He wanted it to last forever, wanted to savor this sweet, wild agony. He lowered the weight of his body onto hers to slow the impatient need threatening to consume them both.

She clung to him, feeling his uneven breath on her cheek, her skin tingling, her body still craving his hands. Her fingers moved hungrily over his heated skin, relishing the tactile feel of heat and fire and texture under her fingertips. She moved under him, uttering soft, muted cries of need and passion. Jordan held her tightly, rocking with her, her anchor in the riptide.

He brushed a gentle kiss across her forehead. Then his lips seared a path down her neck, past her shoulders, into the valley between her breasts. He could hear the frantic beating of her heart beneath his ear, recognized it as an echo of the urgency coursing through his veins. His lips continued exploring her soft flesh, outlining the tips of her breasts with his tongue. As his lips claimed one of the throbbing buds, she arched under him, her cry of need shattering the last of his control.

As he lifted himself above her, she rose to meet him. Calling on the last vestiges of his restraint, he entered her slowly, binding them together in a place beyond the present, beyond time. She melted around him, matching his ardor with her own body and joining in a tempo of exquisite harmony. Then she twisted wildly beneath him, reaching instinctively for the ecstasy that was shimmering just beyond reach. Her body suddenly stiffened, her breath unraveling into soft, fragmented cries. As she called his name, giving voice to their convulsions of joy, Jordan felt his own body dissolve into a series of mind-shattering explosions.

Tempest calmed, the world settled back into its orbit and Jordan rolled to the side, curling her body into the cradle of his.

The serenade of tree frogs hushed, abandoning their nocturnal concert. The moon slipped behind the mountain. In the quiet time that comes before the awakening of the morning, Sarah slept, curled confidently in the cradle of Jordan's arms.

Jordan reached for the patchwork quilt at the bottom of the bed, drawing its folds over them both, moving carefully in an effort not to disturb Sarah. A cool morning breeze wafted in the open window as one by one the stars faded and the black sky began to gray. He lay on his side, watching her sleep. Nothing was more perfect, could ever be more perfect, than greeting a new day with Sarah by his side.

She'd come to him the first time for reassurance, and they'd shared a rare and perfect pleasure. Tonight their passion had burst forth with the fire and brilliance of a nova, searing itself into his soul until it was an inalienable part of him. He knew now that he loved her. She was a part of him, as inseparable from his life as the heart that beat within his chest.

Suddenly an icy wave of apprehension clutched at his insides. Even if she did return his love, could she forgive him when she discovered why he'd followed her to Mountain Springs? Could she love a man who had purposely set out to deceive her, to discover her secrets and expose them?

There would be no story, of course. There had been no question of that since he'd discovered the harm and danger such exposure could do to her. Even if he hadn't loved her and wanted to protect her, he could never have written such a story. He wasn't a writer who exposed all for the sake of a check and a headline. That was one reason he stayed independent, so that he could say no to any editor who insisted on the story regardless of undeserved harm or negative social value. But would she understand that? And most of all, would she forgive him for continuing to hide his deceit? She'd told him all her secrets, exposed herself to him completely. Did she deserve less from him?

Tell her now, insisted the warning voice in his head.

Jordan resisted the urge, panic welling up in his throat. He couldn't. What if she refused to forgive him, sent him away? He wouldn't be able to help protect her. Regardless of her protests, she was in danger. He couldn't ignore his carefully trained observations, his experienced instincts. Someone wished her harm. His confession would have to wait. Surely a fate that had led him to her wouldn't deny him a better time.

Jordan sighed. So many problems to solve. Mountain Springs was Sarah's touchstone. She would never be happy cut completely adrift, traveling the world with him like a piece of flotsam. Strangely enough, he suddenly realized, it was no longer enough for him, either. The old wanderlust had not completely disappeared, but it no longer held the same urgency, the same compulsion. He'd found what he was looking for.

Somehow they'd work it out. He'd take each problem, one at a time, and work through it, beginning with the first and most important—keeping Sarah safe. Unconsciously his hold on her tightened.

Sarah murmured a protest and moved restlessly in his arms. Jordan loosened his grasp, pulling her more closely into the protective circle of his arms, soothing her until her body relaxed in his embrace. His eyes fastened on her lips, still invitingly pink and full from their earlier lovemaking.

How peacefully she slept, so close and trusting in his arms. If he lived two lifetimes he'd never have enough of her. Somehow he had to expose the threat, remove the danger and earn her forgiveness.

Chapter 13

Sarah pulled her car into the shade of an overhanging oak and looked hopefully at the high clouds forming in the southwest. They were, she knew, unlikely to bring either rain or relief from the summer heat. At least not today.

An explosion of jumping grasshoppers danced from the dusty weeds beneath her feet. Sarah recognized their frantic activity as suggestive of her state of mind during the last ten days. She wished it were possible to ignore her scattered thoughts the same way she ignored the insects, but she knew that was impossible.

She began her climb up the path above Hogscald toward Aunt Cinda's cabin, fully realizing it would take all her concentration to win any kind of concession from the determined old lady. But even with the challenge before her, her thoughts returned once again to the single subject dominating her mind—Jordan.

She had seen him only twice since they'd returned from Eureka Springs, although she'd talked with him by phone almost every day. It wasn't the same. She hadn't realized how much she'd come to depend on seeing him, seeing the sharp lines of his face soften when he smiled or his eyes light up when they locked with hers.

Sometimes it seemed the whole world was conspiring to keep them apart. First she'd helped her grandmother can a bumper crop of beans, and then she'd nursed Jimmy Joe through a forty-eight-hour virus. T.J. had asked for her help with a sick foal. Today, when at last she'd found herself with nothing urgent to do, she couldn't find Jordan.

He'd been out of town a lot lately, never saying specifically where he was going. But the Mountain Springs grapevine was in good working order. During the last ten days he'd been reported in Fayetteville, in Rogers and once in Springdale. Just this morning Cousin Mabel had called to inform Sarah gleefully that she'd seen him at the courthouse in Bentonville yesterday. Nosy as ever, she'd blatantly asked her why.

Sarah wouldn't have answered even if she'd known. But that didn't help matters much. She, too, wondered what he was doing. As far as she knew, he wasn't researching another story. And he'd told her the Monte Ne article was completed.

Sarah knew what was disturbing her. How much, if at all, was she part of Jordan's future? They'd never discussed it, except for one offhand mention from him about finding a larger apartment in St. Louis. She knew he maintained a small apartment there but rarely used it. She, on the other hand, was tied there by a teaching contract for the next year. In fact, she'd have to return to St. Louis in a little over a month.

She'd had no doubts about their relationship while they'd been together in Eureka Springs. They'd spent most of their time at the cabin, oblivious of the rest of the world—so close that words had been superfluous. And since then, she reminded herself, they hadn't really had a chance to talk.

She allowed herself a long sigh. Today was probably going to be as frustrating as the last ten days, even if she had escaped the farm for a few hours. She stepped off the path and into the clearing in front of her great-aunt's cabin. She hadn't seen Aunt Cinda since the picnic, but T.J. had. And according to him his grandmother was being as mysterious and contrary as ever.

"Where's your young man?"

Aunt Cinda's strong voice came rolling out the open door even before Sarah reached the stone slab that served as a step to the cabin porch. She hadn't expected to surprise Aunt Cinda with her arrival, but neither had she expected to be greeted in quite this way.

"I don't know," Sarah answered, pulling open the screen door to enter the cabin. Aunt Cinda was in her favorite rocking chair by the great stone hearth. For once she'd discarded her shawl. It was, however, within easy reach—draped across one arm of the chair. "How are you, Aunt Cinda? Today's a scorcher."

"Don't try changin' the subject on me, Sarah Jane. Where's that Jordan fellow?"

"He's out of town, I think."

"Leastways you've stopped denying he's your fellow. That's progress of sorts, I guess," the old woman muttered.

Sarah forced a laugh and bent to kiss her aunt's wrinkled cheek. "You know I never argue with you. You've made up your mind Jordan's my fellow. I can't see how my denying it would change anything. Once you've decided—"

"Ain't me needs to be decidin'. He's your beau. If you want him, that is."

"You approve?" Sarah asked, gently teasing.

"'Course I do. Everybody needs somebody. 'Specially folks like me 'n' you,'' Aunt Cinda said. "Difference is, nobody told me till it was too late. After Udell died, I thought I was supposed to go on by myself. So I'm telling you now, while there's still time.''

Aunt Cinda's voice softened. "It's up to you, child. I ain't one to be interfering with something this important. But I know you need someone of the forever kind—somebody besides a cranky old aunt. Think he'll do jus' fine.''

"I do like him," Sarah said softly.

Aunt Cinda cackled. "You don't fool me, Sarah Jane. That ain't what we called it in my day."

Sarah allowed herself a grin as she walked across the room to the sink against the far wall. "That's not what I came to talk about, Aunt Cinda." Using the dipper from the bucket of water sitting on the counter, she primed the hand pump, then grasped the handle.

"I reckon I know why you're here." Aunt Cinda gave an unladylike snort. "Pump me up a glass of fresh water while you're at it," she added. "Tastes better that way. Sparkling cold, straight from the well. Can't get fresh water straight from the ground in the valley."

"And you don't have to break the ice on the top of the bucket to prime the pump in the wintertime, or pump it up a cup at a time," Sarah returned.

Aunt Cinda sighed. "I know, child. I know. But you gotta admit, there's nothing so good as a glass of fresh, cold well water on a hot day."

Sarah's voice softened. "You're right. And today's one hot day." She carried two glasses back to the hearth and handed one to Aunt Cinda. Then, holding her own glass, she sat down in the chair facing her aunt.

"Things keep a-changin'," Aunt Cinda said, shaking her head in bewilderment. "I remember when my daddy—

that'd be your great-granddaddy—built this cabin right smack-dab on top of the well. Folks around here said he was crazy. But Daddy said it was the newest way. He was right, too. Weren't too long till there was a lot of new rooms being built over wells. Or new cabins. Mama was so proud of that new pump and of being one of the first with inside water. Bet there ain't a dozen left working in all of Benton County no more. Now you just turn a spigot and out comes the water. Hot 'n' cold.''

''You'll find it's a real convenience,'' Sarah told her.

''I reckon I will. Some days these old bones of mine could use a little convenience. But I'm gonna miss this cabin. Lived here since I was six years old, I have. Gertie weren't even born yet. Been here best part of a century. Lots of folks don't go on that long. Much less in one place. The roots are awful deep.''

Sarah patted her hand. ''I know it'll be hard, Aunt Cinda. Especially at first. But things will work out.''

''I know that, child. Matter of fact, I'm looking forward to my new cabin. Done told you that.''

Sarah hesitated. ''Aunt Cinda,'' she began reluctantly, ''about that cabin...''

''What about it?''

''I...I can't find it. Neither can T.J. And time's running out.''

''Horsefeathers. Got plenty of time. Sure don't feel like snow out there today. Done told you it'll be there when I need it.''

''But—''

''But nothin'. You stop worryin' your head 'bout me and tend to your own self. I can still take care of my business. And don't you go thinkin' you gotta hover over me like a old biddy hen, either. I was changing your diapers before you knew your own name. Can do it again, if need be. But I'd rather be diapering your babies. I can diaper them, but I can't be making them. That's what you oughta be concernin' yourself with. Not this old lady.''

"Aunt Cinda!" Sarah's gasp was somewhere between shock and laughter.

"Done told you, Sarah Jane, I weren't born yesterday. Don't need no special sight to know what you're about. It's about time, too, to my way of thinkin'. You can tell me it's none of my business if you want to. And you'll have the right of it. But I sure am interested, if you're inclined to talk. Guess you know I kinda like that fellow."

Smiling, Sarah leaned forward and gave her aunt a hug. "If there was anything to tell, and I wanted to tell anyone, it would be you, Aunt Cinda. You know that. If it was all up to me..."

"He don't feel the same way?"

"I think he does. But I don't know for sure. Not if his feelings are the forever kind. He hasn't said, and I can't read his mind."

"Have a little faith, Sarah Jane. Faith in yourself and in him, too. The good book says it's faith that'll move the mountains. Don't you be forgettin' it."

"I'll remember, Aunt Cinda."

"Good. Now pour me another glass of water. Then we can sit back and talk about other things a while. I do get hungry for a good tittle-tattle now 'n' again. T.J.'s awful good 'bout lots of things, but sometimes a body needs more news than talk of sick horses and haying the south pasture.

When Sarah spotted T.J. coming out of the Co-op the next afternoon, she stopped on the steps of the post office and waited for him to catch up.

"You do any good with Grandmother yesterday?" he asked without preamble.

Sarah shook her head. "Not a lot. All she'll say is she knows her own business. I tried, T.J. Told her neither of us could find the cabin she's talking about. She says it'll be here when she needs it. She does seem a little more resigned to moving, though."

"I guess we'll have to take that as a good sign. I don't know, Sarah. Maybe we should stop worrying about it. She's usually right."

"I know," Sarah said, and laughed at the expression on her cousin's face. "If my not-worried look is anything like your not-worried look, neither of us would be able to fool a fly."

T.J. gave her a sheepish grin. "Yeah, I know. But I can't think of anything else to do."

"Let's give it a little more time," she suggested. "As Aunt Cinda said yesterday, it sure doesn't feel like snow's coming anytime soon. Maybe she's right and something will turn up."

"Maybe," he said. "So, what are you doing in town? Where's Jordan? You're not by yourself, are you?"

"I've got him stuffed in my hip pocket," Sarah said, exasperation creeping into her voice. "In case you haven't noticed, I'm a big girl now. Been able to come to town all by myself for a long time."

T.J. gave a disgusted snort. "I take it Jordan's not with you. Is anybody? Jimmy Joe or Aunt Gertie?" He fell silent when he saw the mutinous look on her face. "Dadburn it, Sarah, you promised you'd be careful."

"Don't you start that foolishness again."

"Well, where is Jordan?"

"Why do you want to know? Going to run and tattle?"

"You can stop baiting me right now," he said. "You know we're trying to help. Besides, Sam's looking for him."

"Sam? What's he want with Jordan?"

"Don't ask me. And stop glaring. Nobody tells me anything. I'm just an innocent bystander."

"Sure you are. You and Bobby McGee. It's probably that fool idea he has that Jordan pushed me into the bull pen."

"Hey, I don't think that," T.J. protested. "Jordan seems like an all-right guy. All I know is, Sam asked me if I'd seen him or knew where he was."

"But you're as ready as he is to try running my business. You and Jordan and Sam."

"Better watch it, Sarah love. You and your own business are sounding more like Grandmother every minute."

"Maybe she has a point," Sarah said heatedly.

"Hey. Where're you off to now?"

"I'm going to see Sam," she called over her shoulder, making a point to ignore the muttered "Oh, cripes!" that floated after her.

Sam didn't seem any too pleased to see her, either. As she entered his office he looked up from his desk, a frown, rather than the smile he usually reserved for her, knitting his forehead.

"Well, Sam, I can see you're real happy to see me."

"'Course I'm glad to see you," he said, giving her a weak smile. "You got some business for me, or just visiting?"

Sarah frowned. Something was wrong. Sam had never been able to fool her.

"That depends," she said. "T.J. said you were asking about Jordan."

"Yeah." Sam hesitated a moment, then turned an innocent face toward her. "I just wanted to talk with him for a minute. He in town with you?"

"No, he's not in town with me. I'm here all by myself." She gave him a speculative look. "What's this all about?"

"Alone! Blast it, girl, I thought we agreed—"

"You mean you, T.J. and Jordan agreed," Sarah returned heatedly. "I didn't. And I want to know what you want with Jordan. If it's about that foolishness—"

"I'm not convinced it's foolishness. You shouldn't be, either."

"It's been two weeks since the rodeo, Sam. Not a thing unusual has happened."

"That's probably because you've behaved yourself and stayed close. Most of the time, anyway."

"But Jordan was your prime suspect, wasn't he? Or the Ewells?"

"Yeah, one or the other."

"So, how's the Ewell clan these days?" she asked him with a feigned innocence.

"Near as I can tell, they're doin' fine. Most of the clan's livin' in California," Sam admitted grudgingly. "But things ain't always what they seem, missy. I'm not through checking yet."

"And Jordan?" Sarah continued relentlessly. "You've found nothing there, either, have you, Sam? There's no deep, dark, secret reason for Jordan to want to harm me, is there? If you'd found anything, I'm sure you'd have told me by now."

Sam moved uncomfortably in his chair, his eyes shifting away from her.

Sarah caught his uneasiness. A flicker of apprehension gnawed at her insides. "You didn't find any reason to suspect Jordan. I know you didn't. You would have told me," she insisted, suddenly alarmed.

"Calm down, Sarah. You're right. There's no reason to think he's the one," Sam said. "But I had to check it out."

"Sounds to me like you might be changing your mind about him," Sarah said in a flood of relief. "Are you actually admitting you were wrong?"

"Maybe," Sam conceded reluctantly. "He's got some persuasive supporters. A lot of people speak well of him. You've been seeing quite a bit of him, haven't you?"

Sarah gave an exasperated sigh. "You know how much I've been seeing him. Far as I know, the community grapevine's in good working order."

"You got no reason to get huffy with me, young lady," Sam growled.

Sarah stared wordlessly, her breath caught in her lungs. Sam had never used that tone of voice with her, not unless— "And you've got no reason to be evasive with me," she said accusingly, fighting back the panic that was collecting in the back of her throat. "You're hiding something, Sam. I know that look. Your bluster isn't going to do you any good."

She forced herself to stop and take a deep breath. "T.J. said you wanted to see Jordan. If you can look me in the eye and tell me that the reason you're trying to find him has nothing to do with me, I'll drop it. If you can't do that, then tell me why. I'm tired of everybody else thinking they know what's the best for me."

"Let it go, Sarah. Ain't no reason..."

Anxiety knotted her stomach when he refused to look up. Now she was sure he was hiding something. "No, Sam," she said. "There's something you don't think I should know about. Neither you nor anyone else can make decisions for me. You of all people know that. Your idea that I shouldn't be told is enough to convince me I should. Just because you feel guilty for not trusting Jordan at first..."

"I never said that."

"You didn't have to...."

"Well, I've admitted I could have been wrong. T.J. likes him, and he's a pretty good judge of character. So's the rest of your family, and Hoyston says—"

"Hoyston!" Sarah felt an ice-cold wave of panic. "Sergeant Hoyston of the St. Louis PD? What has Hoyston got to do with Jordan?"

"Hoyston's my St. Louis contact, Sarah. You know that. And Matthias claims to be from St. Louis. It's just natural I'd check with him...."

Something about Sam's explanation didn't sound right. Sarah clenched her fists until her nails bit into the flesh of her palms. She tried to hang on to the last shreds of her control. "What's going on? Does Hoyston know Jordan? What does Hoyston have to do with him?"

"Oh, hell! Look, Sarah, let me talk to Matthias first. Maybe there's nothing to—"

"Right now, Sam. Tell me what's going on right this minute."

"Sarah—" he began again.

"You can't shield me, Sam," she said, defeat in every word she spoke. "In the end it always makes it worse. You know it does."

Sam's shoulders sagged. The movement spoke eloquently of resignation. With an audible sigh, he reached into the bottom drawer of his desk and handed Sarah a file folder.

Sarah looked from Sam to the folder in her hands. Hardly daring to breathe, she laid the folder on the desk in front of her and lifted the cover.

Photocopies? Newspaper clippings? With numb fingers she shifted through the pile. The headlines, in bold black letters, silently screamed at her: Savannah Seeress Exposed as Fraud. Wall Street Psychic's Insider Source Named. Faith Healer Charged in Boy's Death.

There were others, copies of old clippings dating back nearly a decade. The words in the headlines swam crazily before her eyes. As her frozen fingers shifted through the limsy pieces of paper she could focus on only one line of ype common to each—the centered words beneath each eadline: By Jordan D. Matthias.

Her hands shook as she closed the folder. She fought to ontrol the moisture in her eyes and raised her eyes to Sam. "Hoyston sent you these?"

"No, he didn't. He knows Matthias," Sam admitted. "Calls him a friend and a straight shooter. But Hoyston vasn't the only source I checked."

"Jordan's a—what would you call it—? a psychic-uster?" Her voice trembled.

"Those are all fraud stories, Sarah." Sams voice was un-usually gruff. "It doesn't mean— That's why I wanted to alk to him first. He's got a good reputation. Always makes ure of his facts. Doesn't take anybody's word. Investi-ates them himself..." Sam's voice trailed off, as if he re-lized his explanations were only making everything worse.

Sarah gripped the top of the desk for support and slowly ushed herself to her feet. "I know what it means, Sam." he choked back a sob. "This time I should have listened to ou."

"Now, Sarah, talk to him first. Maybe..."

"I'll talk to him," she said. "I have to, don't I? But here's really not much he can say..."

"I'll admit, it looks like that's what he came here for. But, arah, he might have changed his mind."

"Then why didn't he tell me?" She started toward the oor, then turned back to the desk and picked up the folder. Do you know something, Sam?"

She stopped, her eyes wide and shining with unshed tears. he hugged the folder to her, finally focusing on one incon-equential detail. "I didn't even know he had a middle ame. I wonder what the *D* stands for?" She gave a brittle ugh and slipped quickly out of the office.

Chapter 14

Sarah fought a wave of nausea, paying no notice to the furnacelike heat inside her closed vehicle. She was cold, so cold. Icy sweat broke out on her forehead. She leaned her head against the steering wheel, gulping in deep breaths of hot air, realizing only then that she had entombed herself in the closed car. Her fingers fumbled as she rolled down the window next to her. Then she reached across the seat to repeat the procedure on the passenger side of the car. The folder slid off the seat, scattering the clippings on the floor board.

Fraud. Fake. Hoax. Swindle. Words from the headlines jumped out at her, laughing. How could she have been so wrong?

Sarah dragged her eyes from the scattered papers, looking blindly out the windshield. Waves of heat rose from the paved surfaces, curving and distorting distinct lines into illusory images. Sarah blinked, then recognized the figure walking toward her from the opposite side of the street. In stinctively she turned the key in the ignition. She couldn't talk to T.J. Not now. She couldn't talk to anyone.

The engine coughed once, then roared to life. Sarah quickly steered the car away from the curb, forced her lips into a semblance of a smile and gave her cousin a wave as she drove past.

The numbness that had encased her when she'd first discovered Jordan's perfidy dissolved as she drove the familiar route to the farm. Yet her anguish failed to blank out the vision of his face, loving and tender, as she'd last seen him. False. All false. The memory intensified her sense of betrayal. She tried to create a scenario that could account for his treachery and was forced to admit that there wasn't one.

Jordan had come to Mountain Springs deliberately to find her, to expose her, to add another clipping to his portfolio. The conclusion was inescapable. He'd tracked her here from St. Louis through Hoyston. He'd invaded her sanctuary, her trust, her life, and finally destroyed her last place of refuge.

She gave an empty laugh. It must have been a frustrating summer for him. No exciting mysteries to solve. Nothing spectacular to expose her talents. She'd had a good rest. Not even a hint of a premonition concerning the disaster sitting on her own doorstep. Not that she'd expected one. As usual, her so-called gift didn't operate in matters of self-preservation.

Sarah blinked back the tears blurring her vision. Even without special knowledge, she should have known it was all a lie. The world she'd found in Jordan's arms wasn't meant for her or her kind. She'd had proof of that before.

Jordan had chosen a good red herring in Monte Ne. She wondered if he'd heard of the old resort before arriving or simply stumbled across it in his search for her and seized the opportunity it presented. What did it matter? What did anything matter?

Still, she was grateful for the emptiness of the farmhouse when she finally arrived home. She knew it would take only one look at her face for the family to realize that something was drastically wrong. They would accept her betrayal as their own. She hoped she'd be able to keep the worst of Jordan's sins from them, but in her present state of mind she knew she'd be unable to hide anything. The wounds were too fresh, the hurt too new.

She never wanted them to know how deeply she'd come to care for Jordan, how completely she'd given her heart to him. Sharing this anguish would only cause them pain and would do nothing to alleviate her own. But, dear God, what was she going to do?

Sarah paced the front room, oblivious of the tears streaming unchecked down her cheeks. If only she knew what he was planning, then perhaps she'd be able to make plans—to at least try to protect herself and the family from the worst of the notoriety. How long did she have to prepare? When would his story be published?

The heat of her first anger rekindled brightly, then solidified into an ice-cold rage. To say he loved her—to make love to her—only to add another clipping to his collection. No, that was wrong. He'd never told her he loved her. At least he'd spared her that, but the rest...

Sarah struggled to bring herself under control. Wherever he was, Jordan would return to the cabin sooner or later. She'd go there and wait until he showed up. It would be better to confront him away from Mountain Springs. She'd make him tell her his plans, and she'd tell him to his face exactly what she thought of him.

Her courage deserted her momentarily when she saw his Blazer parked on the road above the cabin. The anguish caused by his betrayal surfaced full force. Desperately she fought to regain control. Her hands, damp with perspiration, clutched the folder that reminded her anew of Jordan's treachery.

The cabin remained silent when Sarah knocked on the front door. With her heart in her throat, she knocked again, louder this time. Seconds later the door was thrown open by Jordan. He was clad only in a pair of well-worn cutoffs, feet and legs bare, water still clinging to his naked chest. The moisture in his hair and the towel thrown casually over his shoulder told the story of his interrupted shower. She blinked, drinking in the sight of him. It took every ounce of willpower she possessed to keep her eyes dry.

"Sarah." He said her name like a caress.

Sarah swallowed, tilting her chin to look up into his face.

He stood aside to allow her to enter, reaching out at the same time to pull her to him. "I was on my way to the farm as soon as I finished showering."

At the touch of his hand on her arm, Sarah jerked back. His hand dropped. She felt his eyes examine her face, saw his startled expression.

"Sarah? What's wrong?"

Mutely Sarah thrust the folder at him, careful to avoid any physical contact. He gave her a puzzled look and took the folder in one hand, opening it with the other. She watched as the color drained from his face.

"Oh, damn!" He looked up, a strange, almost pleading expression in his eyes. "Sarah...I never meant..."

"I'm sure you didn't. When was I supposed to find out? When I read it in the papers?" Her voice was expressionless. It sounded strange, foreign, even to her own ears.

"You don't understand. I didn't mean to..."

"I understand perfectly, Jordan. This is why you came here. You followed me here from St. Louis for a story—an-

other exposé for your files. Isn't that what you do? Write
exposés on psychic frauds? Your credits are impressive.''

"No," he said. "I mean, yes, I write them. But it's just a
sideline. I usually do them on my vacations—"

"Just a sideline! A way to pass a vacation—" Her voice
broke. She turned her back to him, struggling to regain her
composure. She knew the moment Jordan stepped closer,
knew he was reaching out for her. She flinched. "Don't
touch me." She whirled around to face him again. "I
couldn't stand it if you touched me."

Jordan backed away, his hand still extended toward her.

"Why, Jordan?" she asked him. "I trusted you. You
made me trust you. Wasn't that enough? Did you have to
make me fall in love with you, too? Is that how you do it?
How you get all those little nitty-gritty details?" Her voice
quavered. She took a deep gulp of air in an effort to steady
it. "Did I measure up? Make an exciting story?"

Jordan's arm dropped, the knuckles showing white across
the top of his clenched fist. "I'm not— I didn't write a story
about you."

"I wonder why I don't believe you," she said in a bitter
voice.

"Sarah! Look at me. Listen to me. There is no story. Why
would I lie? I've never lied to you...."

"Never lied to you," she repeated dully. "You said you
came here to do a story about Monte Ne. All the time you
were here...were here to... Your dictionary has strange
definitions."

"I did write a story on Monte Ne. I told you, it's scheduled for publication next month. My agent sold it to a
newspaper syndicate."

"It doesn't matter," she said, her voice once again
expressionless.

"No, I guess it doesn't. All right, I'll admit I didn't tell you the whole truth. But I didn't lie. Please believe me, Sarah. After I got to know you I knew I couldn't do that story. I never intended to hurt you."

She stood mute in front of him, her eyes wide, shining with unshed tears. "And pigs can fly. I've heard that before, too."

"I meant it, Sarah. I was going to tell you about this." The folder shook in his hand. "But I couldn't find the right time and . . . and somehow it didn't seem important."

"The right time? I'll believe that part. There's never a right time to tell someone you're going to betray them."

"I didn't mean it that way. It was just that the time we've had together . . . there were more important things to talk about—to do—than discuss some stories I once wrote. Stories that had nothing to do with our relationship."

"Didn't they? I don't see it that way."

Jordan pushed the folder toward her. "Did you read them, Sarah? Did you read any of them?"

She nodded her head slowly. "Some," she said.

"Those people were frauds. Every one of them. Conniving, grasping people taking advantage of others. I know. There's no hearsay in any of those stories. I personally investigated each one of them. They deserved to be exposed."

"And that's why you came here. To personally investigate me. I asked you before—did I measure up?"

"You're not a fraud." He took a deep breath, then stepped toward her. "You're real, Sarah. The realest, most important person I've ever met. I'll be forever sorry you learned about those stories the way you did. My fault. If you'd found out any other way . . . if I'd told you, explained . . . it wouldn't have mattered. It doesn't really matter. In a little while, it won't matter. Not to us. Trust me. . . ."

Sarah twisted away from him, moving toward the door of the cabin. "Trust you?" she said in a tremulous voice. "I already did that."

"Did you, Sarah?" he said in a quiet voice. "Then why are you running away? I haven't betrayed you. Those stories were written before I ever met you. They have nothing to do with us.

"I'll even tell you something I don't have to," he went on. "After I found you, began to know you, I still planned to do a story about you—about a psychic that wasn't a fraud. But when I realized how much it could harm you I discarded that idea, too. Not that it wouldn't make a good story. It could be a prizewinner, but I'll never write it. Please, Sarah, don't run away this time. Don't throw away what we have together. Trust me."

"I . . . I can't. . . ." She gave him an anguished look and slipped out the door, all but running toward the road.

"Sarah," Jordan called, starting after her. He reached the edge of the porch, but then, seeing the panicked look she threw over her shoulder, he stopped. His face was a mask of pain as he watched her jerk open the door of her car. He remained where he was, in plain sight, until he was sure she saw him, saw that he wasn't trying to follow her.

"Think about it, Sarah. Please. I won't follow you now," he called after her. "But this isn't the end. I'll be back."

His shoulders sagged dejectedly as he turned to go back into the cabin. He couldn't afford to chase her, couldn't have her driving panic-stricken on these curving mountain roads trying to get away from him. He'd give her a few minutes head start, then follow at a discreet distance. Make sure she arrived home safely. And he'd given her a little time to work things out by herself before he tried to see her again. He wasn't giving up. She'd understand. She had to understand. Didn't she know she was his whole life?

*   *   *

Jordan avoided stopping at the Shields's farmhouse. He spotted the tailgate of T.J.'s battered pickup by the larger barn and parked the Blazer on the side of the driveway outside the double gate. He wasn't particularly looking forward to this confrontation, but he had no choice. T.J. was the only one who could do the job. If, he reminded himself, he could get him to listen.

T.J. had evidently heard him arrive. He met Jordan at the door of the barn. "Get out of here, Matthias. I've got nothing to say to you. Better, in fact, if you just get on out of town. There's nothing here for you."

It was the type of greeting Jordan had been expecting. Still, he had to try. "I'm going to talk to you. And like it or not, you're going to listen. Then I'll leave," he told the angry man. "I can't get near Sarah. She won't listen to me anyway. So you're elected. Someone has to stay on guard."

T.J. stabbed his pitchfork into the ground. "We'll take care of Sarah. It's nothing to you. Aren't you satisfied yet? Haven't you hurt her enough?"

Jordan grimaced. He'd never intended for Sarah to discover his original reason for finding her the way she had, but that hadn't lessened her feelings of betrayal. The argument wasn't one likely to impress her cousin, either. "I never meant to hurt Sarah, whatever you think."

"You could have fooled me. Anything for a story, right, Mr. Matthias?"

"It wasn't like that," Jordan protested.

"Can't say as I can tell the difference. Sarah, either. You hurt her. Hurt her in the one place where we can't even give her much help. Maybe you didn't do it deliberately. But around here we say the road to hell's paved with good intentions. I reckon it just got a new coat of asphalt. Get out of here, Matthias, before I forget I promised Sarah I wouldn't tear you limb from limb."

Sarah had interceded to keep T.J. from attacking him? Jordan experienced a surge of hope, then realized that she was probably hoping to protect her cousin, not him. "I'm not writing a story about Sarah," he said.

"That don't forgive the intent."

"Look, T.J., this isn't getting us anywhere. Inadvertently, I hurt Sarah. That's something she and I have to deal with—something we'll have to work out together. But even as mixed-up and hurt as she is right now, she doesn't accuse me of trying to physically harm her. I didn't push that concrete block down on top of her. And I didn't throw her into a corral with a mad bull. Someone did. Or do you think they were simple accidents?"

Jordan could see some of the belligerence fading from T.J.'s face. He forced himself to stay quiet, to wait for the man to speak.

"No. I don't think they were accidents. Not that crazy tourist, either. Not now."

"Tourist? What crazy—? Damn it, has something else happened? Is Sarah all right?"

"I'm talking about the trip over Bald Mountain the day I came after her, when you and she were on the bluff. Didn't she tell you about it?"

"No, she never mentioned it," Jordan said, grim-faced. "What happened?"

"Someone tried to run us off the side of the mountain. At the time I thought it was just some damn fool tourist. It was only after... after the others that I..."

Jordan nodded. "I know. One mishap—an accident. Two—maybe coincidence. But the last one, that couldn't have been accidental. And that makes the others suspect."

"Yeah, that's the way I see it." T.J. studied the dusty, scuffed toe of his boot for a minute, the frown on his face an obvious sign of indecision. When he looked back up, Jordan was relieved to see that the animosity in his eyes had faded a little.

"Sooo," he drawled, "what do you plan to do now?"

Jordan let out a slow sigh of relief. "I'm going to Tulsa. You'll have to keep a close eye on Sarah. If you can arrange it, don't let her off the farm by herself. Talk to Sam. He'll cooperate with you. I think he's finally convinced I'm not the villain of the piece. At least not that particular villain. But he can't protect her twenty-four hours a day. The family can."

T.J.'s eyes narrowed. "Tulsa? Sarah ran into trouble there several years ago."

"I know. That's why I'm going. I tried a few long-distance questions. Didn't get the answers I needed."

"Don't go digging around and hurt her any more."

Jordan gave him a keen look, recognizing that he had once again aroused T.J.'s distrust. "Do you know what happened?"

"Not the details," T.J. admitted. "There was a man... The newspapers got hold of her. I think it's all mixed together. It knocked the props out from under her. One week she was happy. A couple of weeks later she came home...injured. It was almost as bad as this time," he added, not bothering to disguise his antagonism.

Jordan winced again, then reminded himself that what was done was done. The job now was to repair the damage. And to protect Sarah. "Did she tell you about the threats?"

Surprise was on his side this time. He watched the color drain from T.J.'s face.

"Threats? In Tulsa? Blast it! She's never said a thing about threats. Sam should have told us, if she didn't."

"Sam doesn't know. Or at least he doesn't know Sarah has an idea who made them. Evidently she goes through this kind of thing every time she's exposed. I promised her I wouldn't tell Sam." Jordan gave T.J. a speculative look. "The threats were involved somehow with the publicity and a hit-and-run accident. I don't know if there was any connection or if there's any connection now. Apparently she didn't tell anyone, not even the police, because she said it was just an idea. She had no proof. It's pretty slim, but at least I can find out if the man's still in jail. And if anything happens while I'm gone..."

Jordan hesitated. If Sarah found out he'd discussed this with T.J., would she consider it another breach of trust? He'd already betrayed her once. But he'd told T.J. too much not to continue. If Sarah added this to his list of crimes, he'd have to deal with that later. Someone had to know. T.J. was the logical one. Besides, he doubted if anything could make his relationship with Sarah any worse than it was now.

"Look, T.J., I promised Sarah I wouldn't tell Sam. But you didn't. If anything suspicious happens—anything—you go to Sam. Tell him what I said about the threats and the hit-and-run driver. He'll have to get the rest out of Sarah."

T.J. gave Jordan a hard look. "It's a pretty slim lead, isn't it?"

Jordan nodded. "Yeah. The Ewells sound more likely to me. But Sam's checking that out."

"If any of them are around here, they're staying well out of sight," T.J. said. "'Course, they know this country like the back of their hands. But if one of them's hanging around here, one of us'll spot him soon enough."

"I wouldn't know a Ewell if I tripped over him," Jordan said. "That's why I'm going to Tulsa. At least I'll be doing something, even if it's only eliminating possibilities. I keep remembering how Sarah looked when she talked about the threats... and then I remember that damn truck, and since both are Oklahoma-connected, maybe... It's not much to go on, but I can't stand just waiting around.''

"Wait a minute," T.J. said. "What did you say?"

"I said it's not much to go on—"

"No, not that. About a truck? What'd you mean?"

Jordan shrugged. "Probably nothing. I've seen an old truck around a couple of times. I can't be sure it was the same one every time. There was one with Oklahoma plates at the ruins the day of the accident. It took me a while to remember that. And that was because I kept seeing it, or one similar to it, when we were in Eureka Springs."

"The same truck? Describe it."

Jordan was a bit surprised, then cautiously optimistic, at the sound of repressed anticipation in T.J.'s voice.

"Older model. Battered. Rusty. Pretty beat-up, in fact. I'm not even sure I can tell you the original color, except it was dark. There was nothing particular to distinguish it from half a dozen others I've seen around, not even the Oklahoma plates—except that it was a little older than most and still running. That's why I think it might have been the same one. Why? Does it mean anything to you?"

T.J. nodded. "It might. That crazy tourist—I thought he was driving an old pickup. But he went by so fast I couldn't tell for sure. What happened in Eureka Springs? Sarah didn't see anything. Why'd you notice it?"

"Nothing happened," Jordan admitted. "I just had the feeling we were being watched. I was probably wrong."

"Jimmy Joe told us 'bout you knowing he was watchin' you. You weren't wrong that time...." T.J. said slowly. "Maybe you aren't this time, either."

"Maybe," Jordan said. "If I can get a name on that hit-and-run driver I can at least check it against vehicle registrations. In the meantime..."

"If it was the same truck every time, that means it's been hanging around here since the first of the summer," T.J. pointed out. "Been careful to stay out of sight most of the time, too. Could be one of the Ewells. They've still got shirttail kin all over the area. Now that I know what to look for, I'll find it—if it's still around."

"Your first priority is watching after Sarah," Jordan reminded him. "If the truck's the right one, it will come after her again."

T.J.'s face sobered. "She's not going to like me babysitting."

Jordan grinned at the apprehensive look on T.J.'s face. It was his first smile since Sarah had left the cabin the afternoon before. He was surprised at how good he felt. Somehow, someway, everything was going to be all right. He had to believe that. First things first, he told himself.

"Take care, T.J., and keep Sarah safe," he pleaded. "I'll be back as soon as I find anything."

"I'll watch out for her," T.J. promised as Jordan turned to leave. "I'll find that truck too—if it's still around."

Sarah walked slowly down the winding driveway to the mailbox. The summer had been a disaster. Aunt Cinda's stubbornness. Caldwell's place being sold out from under T.J. Now her car's sudden breakdown. Luther said it would be another week before he could get the part he needed to fix it. And Jordan. There was always Jordan. Sarah kicked dejectedly at a stone lying in her path. Jordan made the other disasters pale by comparison.

He'd disappeared. Simply vanished. If he were anywhere in the vicinity, it would have been on the grapevine. But no one had said a word. The family wouldn't, of course. They knew what had happened. At least part of it. She knew they were being careful not to mention his name around her. But no one else knew. And no one had said a word about him. He hadn't been seen. That much was obvious. He was simply gone.

Wasn't that what you wanted? she asked herself. Her answer didn't make her feel any better. If he'd cared anything at all, he would have tried—at least once—to see her. No, being right didn't make her feel one bit better.

She opened the mailbox and pulled out a single large brown envelope, idly examining the return address. Some kind of New York agency? It was addressed to her.

Without much curiosity she tore open the envelope, pulled out several photocopied pages and frowned. It wasn't an advertisement. It was then that she saw the words at the top of the first page.

Sarah caught her breath, her eyes blurring. Still, she could make out the words By Jordan D. Matthias. Her hands trembled as she flipped through the three typewritten pages. It was the story on Monte Ne. Quickly her eyes scanned the paragraphs, pausing here and there as a particular phrase caught her attention. She turned again to the last page, hoping to see a message, a note. There was nothing. Just the article.

She forced herself to start at the beginning—reading the words Jordan had written. He'd painted a canvas with words, his description vivid. She could see Monte Ne alive again, alive in a way she'd been able to imagine but never describe.

Then she came to the last three paragraphs. So, she thought, Jordan had identified Monte Ne's historical importance as a forerunner of the planned community. She felt a moment of pride at his astuteness and allowed herself the satisfaction of knowing she had contributed to his project.

Then she remembered that she'd never have the chance to tell him so.

With numb fingers she stuffed the pages back into the envelope and began the walk back to the farmhouse. Would the misery of this summer never end?

Chapter 15

"Do you realize you've been here for breakfast nearly every day this week?" Sarah asked accusingly as she placed the platter of sausage and eggs in front of her cousin. "You never were very subtle, T.J. I know what you're doing."

"What? Eating the best breakfast in Benton County? You bet."

Sarah shook her head. "I know you and Sam have cooked this up between you. When are you going to admit you were wrong?"

"That you cook the best breakfast in the county? When I find a better one, I guess," T.J. said with a straight face. "Come on, Sarah love. Stop glowering and have a cup of coffee. And maybe I'll tell you my news."

When Sarah made no move to join him, he cocked his head to one side. "It's about the Caldwell place," he said teasingly.

"You're not going to get around me that easily, Timothy James. I know they've started clearing a building site down by the road."

"Well, I didn't reckon you'd suddenly gone blind," he returned huffily. "'Course I knew you'd seen the bulldozers. Heck. You can even hear them from here. This is something else."

"All right," Sarah said, pouring herself a cup of coffee. "Go on and tell me what you heard, but you're not changing my mind. Your flypaper act is getting a little old."

T.J. grinned like a magician about to pull a rabbit out of a hat. "Not something I heard, Sarah. Something I did. I've bought the Caldwell place. Signed the papers yesterday."

If T.J. had wanted his announcement to be a bombshell, he'd succeeded. She slammed her coffee mug down the table, choking on the sip of liquid trying to enter her esophagus via the windpipe. Her cousin was behind her chair in a second, administering assistance in the form of several heavy pats on the back.

Weakly she waved him away. "Your cure's worse than the ailment," she said between gasps for breath.

"I'm sorry, Sarah," he said contritely when she finally regained control of her breathing. "I didn't mean to—"

"Surprise me? Or pound me to death?" She gave him a wan grin. "It's okay. I just don't understand how. I mean, I thought the place was sold." Her eyes widened suddenly in surprise. "You're not building—"

"Of course not," he interjected. "I'm buying on a lease-option—everything but the building site by the road and one other." He hesitated for a moment. "Sarah, I'm sorry, but they're also cutting out another five-acre parcel. It's the old homesite between the orchard and the river."

"If anyone was going to buy eighty acres for a building site, it's only good sense to pick the best one on the property," she said hesitantly. "Of course it would be the old homesite. What I don't understand is how you managed to get the rest."

"On a silver platter," T.J. told her earnestly. "Honest. Right out of the blue this lawyer in Rogers calls me. Said the bulk of the property was going to be resold and he'd been instructed to offer it to me before putting it on the open market. I thought it was a joke, but it wasn't. I've got a lease for five years with an option to buy that can be exercised anytime within the lease period for a minimum down payment. And eighty percent of the lease payments apply to the purchase price."

"But who owns it, T.J.? He doesn't sound too smart to me. Are you sure it's legal?"

T.J. laughed. "I wondered the same thing. I think that Rogers lawyer does, too, at least the part about his client not being too smart. But he said he was under instructions. And it's all legal. I had Dad's lawyer look over the papers before I signed." He shook his head. "I don't know who the owner is. A land company holds actual title. I wondered if..."

"You think you know who it is, don't you?"

T.J. grinned sheepishly. "I've got one wild idea."

"Who?"

"I'm not telling you. If I'm right, we'll all know soon enough. If I'm wrong, then nobody can call me a fool. Anyway, according to the lease, I have full and unrestricted use of the land until the building site is surveyed, staked and fenced off from the rest of the property. That means you can go swimming at the river again—legally, I mean. I'm giving you permission."

Sarah looked up indignantly. "You know I haven't been to the river since it was sold. I wouldn't go trespassing on someone else's land unless I—"

"Knew who you were trespassing on."

"I was going to say unless I had permission."

"So now you've got permission. What do you plan to do today? Everyone else is gone, aren't they?"

"Yes. I thought I'd drive into Fayetteville this afternoon. Grandpa said I could use his car. I need to do a little shopping."

"Wait until tomorrow. I'll go with you."

"That's what I meant earlier, T.J. I can't step off the farm without you playing watchdog. It's got to stop."

"I need to go to Fayetteville, too, Sarah. Honest. And your Grandpa's car is air-conditioned. Are you saying I can't come with you?" He gave her a hurt-little-boy look reminiscent of Jimmy Joe.

"You're a poor liar and an even worse actor," she told him. "You don't need to go to Fayetteville."

"And neither do you. So, are you going to stay home like a good girl? Just a little longer, Sarah. Until we're sure."

"I'm sure now." She sighed. "Oh, all right. Maybe I'll go swimming."

"That should be all right. Want to go out to dinner tonight? Maybe catch a movie?"

Sarah shook her head.

"I'll stop by later. Maybe you'll change your mind."

"You mean you'll check on me later."

He grinned. "That's what I said." He picked up the now-empty plate and walked around the table to lay it in the sink. Then, unexpectedly, swooped down to give her a peck on the cheek. "You do fix the best breakfast in Benton County," he said. "Only don't tell Mom I said so. I'd have to deny it."

Sarah couldn't help smiling back. She shook her head as she watched him drive down the hill.

* * *

Jordan had been awake for almost forty-eight hours, but his mind refused to acknowledge his exhaustion. He had only one thought. Get to Sarah. Make sure she's safe.

The frustration he'd felt when he'd finally pieced together the story in Tulsa drained from him as he neared his destination. But even at the height of his anger he'd never believed she'd deceived him intentionally. She was such an innocent. She simply hadn't realized what was going on.

From now on she'd tell him everything. No more ignoring threats or warnings of any kind. She wouldn't have to deal with them. All she had to do was tell him. From now on he'd take care of anything like this.

Turning onto the main street of Mountain Springs, Jordan briefly enjoyed the unfamiliar feeling of homecoming. Not yet, but soon, he promised himself, steering the Blazer into a side street and parking next to the town hall.

As he entered the sheriff's office, Sam looked up from his desk, a dark frown immediately replacing his usual benign expression.

"Where's Sarah? Is she all right?" Jordan demanded.

"No reason she shouldn't be," Sam returned curtly. "Thought you'd left town."

"I'm back," Jordan said, forcing himself to be calm. He'd get no help from the sheriff if he lost his temper now. Besides, it wasn't Sam's fault. He hadn't known, either.

Jordan laid two sheets of paper on the desk. "Here's the fellow you should be frowning at. He's the one after Sarah."

Sam reached for the papers.

"His name's Billy Clyde Jackson. Sarah gave Tulsa police the license number of his car three years ago. He spent twenty-two months in jail on hit-and-run charges and was released on parole last May. He jumped parole."

"Three years ago? That's about the time she came home hurt and scared as an abandoned kitten." Sam sighed. "It was a bad time, but no reason to think it has anything to do with Sarah's 'accidents.'''

"There is if you know the man's a nut case. And know he threatened her. Right in the courtroom."

"Threatened her? She never told me that." Sam's frown turned into a full-fledged scowl. "Why wasn't she warned before he was released? Why wasn't she called into the parole hearing? That's standard procedure with threats."

"They didn't notify her because no one knew she'd been threatened. No one but Sarah. And she chose to ignore it."

"He threatened her in court and nobody knew it? Damnation, Matthias, you're not making any sense."

Jordan almost felt sorry for the man. "Sorry, Sheriff. I'll try a little harder." Jordan dragged his hand through his hair.

Sam seemed to see him for the first time. "You look exhausted," he said, not unkindly. "Well, don't just stand there. Sit down before you fall down and tell me what the hell's going on." He kicked at the leg of the empty chair by his desk.

Gratefully Jordan sank down. At least Sam seemed willing to listen to him. He'd even offered him a chair. "Sarah gave police the license number of the hit-and-run car. Then their only witness gave them the same number under hypnosis. The matching numbers—that's the story that leaked to the press and caused the publicity," Jordan explained.

Sam nodded. "She didn't tell me much about it. It was all over before she came home. I didn't press her. She was in pretty bad shape."

This time it was Jordan who nodded. "I don't know why Sarah went to the arraignment. Jackson originally reported the car stolen, so maybe she wanted to be sure they had the right man. Anyway, she was there. Jackson may have seen and recognized her. There were a couple of photographs in one of the papers. Maybe he didn't see her. But something set him off. He went completely crazy. They had to drag him out of the courtroom.

"I talked to one of the officers who was there. He said Jackson was screaming and yelling and calling down vengeance on the devil's disciples who interfered in his work for the Almighty. But no one realized it was directed at Sarah, because no one knew that she'd been receiving threatening phone calls and crank letters about her 'devil's work.' I had to drag it out of her, and then only a little bit of it. I didn't even get his name from her. That's why it's taken me so long to get back."

"She told you this guy threatened her? She never told me." Sam's expression was growing darker by the moment. "Neither did you. If I'd known, I could have checked it out a long time ago. Damn it. She nearly had me convinced she was right and I was wrong...."

"I'm sorry, Sam. Once, when we were talking, she mentioned threats. After what happened at the rodeo I made her tell me more. I promised her I wouldn't tell you because she insisted it wasn't important. Said you'd just be off on another wild-goose chase. I think she really believes it isn't important. And I thought it was a long shot, too. The Ewells sounded like better prospects."

Jordan shut his eyes for a moment, struggling to keep his frustration under control. "But now I'm convinced he's the one. I talked to a couple of the inmates, too. He was still muttering threats when he was released. It all fits."

"Damn it all. She needs a keeper."

"She's got one."

Sam's head snapped up. Jordan met his eyes without flinching. After a long moment Sam slowly nodded his head, then turned his attention to the set of mug shots.

"I don't think I've seen him around. Stands to reason he'd keep out of sight, though."

"I understand he's about sixty pounds heavier. Prison must have agreed with him."

"Then maybe we'd just better see he goes back." Sam studied the pictures again. "Heavier. Fuller cheeks, jowls. Maybe..." He pushed back his chair and stood, the paper still in his hand. "I'll find him. What are you going to do?"

"I'm going to find Sarah and wring her foolish little neck. Then I'm going to marry her, if I can convince her to have me."

"Now see here, Matthias—" Sam protested.

"And you'd better start calling me Jordan. I'm going to be around a lot."

Both men were still staring at each other when the office door slammed shut. Jordan turned as T.J. stepped into the room.

"Thought that was your Blazer," he said, nodding at Jordan. "You're just in time. I think I've found the pickup."

"What pickup?" Sam demanded.

"The truck I think nearly ran Sarah and me off Bald Mountain. The one Jordan may have seen at the ruins. Maybe the same one that followed him and Sarah to Eureka Springs," T.J. said smugly.

"Stop showing off," Jordan told him. "Where'd you see it?"

"Luther just towed it in to his place with a broken axle. The guy driving it is there, too."

Jordan grabbed the paper from Sam's hands and thrust it at T.J. "Is this the man? He may be a little heavier now."

"What's his name?" Sam asked at the same time.

"Name's Jackson. Lenny Jackson," T.J. said, studying the mug shots. "These look something like him, but I don't think it's the same man. The guy at Luther's is younger."

"Younger brother," Jordan said explosively. "Lenny is Billy Clyde's baby brother. Billy Clyde won't be far away." He turned his attention to T.J. "Where's Sarah?"

"At the farm. I put her car out of commission. She may be at the river. She said she might go swimming."

"Alone?"

"Sure. It's almost part of the farm. Why? What's going on?" Jordan was already halfway out the door.

"Jordan, wait," Sam yelled after him. "Take T.J. with you. I'll take care of Lenny and meet you at the farm. Go on, T.J. He can tell you what's happening."

Sarah gave her wet hair one last wring, flipped it over her shoulders, then picked up her towel and the basket containing her empty thermos and her half-eaten sandwich. She glanced around the grove one more time. Her swim had cooled her off but had done little to refresh her spirits.

What did she expect? she asked herself. Everything here reminded her of Jordan. The shady oak where they'd spread the quilt, the old tree snag that had marked her starting point the time he'd challenged her to a race, even the river—everywhere she looked she could see Jordan.

She remembered the way he'd tossed his head, scattering droplets of water that had caught the sun like shining diamonds—and the effortless way his body had cut through the water, swimmer's muscles rippling under the skin. She could see the long lean length of him stretched beside her on the quilt, his eyes alight with laughter, his mouth tender and inviting.

Gone. All gone now. Because she'd been afraid to trust her own heart. Because she'd been afraid to trust him!

He said he'd be back, she reminded herself.

But that was a week ago, some perverse demon told her. You've no one to blame but yourself. You sent him away.

Sarah sighed and began slowly walking up the hill. Somehow life's complications had gotten the best of her. Nothing mattered much anymore. Not without Jordan.

From the orchard at the top of the hill she looked down at the river. Maybe she should go back to St. Louis early. She certainly wasn't doing herself or anyone else any good here. Aunt Cinda was hardly speaking to her. T.J. wouldn't let her out of his sight if she left the farm. Even Jimmy Joe was avoiding her. Her depression was catching.

Sarah moved back onto the path that led through the woods, then crossed the pasture to the barbed-wire fence along the roadway. She paid no attention to the car moving slowly along the road, waiting only until the dust settled before crawling through the fence to the road.

She looked up when she heard the car turn around and head back in her direction. As it rounded the bend that hid the driveway to the farm, it pulled to the side of the road and stopped. She walked slowly toward it, fully expecting the driver to ask directions. It was easy to get lost on the unmarked back roads if you didn't know the area.

The door on the driver's side of the car opened, and the driver stepped out. Sarah felt a fleeting sense of familiarity at the sight of the large man approaching her. Several feet in front of the car he stopped, apparently waiting. Sarah continued toward him. She was less than ten feet away when she looked up into his face.

"Remember me, missy?"

She froze at the sound of his sibilant voice.

"I sure wasn't likely to forget you." He took a step toward her. "'Course, I have good reason to remember you. You and your devil's works."

Her eyes widened in recognition. Dear God! Jordan, T.J., Sam—they had been right. That was the only thought she allowed herself before instinct took over. Then she dropped the basket and towel and ran.

The man was between her and the farm. On the road or the driveway he'd overtake her in the car. The pasture between her and home was all open land. No place to hide. Those facts flashed through her mind, one after another.

She climbed the bank and slipped through the barbed-wire fence. She heard him holler, then start after her.

He'd put on weight since she'd seen him three years before, was probably out of condition, but he was still a big, strong man, and he had the determination of the demented on his side. She'd told Jordan he was crazy. She just wished she'd known how crazy. As her mind played with her thoughts, her feet raced along the pathway at the edge of the pasture.

She stopped once, looking over her shoulder. He'd cleared the fence and was halfway up the path she'd just run. Sarah took a deep breath, pressed one hand to her aching side and ran for the woods.

The woods were her only chance. Get off the trail and find a hiding place. If she could get far enough ahead of him, maybe he wouldn't see where she left the trail. She looked behind her once again. Thankfully, he wasn't yet in sight. She angled off the trail, circled a bramble thicket and, trying not to disturb the foliage, crawled into the grove of sassafras trees and honeysuckle vines.

He was on the path in the woods now. She could hear him coming closer. Would he be able to tell where she'd left the trail? He was muttering under his breath, misquoting scripture verses, calling down damnation on the minions of Satan.

Sarah lay as still as her laboring lungs would allow, hoping she was low enough against the ground for the tangled brush to hide the white flag of her blouse. She shouldn't have stopped here, but she had to rest. Just for a moment or two.

She tried to ignore the stabbing pain in her side, listening for the sounds that would tell her he'd passed her hiding place, that he was still following the trail. She knew he wouldn't be fooled long. When the path dead-ended at the river, he'd realize she was making her way through the woods. But it might give her time to make it to higher ground. This thicket was too close to the trail.

The man was still following the trail. If he'd left the path she would have heard the sounds of breaking branches and the shuffling of his feet through last year's leaves. Cautiously she raised her head. He was almost to the bend in the path. Once past that, he'd be out of sight and she could move.

Keep going, she urged him silently. Stay on the path. Just a little longer. As he moved around the bend, she cautiously began to crawl from the thicket, pausing every few moments to listen for the sounds of his return, praying she wouldn't hear them. Slowly she stood upright and looked around for a route. Then she began to move uphill.

Chapter 16

Jordan lapsed into tight-lipped silence after telling T.J. the results of his investigation in Tulsa. At any other time, he knew, he would have found the young man's colorful expletives humorous. But at the moment all he could do was agree with the sentiments he expressed.

He no longer had any doubts they were dealing with a madman. The presence of Lenny Jackson in Mountain Springs confirmed it. Billy Clyde would be somewhere close. He could only hope that the man had not located Sarah. Or that he was too much of a coward to try anything alone.

Jordan slowed the Blazer to make the turn off the highway, then immediately resumed speed. The trailing dust cloud thrown up by the speeding wheels lingered in their wake. It seemed to take forever to travel the few miles from the highway to the driveway of the farm.

He drove up the winding driveway, stopping in the turn-around area by the side of the house. There he sat waiting, grim-faced, his hands still on the steering wheel.

T.J. had said little after exhausting his supply of epithets. Now he looked at Jordan expectantly. "Aren't you coming in?"

"Not now," Jordan answered curtly. "Just see if she's here." He couldn't dismiss the nagging thought that told him she wouldn't be.

"There's no one here," T.J. confirmed a short minute later, jumping back into the front seat. "If she's gone to the river, we can drive partway. It'll be quicker by road."

Jordan nodded his agreement, already turning the car in the driveway as T.J. slammed the passenger door. The feeling of urgency persisted.

They saw the strange car parked at the side of the road as they rounded the first bend. Jordan braked in front of the vehicle, and both men jumped from the Blazer. In unspoken agreement they moved in opposite directions—T.J. toward the parked vehicle, Jordan along the road in the opposite direction.

"It's locked," T.J. said, rejoining Jordan. "No sign of the driver, and it's got Oklahoma plates."

Jordan nodded, continuing to walk the roadway, searching for anything unusual. Then he spotted the abandoned basket and towel and froze.

His eyes searched the landscape—the recently mowed pasture, the hay stubble showing yellow through the green of the new growth and the silent, stoic trees of the woodlot in the distance. There was no sign of life—no sign of Sarah—and nothing to indicate what events had caused her to abandon her belongings in the ditch. Nothing but their mute testimony and the empty car.

"The woods—she'd make for the woods!" Jordan managed to say the words in spite of the rage choking his voice and the fear clutching his heart.

Both men began to run.

* * *

Sarah left the cover of the thicket cautiously, not wanting to alert the man to her location. If he'd only remain out of sight until she reached the other side of the hill, she might have a chance of remaining hidden.

Staying low to the ground, stopping every few seconds to listen for sounds that would warn her of his approach, she moved up the ridge. She pushed through the tangle of undergrowth in her path, paying little heed to the briers tearing at her bare arms or the limbs slapping her unprotected face.

Just a little farther, she promised her tired body. Only to the top of the hill and over the crest. Then she could rest for a minute. She would be safely out of sight.

She stopped again, hugging the ground, the dusty smell of dried leaves in her nostrils, and listened intently. The unnatural stillness of the woods testified to the invasion of abnormal elements. No chattering squirrels, no singing birds, not even a breath of wind rustling through the high limbs of the trees, broke the deadly silence surrounding her.

Cautiously she raised her head, surveying the terrain above her, estimating the time and effort she would need to reach safety. The brushy undergrowth continued another ten feet up the slope before thinning out along the rocky ridge line. Her only chance was to reach the other side of the hill unseen. She allowed herself another moment of rest, then warily began moving toward the crest.

The quail were her undoing. They exploded in a combination of sound and fury from the thicket in front of her, a sudden whirl of wings in her face. Sarah automatically recoiled. On the trail below she heard a roar of rage, then the ominous sounds of crashing underbrush. With no time to catch her breath, she began scrambling toward the top of the hill.

Her gasps of breath were labored, her lungs burning in their need for air as she ran through the boulders that marked the crest of the hill and began her descent down the other side. She ignored the burning fire of her scratches and the welt on her forehead. Between her gasps for air she could hear the man still behind her.

Sarah estimated it would take him several minutes to reach the top of the hill. She had a little time to take cover, but her options were limited. There were no woods on this side of the ridge. The timberland gave way to a rocky, rolling pasture, its blanket of green marred by occasional outcrop of granite and the untamed growth that surrounded them.

She could see only two possible hiding places—one a tangle of blackberry bushes surrounding a shelf of rock protruding from the hillside, the other a narrow stretch of small trees and bushes growing along a deeply eroded gully.

She chose the thicket, knowing the gully was more logical but hoping the inhospitable environment of briar and bramble would discourage close inspection.

Her hunter was making no effort to disguise his progress. She could hear the crackling sounds of breaking limbs and twigs interspersed with grunts, growls and an occasional blasphemous phrase as he moved closer to the top of the hill.

Sarah circled the copse, dropped to her knees and entered the tangle of berry vines from the low side of the hill. No crushed underbrush or broken limbs would betray her presence from the top of the ridge. Carefully she crawled toward the center of the thicket.

A shallow indentation in the ground, protected by an overhang of rock at the base of the largest boulder, offered the best cover. Wearily she wriggled her body into the slight protection of the hole and lay still, every muscle tense.

As nature adjusted to the alien presence in the thicket, the twittering of sparrows and the faint scurrying noises of small ground rodents resumed—a welcome indication that, for the moment, she was safe. Sarah's racing pulse and labored breathing slowed. Perhaps she had outwitted him after all.

How she wished she'd listened to Sam and Jordan. Especially Jordan. She'd been wrong—wrong about so many things. She knew it now. And she'd probably never have the chance to tell him. The man from Oklahoma would see to that. She had no illusions about him. He was dangerous.

"Sarah won't stay on the trail," T.J. said as the two men, still running, entered the woods. "She knows it dead-ends at the river. Watch for any signs of someone leaving the path."

Jordan nodded, not bothering to answer as they raced along the narrow path. He forced himself to repress his memory of the last time he and Sarah had been together at the river. He had to find Sarah. That was all that mattered now.

They spotted the broken underbrush at the same time. Jordan let out an oath. Sarah wouldn't have done that. It meant Jackson knew she'd left the path and had followed her.

Now Jordan took the lead, following the trail of trampled brush with his eyes as he plunged headlong up the hill, taking shortcuts across the rough terrain whenever possible. T.J. was only a step behind him when he reached the area where the underbrush began to thin.

Both men stopped, eyes searching the open space at the top of the hill for any sign of Sarah. They spotted the man at almost the same time.

"There he is," T.J. yelled, pointing toward the crest of the hill.

Jordan raced toward him, but at T.J.'s cry Jackson changed direction and began running parallel to the top of the hill. T.J. lunged after him, felling him with a tackle around the knees. Jordan heard Jackson hit the ground and the air leave his lungs in a *whoosh*.

"Where's Sarah?" Jordan demanded, standing over the fallen man with clenched fists.

Jackson was gasping for breath, still unable to speak.

"He didn't catch her," T.J. said, calmly flipping his victim onto his stomach and twisting his arm behind his back. "Go on after her."

Jordan looked anxiously from the man on the ground to the top of the hill.

"Go on," T.J. urged him. "I've got him. We'll wait for Sam. I reckon you've got about fifteen minutes."

"He won't give you any trouble?"

"Him? Naw. He's finished. Get going. She'll be hiding in the most unlikely place."

Jordan nodded, giving T.J. a grateful look, and began moving away.

"She ought to be glad to see you," T.J. called after him. "Don't screw it up this time."

Sarah continued her still, silent wait. Was he searching the gully? No. It was close enough to her hiding place that he would have disturbed the birds. But he'd had plenty of time to make it to the top of the ridge. Was he standing on top, trying to decide which way to go? She could imagine him watching, waiting for any sign, any movement that would give away her hiding place. Despite the heat of the day and the perspiration running down the side of her face, she couldn't suppress a shiver.

Seconds crawled by like minutes. The minutes took longer. Still Sarah waited, alert for the cessation of natural sounds that would warn her of approaching danger. Where was he? Could he have fallen? Or turned back? Not likely. She would have to wait him out.

Gradually her tense muscles began to uncoil. She was beginning to think about easing out of the hiding place for a quick look when the birds sounded the alarm. Their sudden commotion was followed by a voice calling her name. Sarah held her breath, afraid that even that shallow sound would give her away.

"Sarah?" the voice called again.

She squeezed her eyes shut. *You can't run away this time,* she told herself. *Stop imagining Jordan's here. Stop imagining you hear his voice. You're all alone. You sent him away.*

Sarah made herself open her eyes. If the man from Oklahoma wasn't bluffing, if he'd really found her, she'd face him. She was tired of hiding.

"Sarah?" the voice called again. "You can come out now. Everything's all right. T.J.'s got Jackson."

Jackson. Yes, that was the man's name. But that couldn't be—

"Please, Sarah." His voice was more desperate now. "Please answer. If you don't want to see me, I'll go away. But please tell me you're all right."

Sarah was already crawling along the tunnel through the bramble. She didn't give herself time to think about it. She'd heard his voice, recognized it calling to her. She was going to him. Seconds later she was in Jordan's arms.

Jordan held her against him, his arms completely enfolding her as if to prove she was real. He'd been so afraid—afraid for her, and afraid she'd never let him near her again. She was here now, but once she realized she was safe, would she send him away? Would she ever trust him again? Would she give him another chance?

Sarah tilted her head to look into his face, saw the cold desperation in his face. "Jordan," she began, "what are

you doing here? And how did you know—?'' She shook her
head, pushed at the limp hair hanging over her eyes and saw
his eyes glint dangerously. Her own widened as she tried to
pull away. Jordan held her firmly with one arm. With his
free hand he brushed back the hair and traced the welt on
her forehead with a gentle finger.

''Did he—?''

''I got slapped by a branch,'' she told him breathlessly.
''I'm all right, Jordan. Honest. Just a few scratches from
briers.''

Jordan nodded, a muscle quivering in his jaw as he resisted the impulse to let his lips brush the welt. He stood for
a moment, still holding her against him, then reluctantly let
her go and stepped back. ''We can talk later. It's enough
that you're safe now. Besides, it's a long story....''

Story! She stiffened at the word and turned her back to
him.

''The cavalry will be coming over the hill any minute,''
Jordan told her. ''T.J.'s anxious. He blames himself for
telling you it was okay to go swimming.''

''That's ridiculous. He's not my keeper. What does he
think he could do? Keep me tied to the farm?''

Sarah's head swerved at Jordan's sudden laugh. She gave
Jordan a suspicious look. ''Did he—?'' she began.

''If it wasn't for T.J., we might not be here,'' Jordan said
quickly. ''He spotted Jackson's brother. And just in time.
That's when we knew Billy Clyde was around.''

''I still don't understand....''

''We can sort it out later,'' Jordan told her. ''Promise me,
Sarah, that when this is all over you'll hear me out.''

Sarah didn't answer, but at least, Jordan reasoned, she
hadn't said no. He was afraid to ask again. He didn't have
another chance, anyway, as his name sounded from up the
hill and he looked up.

''Here comes your cousin,'' he said flatly.

* * *

"I don't understand why Cinda didn't warn you," Sarah's grandmother complained after they'd all returned to the farm. "She's supposed to know these things."

The fact that her grandmother had broached the subject in front of Jordan told Sarah how completely he'd been admitted to the family's inner circle. Her eyes sought his as she wondered if he understood. The intensity of his gaze made her heartbeat quicken. She forced herself to look away.

"You know it doesn't always work that way, Grandma," she said. "My guess is that she didn't get a warning because everything was going to work out okay. It did, you know. I wasn't hurt. I'm fine."

"But you said you'd be able to tell if Cinda needed anything," her grandmother protested.

"That's different. It's true we can usually contact each other mentally. If she needed me for anything, she'd let me know. I could have called for her, too. But she wouldn't have been able to do anything to help today. So I didn't. Do you understand?"

They were still in the midst of explanations when Sam arrived at the farm. After assuring himself that Sarah was unhurt, the sheriff had taken Billy Clyde back to town to join his brother.

"What happens now?" Jordan asked.

"Billy Clyde goes back to Oklahoma for parole violation," the sheriff said gruffly. "I don't have anything to hold Lenny on. But I'll put the fear of the righteous in him. Don't think he'll stay around, either."

It was better, Sam explained over Jordan's protests, to send them back to Oklahoma. But the authorities would be alerted. And the next time Jackson was released, Sarah would be told.

Sam had been able to piece together most of the circumstances surrounding Sarah's near-accidents. Jordan was

unable to suppress a shudder when he discovered how larg
a part chance had played in the summer's events.

Billy Clyde had discovered where Sarah lived, and on
several occasions, including the trip to Monte Ne, had ac
tually followed her from the farm. The brother had also
tried to follow her and Jordan to Eureka Springs. He'd los
their trail temporarily then spotted them later on their sight
seeing trip in town.

But, according to Sam, the two most dangerous inci
dents, the trip across Bald Mountain with T.J. and the in
cident in the bull pen, had both occurred because th
brothers had spotted Sarah by accident and taken advan
tage of the circumstances. It couldn't be proven, Sam ad
mitted, not without a confession, but he was satisfied tha
that was what had happened.

Jordan clenched his teeth at the thought of how clos
Sarah had come to real harm. Jackson would never get nea
her again, not if he had anything to say about it.

Dusk had fallen when the explanations were finally fin
ished. T.J. left shortly after Sam, taking Jimmy Joe wit
him, hoping to distract the boy from the day's excitemen
with the promise of a movie.

The grandparents excused themselves a short time late
finally leaving Jordan and Sarah alone. Sarah moved to th
old-fashioned swing on the front porch, an apprehensiv
Jordan following. She had welcomed him on the hillside
but he wasn't sure she was ready to accept him as easily into
her life. She would have to, he told himself. He wasn't giv
ing up. He needed her.

"Jordan, I'm sorry," Sarah said, her voice shaking wit
trepidation. "I should have listened to you."

"It doesn't matter. I'll admit those two were unlikely,"
Jordan said. "Even with the pattern, it was hard to recog
nize. The motivation was there, but not easy to identify

And after putting it all together, coincidence played a big part in the attacks. I can understand—"

"No," Sarah interjected. She had to make him understand. "I didn't mean that. I'm talking about that day at the cabin...the stories. I should have listened to you then. I was—"

Jordan didn't wait to hear any more. He pulled her against him, resting his cheek on the top of her head. "Thank God," he whispered. "I was so afraid...just talking on and on because I was afraid to ask if you could ever forgive me for hiding..."

"No, you were right. I should have trusted you."

"Hush, sweetheart," he said, pulling her into his arms. "It doesn't matter now. I love you."

Sarah leaned against him, almost frightened to be so happy. He loved her! He'd never said that before. Only a few short hours ago she'd believed she'd never see him again. Shaking, she buried her face against his chest.

Jordan held her tightly, his own arms trembling. "You have to marry me, Sarah. I can't imagine my life without you."

Sarah's breath caught in her throat. She couldn't speak, but her answer was in her eyes. Her look of happiness made Jordan catch his breath. He captured her lips with his in a passionately tender kiss that promised forever.

Sarah wound her arms around his neck, holding him as she'd never thought to hold him again. Even her dreams, the dreams that had tortured her because she'd thought she'd lost him, faded in contrast with reality.

Jordan explored her face with his lips, kissing her eyes and each freckle across the bridge of her small upturned nose before once again capturing her lips.

He raised his mouth, drew a ragged breath and lifted her into his lap. "How soon, Sarah? Later this week? How long does it take a to get a license in Arkansas?"

Sarah looked at him, dazed, still caught in the whirlpool of sensation he created each time he touched her. "This week? But, Jordan, I have to be in St. Louis in two weeks."

"I know, love. If we get married this week we should be able to squeeze in a week's honeymoon. I've already got a hold on a large apartment. I think it'll do. It's not far from your school. But if you don't like it, we'll find another one."

Sarah looked at him, a disbelieving look still on her face.

Jordan groaned. "Am I going too fast? Do you want a big wedding?" He sighed. "I'm sorry. I don't mean to bulldoze you. I like your family. I want them to like me. It's just...I want you so much, and I don't think they'd approve of us living together without making it legal. But if you want more time, or a big wedding...somehow I'll manage to wait."

"I don't care about a big wedding. But what about you?" Sarah couldn't suppress the doubt in her voice. "You'll be off on another story somewhere. I'm committed to teaching next year."

Jordan shifted her in his lap. The expression on his face was one of amazement.

"I'll be staying with you. In St. Louis. Dear heaven, do you think I'd let you out of my sight after what's happened? Sarah, you're the most important part of my life. I've always traveled because I had nothing better to do. Now I do."

"But—but what will you do? How can you work if you stay in St. Louis?" Sarah held her breath.

"I've got a book contract that will keep me busy for most of the year. After that we'll plan what to do next. Together. We'll also have the year to build our house. Then it will always be here, waiting for us to come home no matter what else we decide."

"Here? We're going to build a house here? In Mountain Springs?" Suddenly she understood. "You! You bought the Caldwell place!"

"Of course I did. It was the perfect solution. We get our dream house. Aunt Cinda gets her new cabin. T.J. gets his horse ranch and..."

Sarah tried to understand what he was saying, but too much was happening too fast. "Cabin? You mean—"

"The cabin down by the main road. That's okay, isn't it? I figured it would be close enough to keep an eye on her and yet she'd have her privacy. Didn't she tell you?"

"Tell me?" Sarah was now completely bewildered. "You mean she knew? But how? She described her new cabin at the picnic. I thought that was the first time you met."

"It was. Aunt Cinda dreamed up her cabin without any help from me. But after she described it, it seemed like a good idea. I went to see her after we got back from Eureka Springs."

"You were awful sure of yourself."

Jordan raked his hand through his hair in the nervous gesture she'd come to recognize. "No, I wasn't. I only knew what I wanted. And I hoped if I showed you I could help you it would count in my favor. The cabin's a business proposition—it and a half-acre lot in exchange for Aunt Cinda's forty-acre mountaintop. With the timber, it's a fair exchange. It all happened before you discovered... Please, Sarah, don't be upset. I was only trying to help...."

"Upset! Oh, Jordan, it's perfect." She stretched to find his lips. "I love you," she whispered against his mouth. She felt the leashed hunger in his touch as once again she lost herself in the magic of his kiss. She had a fleeting moment to wonder if Jordan had any idea how large a wedding her family could arrange in just three days. It was her last coherent thought for a long, long time.

* * * * *

Keepsake

◇ *Harlequin Books*

You're never too young to
enjoy romance. Harlequin
for you . . . and Keepsake,
young-adult romances
destined to win hearts, for
your daughter.

Pick one up today and
start your daughter on her
journey into the wonderful
world of romance.

Two new titles to choose
from each month.

1989
IS THE YEAR
OF THE MAN!

What makes a romance? A special man, of course, and Silhouette Desire celebrates that fact with *twelve* of them! From Mr. January to Mr. December, every month spotlights the Silhouette Desire hero—our **MAN OF THE MONTH.**

Sexy, macho, charming, irritating…irresistible! Nothing can stop these men from sweeping you away. Created by some of your favorite authors, each man is custom-made for pleasure—*reading* pleasure—so don't miss a single one.

Diana Palmer kicks off the new year, and you can look forward to magnificent men from **Joan Hohl, Jennifer Greene** and many, many more. So get out there and find your man!

Silhouette Desire's

MAN OF THE MONTH …